ALL TIDE UP

ALEX CAY

ALISTERN PRESS
DALLAS

Library of Congress Cataloging-in-Publication Data has been applied for.
ISBN: 978-1-940221-09-0

For Gigi, thank you for passing on your wonderful sense of humor.

CHAPTER ONE

SVETLANA TAKITOV HAD JUST reached her fourth fake orgasm when a loud bang at the front door broke her concentration and stirred an emotion she didn't often feel: concern.

Dillon West, the beautiful but recently struggling actor she'd chosen for the tryst, peeled himself off her back and kneeled upright. With a wiry build and close-cropped, blond-frosted hair, he looked like a meerkat listening for a predator.

Svetlana rolled her eyes. At least it was a pretty version of the glorified rodent.

A second bang sounded and then a loud boom, as if the entire entrance had exploded.

"What the—" Dillon hopped off the bed, untied one of Svetlana's wrists and wrapped the silk Missoni scarf around his waist. Then he squeezed past the tripod and reached for the doorknob.

"Wait. The other one," Svetlana said in a sharp Russian accent as she twisted her still-tethered wrist.

"Shh." Dillon put a single finger to his lips and slipped out the door.

"Bastard," Svetlana hissed.

A moment later, a series of shouts erupted from the great room, the words echoing off the condo's wall of glass and back toward the master bedroom.

The strange thing was not the shouting. At least not to Svetlana. She'd had her share of bad boys in the past. No, what was odd was that the yells started in Russian with words like *zadolžat'* and *ubit'*: owe and kill. It sounded like three different voices, not counting Dillon's—which was much higher than the others—and two of three sounded almost identical.

Svetlana strained to make out the rest as she went to work on the second knot. Dillon had pulled this one too tight, though. There was no way Svetlana could untie it with her single free hand. Not without risking a tear in the Missoni.

The yelling switched back to English, as Dillon said, "You heard the judge, I'm innocent!"

"Fuck the courting. You are coming with us."

"Wait, I—" Dillon's sentence was cut off with a sickening thud. Then a thump, as if Dillon had crumpled to the new shag Berber carpet. The one that she'd convinced him to install for the second scene.

The condo fell silent and Svetlana froze.

The men started in Russian again, one of them saying, "Look for any cash or valuables and meet us at the car."

Two crackling noises and a rustling sounded in the living room and then the kitchen.

Svetlana searched furiously for anything to cut the scarf with, but there was nothing sharper than her chrome-plated vibrator anywhere within reach. The only item that could even classify as a weapon was the brand new Babolat AeroPro tennis racket that she had strategically placed inside the camera's frame of view at the edge of the bed.

The footsteps neared, along with a muffled humming. One of the Russians was eating something.

Svetlana stretched and torqued her body as she reached for the racket. Her fingertips brushed the purple taped grip, but she remained a full inch from success.

Typical.

The man neared the bedroom, chomping and humming. The door flung open, sending a rush of cool air from the hallway and creating a thin layer of blonde goose bumps across Svetlana's naked body.

Seeing this, the man froze squarely in the doorway, feet planted, one hand hanging low and gripping a thick pistol, the other hand to his mouth holding the remnants of a piece of fruit.

One of the fresh mangos that Dillon was supposed to eat off her belly in Act Three.

Bastard.

In a single fluid motion, Svetlana lunged for the Babolat, took hold of it—no doubt giving the man a look of a lifetime from his vantage, and keeping him paralyzed in mid-bite—and then twisted her body, as she yelled and thrust all of her hundred and seven and a half pounds into hurling the Babolat across the room and toward the man.

End over end, the racket surged from Svetlana's hand and straight into the man's face. The force of the custom designed, state of the art, composite construction connecting with the mango shoved the oversized pit straight down the man's throat. First he dropped the gun, then he spun around in total panic—two, three, four complete circles, and his expression grew more animated and deeper purple with each turn. Until finally, he gagged, snorted a strand of mango from his nose, and fell with a booming and terminating thud.

The good news was that in her final lunge, Svetlana had loosened her tethered wrist.

The bad news? She had torn, and therefore ruined beyond repair, the second Missoni.

Saquish Head, Massachusetts

Patrick Finn woke to the sound of the crashing Atlantic surf, a bit louder than most days, and the comforting warmth of his pillow mate's breath. Almost magical, Finn thought. Except for one small detail. The breath smelled like the ass-end of a dog.

Maybe because it was.

Finn turned his head away and, with a wince, cut his squinted eyes back to the other side of the bed.

Hobey, Finn's recently rescued English Bulldog, lay sprawled, legs open and head lolled, in labored breathing. The muscular ball of a dog gulped in a mouthful of air and passed another round of wind.

Best alarm clock in the world, Finn thought as he swung his six and a half foot frame off the side of the bed and to the floor.

"Storm coming, pal. Let's go secure the fort."

Hobey sat up, burped, then hopped off the bed. A bit top-heavy, the dog fell onto his side and skidded across the hardwood and into the wall. Head first.

The poor thing had the grace of a three-legged pig.

Finn grabbed his phone from the dresser and clicked it on to check for messages, but as usual there was no cell signal.

He loved this place.

His house, more of an upscale cabin, really, sat at the very end of what was called Saquish Head, a peninsula that extended between Plymouth Massachusetts and the rest of the Atlantic. With a single option for entrance being the Powder Point Bridge, seven miles north of Finn's abode, traffic was minimal to say the least. He figured the nearest cell tower was about six or seven miles west, and on the mainland.

A few minutes later, coffee in hand, Finn led the beast out the front door. Cool and damp outside and with a thick cover of steel gray clouds above the Atlantic as far as one could see, it confirmed Finn's suspicion of the oncoming storm.

Hobey waddled down the sandy path toward the beach, stopping only to fertilize a grassy patch before cresting twin sand dunes and disappearing.

Finn followed over the dunes and found Hobey eating a beached crab, shell and all.

"Just in time!" Larry Kratt, Finn's neighbor from about thirty yards down, called from behind. Known around these parts as Lobster, the man strained his rickety frame as he pulled a large, bright red Radio Flyer wagon through the sand. Water splashed out of the back as he tugged it along.

"For?" Finn took a sip and stood tall, but couldn't make out what Lobster was talking about. He'd offer to help, but Lobster would only be offended. He was the type to do it himself, he *didn't care how damned old he was.*

"I finally did it, and today's the day. Glad you're here to witness the act of kindness, Patrick." Lobster tripped and fell, one knee digging into the sandy path.

"Mr. Kratt? Do you need—"

"Can do it myself, thank you." Lobster stood and brushed the sand off his bony knee.

"A bit cold for shorts this morning, wouldn't you say?" Finn held the large mug with both hands.

"Not if I'm going in." Lobster waved a finger toward the water.

Finn was about to ask, but then the man's cargo came into view.

Inky black, its head was huge, about the size of both Finn's fists pressed together, and its claws could hold a ten pound medicine ball. The largest lobster Finn had ever seen, its bulbous body was nearly the size of Hobey's.

Speaking of…

The dog wandered over, thrust his overbite chin up to the lip of the wagon, and sniffed with his all-but-useless nose.

"Careful fella'. One snip could take a paw clear off." Lobster smiled at Finn. "Beauty ain't she?"

"Adorable. Where'd you get it?"

"It was our anniversary last night, you know that?"

"I'm sorry, I didn't realize…" Finn's words trailed off as he scolded himself for forgetting. Leaving ol' Lobster all by himself last night while Finn finished up late at the office.

"Yeah, well, every year we would go to dinner at the Fish Whistle, up there in Duxbury. Special spot to us."

"I remember," Finn said.

"So, not to break tradition, I went anyway. You know, to celebrate."

"That's lovely," Finn said.

Lobster waved him off. "It was terrible. Sitting there all alone, thinking of our forty years together."

Finn stayed quiet and nodded. Gene Kratt, Lobster's wife had died in a terrible freak accident late last year when her bible study group had made a field trip to the local salt water taffy factory. As the entourage made their way across a catwalk poised over the large vats of taffy, Mrs. Kratt lost her footing. She slipped under the rail and plunked straight into the Molasses Mint without as much as a peep. Being at the back of the line, nobody even noticed. Then, at the end of the tour, when the women were given fresh samples of the taffy, one of them unwrapped the wax covering of her treat to find Mrs. Kratt's King James Bible bookmark. Then Judy, their bible study leader admitted, "Mine does taste like hair spray."

It was then that they noticed the coloring of the taffy was a bit *too blonde.*

The plant manager assured them that the heating processes would have killed any kind of germs that could have been transferred into the taffy along with Mrs. Kratt. They would all be just fine.

So, the group of ladies voted right then and there to buy the whole lot of fresh taffy, figuring it was like eating the body of Christ, in a way. Now, in great reverence and respect, they serve

Gene's Molasses Mint at every Bible Study gathering.

After the initial shock and being the good Christian man he is, Lobster decided not to sue. Instead, and in deep grief, he sold his crab fishing operation and retired. Now, he mostly just roams the beaches each day, as if waiting for his own time to come.

Lobster continued, "But Lenny was still there." He waved his shaking finger at the lobster whose back was so bulbous that half of it protruded from the water. "Up to forty-eight pounds they said."

Doing the quick math of twenty-five dollars a pound in his head, Finn said, "Are you telling me you paid twelve-hundred dollars for a lobster?"

"Eleven-hundred and seventy-five, to be exact. They gave me a bulk discount." He beamed. "And a serving of bread pudding on the house."

"That was generous."

"You betcha."

"How old is he?"

"That's the thing, see? It's not a he." Lobster gave a long nod with terse lips.

"How do you know?"

"Been around crustaceans as long as I have, you get a sense of these things, son. Should'a been named Linda."

"Then how old is Linda?"

"That gadfly Shaunessy claimed she was over fifteen when he caught her, and she's been up at The Whistle for almost a decade now, believe that?"

"Hard to believe," Finn agreed. He'd heard Lobster talk about Shaunessy before, how the kid had been trained to catch crabs by Kratt himself before branching off and starting a large lobster fishing operation up in Maine and taking two of Lobster's best men with him. *Imagine that,* he'd say, *not just taking two of my best crabbers, but making them lobstermen, too! It's blasphemous to kill such beautiful creatures!*

Lobster shook his head. "Poor thing's missed the prime of her life."

Kratt's affinity for lobsters had delved into the realm of disturbing.

Finn took a gulp of warm coffee and said, "You think being in a tank for so long has changed her? You know, made her... domesticated?"

"A gal like this one is a warrior, let me tell you. She'll be eating fresh grouper by the end of the day."

"If you say so."

"Let's get her in then!" Lobster clapped once and took hold of the wagon handle, started pulling again.

The sound of a vehicle rumbled up behind the houses, and a cloud of dust rose from the road.

"Well, if it ain't a party now." Lobster put a hand on his hip. "That Nikki?"

Sure enough, the white Ford 150 pickup truck of Finn's long-time and trusted assistant at his namesake agency, Finn Sports, Nikki O'Callahan rounded the bend and came into view. She was out of the truck and down to the beach in thirty-seconds flat, heels in hand. "Patrick, you gotta' get a land line, you're killing me."

"Not possible." Finn took a sip of coffee, impressed that she spoke a whole sentence without swearing.

Hobey waddled over and Nikki bent low as the dog rolled over, let her pat his belly. Brave dog. Though Nikki was all of four feet eleven inches, she carried herself like a Navy SEAL—wiry and jagged at the edges. Finn wouldn't dare put himself in the position of mercy with her.

As Finn had that thought, Nikki glanced up at him, and in her distinct Boston accent she said, "You're telling me they can run fiber optic cabling across this fuckin' ocean and all the way to China and you can't get a simple fuckin' telephone line out here?"

One clean sentence in a row's not bad. "You mean Europe?" Finn said.

"You fuckin' with me, boss?"

Key word, *boss*. "Relax, I'll look into it."

"Fuck is that?" Nikki stood and peered at the giant lobster.

"That, is a beautiful creature who has been wrongly imprisoned for half of her life." Lobster shook his head.

"It looks like it was exposed to something. Like, radiation." Nikki took a step back.

"Well, it's time this angel headed back to her natural environment, one where she can roam free and enjoy the pleasures of God's planet."

"Well, the part with an ocean anyway." Finn smiled.

Lobster made a face, then said, "You gonna' help with this, or what?" Then he dragged the wagon through the sand and down to the water's edge, where a small back eddy swirled between two rocks protected from the waves of the ocean.

As they followed him, Finn explained to Nikki about Linda the Lobster.

"Ready?" Lobster asked.

Finn placed his mug on one of the rocks. "What are you—?"

"Just lift and dump her in, it'll be like a water-gasm for her."

"She's been stuck in a room-temperature restaurant tank for years. You think this is such a great idea?" Nikki asked.

Finn put up both hands. He'd already tried to reason with the man.

Lobster waved Nikki closer. "Come on missy, may need you, too. Just watch your fingers. Don't want that to be Linda's first meal, she needs proper protein from the ocean."

"Your concern for me is touching," Nikki said.

"One…" Lobster grabbed the edge of the wagon.

Finn sidled up next to him and took hold of the other side.

"Two…"

Nikki held Hobey's collar and kept a good five feet behind Finn.

"Three!"

The men heaved the wagon over, and with a rush of water, sent the giant lobster into the swirling pool between the rocks. Linda slid to the bottom, bumped against a mound of shells, and slowly turned belly up.

Finn made a move to help her, but Lobster put out a stiff arm and stopped him. "Give her a moment, she's probably all tingly from the sensation, the glory of it."

"He can't be serious," Nikki said.

Linda the Lobster proceeded to float all the way to the surface, and her yellow and black belly bobbed there, like a danger buoy.

"Now what?" Finn asked.

"Wait." Lobster stared at the creature with an intensity that Finn had never before seen on the man's face.

Then, without the slightest warning, Linda flipped herself back over and, face out of the water, her tentacles in spasm, seemingly stared straight at Finn with those black beads for eyes. Then she swept her great tail and exploded out of the pool and into the vast ocean.

"Yipee!" Lobster jumped up and down, held a hand up for a high five that Nikki ignored, then leaned over and hugged Finn. Being half his size, Lobster's arms reached around Finn's belly and his face tucked into his chest. "Thank you for helping with such an important step to rebalancing the eco-system. The both of you."

"I didn't do anything," Nikki said.

Lobster pushed from Finn and pointed down at Hobey. "I was talking to him."

Then, without another word, he spun on a heel, grabbed the handle of the empty Radio Flyer wagon, and dragged it across the sand toward his house.

"Why do you live out here with these people?" Nikki asked.

Finn shrugged. "It's peaceful."

"What a shame." Nikki peered out to the water. "That thing could've even fed you."

Finn finished his coffee. "So, did you need me, or just come out to bust chops?"

"Shit. In the excitement of freeing Willy, I almost forgot."

"Forgot what?"

Nikki ran a hand through her hair. "So, that Svetlana? The walking tennis disaster that I tried to warn you away from, but all you men are the same and once you see a pretty set of—"

"I recall," Finn said. Svetlana Takitov, the twenty-three year old Russian tennis phenom Finn had signed in hopes helping her rise in the tennis circuit and maximizing her worth in sponsorships. Just like *Maria Sharapova*, she had said. As it turns out, Svetlana—who was quite a tennis player—was also a bit more abrasive and rumored to be a whole lot more...as he had considered the description to Nikki...*libidinous* than Ms. Sharapova.

Thus far, with a few dozen men but zero major championships under her belt, Svetlana had yet to land one single sponsorship. The lone company that had contacted Finn about promoting Svetlana as the face of one of their products was Glaxicorp Pharmaceuticals, who was pushing a new ointment for herpes.

Now, Finn had dumped over fifty-thousand bucks into the leggy Russian, getting her into tournaments and setting her up with the latest and greatest equipment, including a pair of custom-made Babolat rackets that had cost over a grand each. All this, and with her latest wrist injury—*how did she get so many of those, anyway?*—she'd failed to qualify for either Wimbledon or the US Open this year.

In short, Finn's investment was being flushed down the toilet.

Nikki said, "Well, they just found a stiff in Dillon West's condo on South Beach. You know, that little prissy actor?"

"The kid that burned down the nightclub?"

"None other."

"Who could forget?" Dillon West was once the heartthrob of America. Then he made a terrible career move by agreeing to star as the main spokesman for the Tea Party in the last election.

Hollywood dropped him like a moldy bag of coke. Then, to rub salt in his own wound, the kid had somehow caused an accident that burned down a Hollywood hangout in Miami.

He hadn't been able to find work since. "Who's the stiff?"

"Some Russian named Petr, that's all we know."

"So, what, because he's Russian they're assuming Svetlana is involved?"

"That, and…she *may have been* caught on a security video of the back stairway leaving ten minutes after neighbors had complained about loud yelling coming from Dillon's place."

"Sounds weak. She could've been at anyone's condo."

"As her history suggests." Nikki smirked. "But, they found… evidence of hers in Dillon's bedroom."

Finn sat down on the rock and exhaled. "What type of evidence?"

"Panties, for one. Monogrammed of course, with the oh-so-modest moniker of your little blonde princess. *Svet.*"

"That it?"

"Let me think." Nikki held a finger to her lips and gazed up to the sky, a big show of pensiveness. Then she said, "Oh! That, and a tripod."

"Lovely."

"Yep. And now Dillon's missing and so is she."

"Great," Finn said. "Another client, another dead body."

"That's still not the best part," Nikki said in a singsong voice.

"Don't tell me," Finn said. "The tape."

Nikki held her hands out wide as she said, "You got it. That's gone missing, too."

CHAPTER TWO

MILOSEVIC AND JAKOV POPOV SAT in their condo kitchen at the wrought iron table they'd stolen off a Starbucks patio in Coral Terrace two days earlier. The anti-theft chain that they had snipped using a pair of industrial bolt cutters—ones they'd stolen from a Lowe's as a means to attain the table—was now being put to good use, wrapped around both legs of the whiny little actor named Dillon.

Dillon lay motionless on the kitchen floor between Milo and Jak, staring up at the ceiling.

Milo gazed out the window overlooking the so-called wildlife preserve that constituted the condominium's back yard. In truth, the preserve was no more than a thick layer of cattails over marsh, a perfect habitat for alligators and snakes, but not much more. No wonder the homeowners had just packed up and left, abandoned the place. Who the hell could expect to get their investment back in this market from a house that was situated at the center of a glorified swamp?

One man's loss is another's gain, though. And so, Milo and Jak had slipped into the place one day last month and taken up residence. No electricity on the whole street, and they'd yet to spot a neighbor. Surprisingly, they had running water.

Jak glanced at Dillon and back to Milo, as he said in Russian, "I wrote a new poem. A tribute to our fallen comrade, Petr."

"I don't care," Milo answered. He needed to figure out a way for them find Svetlana, reap their bounty. Writing poems, writing anything for that matter would never net them a dime.

"This one is different. You would like it." Jak drummed his thick fingers on the table.

Milo shrugged.

Jak continued, "It is still about Mother Russia, of course. But it is in this new style I have been experimenting with, called Haiku. It's Japanese."

"Five syllables, seven syllables, five. I know what Haiku is."

"Not syllables, brother. Sounds. They are different."

"Whatever."

Dillon turned his head. "Can you guys at least talk in English? It's so boring laying here."

"Shut up or I will shoot you in the mouth," Jak said in English. "How is that?"

Dillon turned his head away, sullen.

Jak cleared his throat, and back in Russian said, "It goes like this,

Mother, we are your lambs.

In your fruits we feel freedom.

Your mango is for our slaughter."

"The last line does not fit, too many syllables," Milo said.

"I told you, sounds not syllables." Jak began to count off the sounds in each line and Milo interrupted him.

"We need to find Svetlana, not talk about Haiku."

"It soothes me."

Dillon said, "If you're going to continue in Russian, can you at least feed me? I'm chained up like a goat and starving down here."

"It is your fault we are in this situation. You don't deserve food," Jak said.

"You guys better hope this bump goes down. I have a photo

shoot with Master Bait fishing magazine next week. It's like a centerfold and everything."

"I said shut up." Jak stood and yanked the pistol from his chest holster.

"Feed him something," Milo said. "I need quiet to think."

Dillon turned to Jak and said, "Great. Do you have any, like, protein powder and almond milk? You know, for like a smoothie. Maybe fresh strawberries or blackberries, too? And whey protein would be best if you have that. It tastes *whey* better than soy. Get it?"

Jak walked across the kitchen and opened the party cooler they'd stolen from Target. He pulled out a bag from the icy water and shook it off. From the bag, he drew out a small hunk of pinkish gray meat and a piece of bread.

"Bread gets stale on ice, you know. You should just leave it out," Dillon said.

"Then it would mold from the humidity," Jak said, tossing Dillon the food.

Dillon sat up, propped his back against the table leg, and took the food. "What is this, anyway? Baloney?" He inspected the meat.

"Beef tongue."

"Oh barf." Dillon reached up and placed the meat on the table, but it fell through the slats and landed on his head.

Milo reached over, fetched the meat from Dillon's hair, and took a bite of it. He said with a half-full mouth, "You are sure this act of sex was being filmed?"

"Of course, I was in it," Dillon said while chewing his bread.

"And it is of good quality? You can tell it is Svetlana?"

"It was epic. She even meowed a couple of times, you know, in response to my primal growl. It'll be worth a fortune, I'm telling you. But like I said, I have no idea where she went. I'm of no use to you. I gave you the million dollar idea, so now you should just let me go."

"I think you do know," Milo said.

"C'mon man, I told you a thousand times. I'm sorry. I'll help you start a new club, talk it up, you know? Make it the place to be seen."

"I don't want the club. I want the money."

"I can't help you." Dillon shrugged as he popped the last bite of bread into his mouth.

Milo's phone buzzed on the counter across the kitchen. He got up and answered it in English, "What have you found?"

The female voice on the other end gave him the information he'd been hoping for and more. Much more. The excitement cleared Milo's mind. So much so, that he didn't need to bother writing it down. It was instantly locked into his memory. Thanking the helper, he promised to look her up the next time he was in Albany, New York.

Of course, that would be never.

Milo ended the call and turned to Jak.

Jak said, "So? Who was this?"

Milo said, "A little bird." Then he turned to Dillon. "It appears our friend here has more of a background than that which came out in the trial."

Jak said, "He's adopted. We already know this."

"In fact, he is not adopted. Isn't that true, Marcus?"

"Who is Marcus?" Jak asked.

"Shit," Dillon said.

"His real name is Marcus Goldstein, not Dillon West. That was fabricated for his *Hollywood career*."

"Goldstein? He sounds Jewish," Jak said.

"That's because his parents *are* Jewish. They live at 333 West 72nd Street in Manhattan. His father is a dentist and his mother is Dr. Goldstein's assistant."

"What do you want from them?" Dillon said.

"It isn't what I want from them, Dillon. It is what I want to do to them." Milo walked over and leaned down low as he continued, "I want to drill each and every tooth from your mother's mouth before having Jakov here pull each of your father's teeth."

Jak said, "I'm very good at pulling teeth. If you don't count that liquor distributor. But his gums were—"

"And then," Milo said, cutting his brother off. "I will shove all those teeth down Dillon here's throat…"

Dillon gulped audibly.

Milo finished, "Until he chokes to death."

"That would make for a lovely poem. Or Haiku. Either one," Jak said.

Dillon looked to Jak and back to Milo. "What do you want me to do?"

Milo drew out and tapped his Glock pistol against the steel table. "I want you to help us find Svetlana."

Dillon nodded vigorously. "I can do that."

Milo smiled. "I thought you could."

Finn shifted into neutral and pressed a button to disengage the Jeep's four wheel drive as they reached the Powder Point Bridge. Nearing civilization, Finn's phone buzzed in his pocket. He drew it out and looked at the screen. Seventeen missed calls.

"Go ahead," Nikki said. "Say it."

"Congratulations. You beat my mom."

"Dammit. How many?"

"She called nine times to your six. But she smoked you in messages. Five to one."

"Why would she leave five messages?"

"She's a mom. Free pass. You, though. Six calls, really?"

Nikki wrinkled her nose. "You're like a giraffe. Thought I might get lucky, catch you in the path of a cell signal."

"Excessive."

The other two calls were from Lindsay Blake, Svetlana's new

publicist. Finn had met her once and talked to her a few times on the phone about Svetlana. In fact, he was the one who had introduced them, after meeting her at the gym.

But no call from Svetlana.

Finn dialed her number and the call went straight to voicemail, so he asked her to call him back and hung up.

Next, he dialed Lindsay's number and waited as traffic bottlenecked at the end of the bridge. The wind was whipping now and made the soft top of the Jeep rattle.

Lindsay answered after three rings, "Patrick, thought you'd never get back to me." She was out of breath.

"This a bad time?"

"Power yoga, I'm fine. Where the heck is Svet?"

"I was kind of hoping you could tell me." He imagined Lindsay standing there in her yoga tights with her long red curly hair and freckles. She was the kind of woman who looked best without all the makeup. Natural and God-molded.

"All I know is that I get a call from Dillon West's agent about an hour ago, demanding I force her to come in and make a statement."

Nikki held up her hands inquisitively, and Finn shook his head as he headed to Route 3, toward Boston. "Where's Dillon?" he asked.

"Nobody knows."

"Okay, look, I have an idea. I'll call you back in five."

"Patrick, don't leave me out. I'm connected to this little mess and it's my name too. I want to be kept involved."

"I'll call you back, promise." He hung up, then scrolled his address book until he came to the American Express number. He pressed dial and a girl with a distinct Indian accent answered claiming her name was Margaret. Finn suppressed a smiled as he said, "I need to know my last three transactions, please. On the additional card."

Nikki pushed all the way back against the window and crossed her arms. "You fuckin' kidding me, or what?"

Finn slowed to the stop light and held up a hand to quiet her.

Nikki continued as Margaret placed him on hold to search the transactions. "Let me understand this, you gave Svetlana a credit card? *Our* company credit card? Are you out of your fuckin' mind?"

Finn whispered, "Look at it this way, now we can track her movements, see where she is and find her."

"At a pretty penny, I might add."

"It won't be that bad."

Nicki slapped the dash with an open palm. "You're fuckin' her, aren't you? Those Russians are unbelievable."

"Relax, I'm not…sleeping with her."

"No, but you want to."

Finn moved to answer, but with an inhale he hesitated just the barest of moments. It was enough.

Nikki shouted, "I knew it! God, you men are all the same."

Finn said nothing. He waited for Margaret to come back on the line while a lovely classical tribute to Guns N' Roses' *Welcome to the Jungle* played in the background.

Nikki didn't back off. She said, "I hope she buys like a dozen pairs of those Jimmy Choo shoes, and some Kate Spade shit, too. Hell, I hope she buys a whole floor of Saks perfume…"

Finn blocked the rest of Nikki's little tirade out as Margaret returned with the information on Finn's account. As she told him what the purchases were, his knee-jerk was first to faint, and then to ask how the hell she was able to charge these items without notifying the person responsible for the account. But he realized that this was American Express. The Platinum Card. They prided themselves on not interfering with the customer's experience, no matter how extravagant.

Feeling a bit numb, Finn thanked Margaret and hung up the phone.

Nikki raised her eyebrows and said, "I hope it was a fur fuckin' coat."

"Not exactly," Finn said.

"Worse?" She smirked.

"It seems…" Finn tried to collect his thoughts on this one, honestly unable to believe it was true, as he said, "Svetlana chartered a Gulfstream…at the cost of five thousand dollars per flight hour."

Even Nikki had no words, as Finn finished, "To Christmas Island. On the far side of Australia."

CHAPTER THREE

AFTER A QUICK STOP BACK AT FINN'S house and then Nikki's place south of Boston for each of them to pack a bag, then a short call to Lindsay and also Svetlana's hairstylist, Jon LaChapelle, they all agreed to meet at Miami International Airport after the first leg of Finn and Nikki's flight.

En-route to the Indian Ocean.

What was another couple of plane tickets, Finn figured. At this point, he was in Svetlana Retrieval Mode, soon to be in Svetlana Damage Control Mode, and then hopefully he would find an entrée into Svetlana Repair Mode. Finn's investment in the girl was evaporating. Well, no, actually, at her own initiation, his investment in Svetlana was growing and the likelihood of Finn ever recouping—forget about making any profit on—that investment was circling the drain.

Good news was that they'd beaten the rush of media that would no doubt descend on Saquish Head. As it was, the story was on a continuous loop on all the networks, blaring on every television screen at the airport. Dressed in a threadbare Phish t-shirt from about 1985 and a pair of khaki cargo shorts, Finn topped the look off with a pair of rose-colored John Lennon sunglasses.

Not a chance he'd be recognized by anyone.

Stuffed into an economy seat in row 37, Finn shut his eyes after takeoff and tried to push away all the thoughts and theories around what must have happened in Dillion's apartment. He'd get the real story from the source herself, Svetlana. Still, he couldn't help but kick himself for agreeing to give the girl so much rope in the first place. He should have insisted that she remain on the rigid two-a-day training regimen that tennis-coach extraordinaire Micky Bellini had outlined for her. It would have kept Svetlana out of the nightclubs and focused on her core competency, tennis. Maybe then she would have qualified for the Aussie Open. Hell, she hadn't even qualified for the Israel Open. Instead, she'd been non-stop gossip for the paparazzi.

Not the ideal way to maximize corporate sponsorships.

Nikki, who was seated directly behind Finn due to the last minute purchase of the seats, leaned forward and said, "Look at it this way, you got a shitload of miles on your Amex Card for that flight. Probably even paid for these."

"Very helpful, thank you."

"I bet she racked up enough to pay for her next trip to Vegas."

"Very insightful, I appreciate it."

She patted his shoulder through the opening between the seats. "Always here for you, boss."

She sat back and then forward again. "Remind me why we're laying over in Miami and picking up the publicist and hair stylist?"

"Lindsay thinks it'll be easier to convince Svetlana to come back to the States if we have her and Jon's influence and support."

"I could convince her in about two minutes flat." Nikki made a face.

"You are quite persuasive, I admit."

She smiled at the sarcasm. "LaChapelle is high maintenance, if you ask me. And that Lindsay isn't all she's baked up to be, either."

The twenty-something girl seated next to Finn rolled her eyes at him and placed a huge pair of glossy orange headphones over her ears, making her look like an exotic rainforest beetle.

Finn turned back to Nikki, "Why do you say that?"

"For one, I don't trust anyone who doesn't color her hair. I'm sorry, but, if you're anywhere north of thirty and you don't bother to touch up, you know make an effort, then I figure that you figure that you're too good for it. For the rest of us."

"How do you know she doesn't? Her hair is pretty red."

"The roots, it's obvious. They're *au naturale*."

"That all?"

"No. I also don't trust anyone who does yoga naked."

Finn spun around and peered at Nikki through the seats. "Naked?"

"Yeah, she says it's invigorating. Allows for the negative energy to exit and the positive to enter her conscious and subconscious. Some yin-yang bullshit."

"Naked."

"Oh boy, here we go. I gave you an image and now the rest of your day is ruined."

"I wouldn't say ruined."

"Forget I mentioned it."

"Hard to forget something like that."

She exhaled. "And how exactly is hairdresser Jon going to help?"

Finn said, "You know how tight she is with Jon, I'm surprised she didn't stop and pick him up on the way."

"But *we* are."

"Just go with it, would you?"

"Do I have a choice?"

"Not really."

Nikki huffed and sat back, didn't say another word. Fine with Finn, he needed to clear his mind, rest for a bit. It took a few minutes, but he eventually was able to do both. When they landed two quiet hours later, Finn suggested they go find food and maybe some snacks for the next leg of the flight. That one would take some twenty hours.

"Can you survive that long, without a grocery store?"

"Very funny," Finn said, searching the terminal for anything substantial. Like a Chili's or TGI Fridays. He was suddenly feeling famished and needed to get some solid nutrition, and fast.

Nikki pointed ahead. "Ever been to the Corona Beach House?"

"Sounds delicious."

Settling into a table near the front, Finn sent a text message to Lindsay and Jon, letting them know where he and Nikki were, in case they'd arrived at the airport early for the flight. Then he perused the menu and made his choice. Well, *choices*.

A young waitress named Cheryl arrived to take their order. Nikki asked for a chicken Caesar salad and—*when in Rome*—a Corona Light.

"Watching your figure?" Finn asked.

"One of us should."

Cheryl turned to Finn and Nikki said to her, "You're gonna need a pen, honey."

"I have a good memory," Cheryl said.

"It better be like Mensa good with this guy ordering." Nikki thumbed Finn.

"What's that mean?" Cheryl asked.

"Ignore her." Finn pointed at the menu and said, "I'll have a chicken wrap."

"A healthy start, impressive," Nikki said. "But, what...no appetizer?"

Finn gave her an annoyed look and pointed to menu again. "And an order of nachos."

"Okaaay." Cheryl twirled a strand of her hair with a finger.

"Make those chicken nachos."

"Got it," she said. "Something to drink with all that?"

"Hold on." Finn dragged his finger to the other side of the menu and said, "Also, a Philly Cheesesteak."

Cheryl raised her eyebrows. "That's like, a lot of food, you know. The portions here are pretty big."

"Trust me." Nikki held up a hand.

Finn said, "And how about a grilled cheese? Oh, and an order of fries."

"The cheesesteak comes with fries."

"Then an order of onion rings."

"Got it." Cheryl looked to be mulling the list over in her mind.

"And…" Finn continued, "a half dozen tequila wings. Make those spicy. And some BBQ sauce, too. I'll put that on the cheesesteak."

"Hold on." Cheryl walked off, shaking her head.

"I think you scared the poor thing," Nikki said.

Finn was about to answer her, but Cheryl returned, pad and pen in hand. She said, "So that was…"

Finn repeated it all and said, "Oh, and a bucket of popcorn. You'll have some of that, won't you?" he asked Nikki.

"Probably not."

"That's okay." Finn flipped the menu over. "You having dessert?"

"Wasn't planning on it."

Finn said, "How about a Corona Cancun Brownie Sundae to top it off?" He peered at Nikki over the menu. "You can have a bite if you want. Or anything else, of course."

"Sounds delicious, all of it. Really."

Finn handed over the menu. "And a Corona for me, too."

"Hers is a Light." Cheryl pointed the pen at Nikki.

"Better make mine a heavy."

Cheryl walked away and Nikki said, "Jesus Patrick, you just ordered enough food to feed, like, the whole flight."

Finn glanced down at himself. "I probably add up to a full row of passengers, wouldn't you say?"

"We should alert the pilots, tell 'em to shove an extra few gallons of fuel in the plane."

"Nah, I'm seated in the back, keeps the wings up."

She shook her head. "You need to think about cholesterol and trans-fat and all that shit."

"Trans-what?"

Cheryl returned with the beers and said, "I forgot to ask, do you want that all brought out together?"

Nikki said, "You have a trough? That'd work."

Finn said, "Just bring it out as it's ready, that's fine."

She walked away again, shaking her head.

"Traumatized for life."

Finn shrugged. "What did I do?"

Before Nikki could answer, a high-pitched male voice said, "I'm not eating in there."

Finn turned to see Lindsay and Jon walking up to their table. Lindsay had a puffy, flower-print duffle slung over her shoulder and was wearing almost no makeup, as usual, and looking great. Jon, wearing black and gold oversized sunglasses, rolled a full-size carry-on suitcase—bright purple—behind him.

Lindsay greeted and shook Nikki's hand, then leaned over to Finn and gave him a peck on the cheek. "Patrick, always nice to see you."

Her voice was the perfect pitch for a lady and a bit scratchy, and she smelled like lavender and the spice of habanero. Though maybe the heat was coming from the kitchen.

Jon kissed Nikki on both cheeks and blew a kiss to Finn. "Hi there, big boy." And he waved.

"Hey Jon." Finn pulled up a couple of seats for them, and they sat, Lindsay closest to him.

Finn pointed at the purple suitcase. "Jon, you know we're only going for a night, right?"

"Oh it's mostly shoes. You know, island wear is so difficult."

Nikki looked at Finn and raised her eyebrows. *See?*

Jon leaned forward and whispered, "So, trouble has found our girl again?"

"Sheer coincidence, I'm sure." Nikki rolled a tongue inside her cheek.

Jon glanced at her and continued, "You have to admit, though, it's all so exciting. Everyone is talking about it."

Lindsay sighed and said, "They're talking about a possible sex tape, not the murder."

"I know, I know! It must be hot, too." Jon sat back and waved a hand. "Well, if you're into the straight thing."

Finn turned to Lindsay. "Any evidence whatsoever that there was a camera there yesterday, not just a tripod to fuel all this speculation?"

Nikki said, "Are you kidding? I bet that little perv, Dillon, films everyone he's with."

"Either way, we have to convince her to come clean," Lindsay said. "Damage control begins with culpability. Then we can begin re-building Svetlana's brand."

"Her brand? What, like Dexter?" Nikki said in full sarcasm.

"We don't know she was involved in all that," Jon said.

"Seriously?" Nikki snorted. "I figure Svetlana's fuckin' some washed up actor and his friends, and it gets out of hand, probably drugs involved—"

"Whoa, whoa, whoa." Finn put up both hands. "All we know is that she was in the building. Presumably, yes, up in that apartment with Dillon, doing…God knows what. But that's it. We'll find out the rest when we locate Svetlana, okay? Until then, let's keep our theories to a minimum and to ourselves."

And before anyone could respond to that, Cheryl and three other waitresses returned with endless plates of food.

"Christ, Mary," Jon said. "You shouldn't have ordered for us."

"We didn't," Nikki said.

The table wasn't large enough to hold all the plates, so Cheryl pulled another over and pushed it against the first.

Lindsay ordered a white wine and Jon just scrunched his nose and shook his head.

Finn offered to share his food, but nobody took him up on it, so he dug right in, eating the chicken wrap in two bites and the grilled cheese in four.

"My heavens," Jon said, putting the tip of a finger on his lip. "Where do you put all that?"

Nikki, chomping on her salad, said, "I told him he needs to cut down. Cholesterol and all."

"It's not like he's fat," Lindsay said, leaning back and giving Finn a long looking-over. "Actually, looks like he's in solid shape. Just big."

Finn finished his bite, swallowed, and said, "I am able to hear you while eating. The auditory mechanism doesn't shut off."

"We just love you, Patrick. We're concerned for your health and well-being." Nikki tipped her Corona to him and took a swig.

"I think it's kind of hot." Lindsay winked. "Like a great big bear."

"Well...thank you." Finn glanced at Nikki who performed a gigantic eye roll for him.

Jon spread the fingers of his hand, finger still on the lip. "I'm just in awe."

Finn finished most everything, including a second Corona, leaving just a single onion ring as a gift to the gods and taking the box of popcorn for the flight. When they boarded, funny enough, the girl who had been seated next to Finn on the first leg must have stayed in Miami, as Lindsay ended up booked into the seat next to him.

Nikki thought it was *just lovely*. That Finn and Lindsay *could spend the whole flight talking about the wonders of The Universe and the power of quantum physics and the secret to global peace and happiness.* Then she pretended to jam a finger down her own throat and said, "I'll be asleep behind you."

Meanwhile, Jon had somehow been upgraded to First Class.

"Happens all the time," Lindsay said.

After the plane took off, Finn logged onto the Internet with his tablet computer to read about Christmas Island. He wanted to get a sense of the landscape and culture before they got there.

Interested too, Lindsay flipped up the armrest, which both blocked Nikki's view from behind them and allowed Lindsay sit closer to Finn. Presumably to see the screen in his lap better, but she also touched his arm a number of times. Her hand was warm and her touch transferred a certain amount of energy each time she did it. After soaking enough in about Christmas Island, they talked all the way to Miami, discussing everything from Finn's days as a semi-pro hockey player to Lindsay's practice of yoga—nothing about the naked bit, too bad—to Finn's former profession as a high class bounty hunter. Pretty much everything but Svetlana.

Within an hour of the second take-off, and after dinner service —yes he ate again—both Finn and Lindsay had drifted to sleep for the night.

"Are you sure this is where she will be?" Milo said to Dillon as they boarded the third flight of the day. This one to an Australian city named Perth. Milo had never even heard of the place before today. But it was the only way to get to this stupid island that Svetlana had fled to.

"I told you, Svetlana won't trust anyone else with this...project. Her man is on Christmas Island." Dillon slid across to the window seat. "Can I sleep on this flight, please? No more questions. Your moods are like draining me."

"You have not seen me angry yet."

"Ugh." Dillon pulled the Yankees cap he'd bought at Miami International down low and leaned his head against the window, then closed his eyes. "Give it a rest, dude."

Meanwhile, Jak pulled out a small journal and pencil from his black canvas backpack and slid across to the middle seat. "I will write a poem about Christmas."

"That sounds nice," Milo said.

"Really?"

"Sure, but do me one favor."

"What is this?" Jak asked.

Milo turned up his collar and closed his eyes. "Don't fucking read it to me."

"Let me understand this," Nikki said as the four of them made their way through Sydney customs and toward the next flight to Perth. "It's gonna take us five separate flights and almost fifty hours to get to this fuckin' island?"

Finn, who had tried to call Svetlana again the moment they landed—no luck, he hung up—did the math. "Fifty-two hours to be exact."

Nikki said, "I don't get it. My phone says this place is just south of Hawaii, somewhere in Pacific Ocean paradise."

Lindsay said, "That's *Kiritimati*, which is nicknamed Christmas Island. Different place. Way too small to hide there. And nothing to do but fish. The original Christmas Island is a colony of Australia, a place where refugees are held. I'm sure you've seen it on CNN."

"That fuckin' Svetlana," Nikki said.

"Girl knows how to party," Jon called over his shoulder as he wheeled his bag a full two strides ahead of the others. The word *party* came out with about four syllables.

"Aren't you chipper?" Nikki said. "Comfy up in royalty class?"

"How'd you get upgraded anyway?" Finn asked.

"I have a little secret," Jon said. "Well, I'm being modest. It's really not so little."

"Gross," Nikki said.

Jon laughed. "First, I find the flight attendant in charge up at the desk."

"And?" Finn readjusted the strap of the duffle on his shoulder as they walked.

"And then I give her a big juicy compliment. Like, *oh, I love that brooch, where did you find such a treasure*? And then I usually squeal a little." He waved a hand. "Works every time."

"Maybe I should try." Finn glanced at Nikki.

"I'd love to see that," she said.

Lindsay scrunched her face. "Won't work for you."

"Why not?" Finn asked.

"You're a bit, too, how should I say…masculine."

"Oh sister, he's like a tower of testosterone," Jon said.

"So?" Finn asked.

Lindsay put a hand on Finn's arm as they approached the gate. "So, they'll think you're hitting on them. With Jon, he's just telling them how great they look, you know, allowing them to be fabulous without judgment or competition."

"I think I'm starting to understand why he and Svetlana get along so well."

"Just watch," she said, as Jon walked straight up to the desk ahead.

Before the rest of them even reached the counter, the flight attendant was handing Jon a new ticket. "You'll be in seat 2A, how's that?"

"Divine," Jon said as he touched his own hair. "And I'll be doing my highlights like yours from now on."

The flight attendant actually blushed.

"Jesus, he's a machine," Finn said.

"An animal," Lindsay agreed.

After the flight to Perth, the four of them caught a jumper plane for the last leg to Christmas Island. It was a quick and wordless flight and as the plane made its final approach, the wing dipped to one side to reveal a perfect view of the entire island. With short stretches of beaches between rocky cliffs, and tiers leading to a plateau at the center, the island resembled a giant grass and rock wedding cake.

He checked his watch.

In all, it had taken Finn and company a total of two full days to make the trek all the way there from Boston. It was now Tuesday.

He hoped Svetlana hadn't left yet.

As the others deplaned, Finn registered his phone to the Telstra mobile network and checked his messages. Three more calls from Mom and a few agency business related messages, but nothing from Svetlana or anyone else.

Well, except for the seventy-three unknown or blocked ID numbers that had called without leaving messages. All from the States.

Paparazzi.

Finn tried calling Svetlana one last time. Nothing.

While still seated, he sent a text message to American Express and waited. A responding text came back within seconds detailing the last five transactions made on the account: four in various airports—all Finn's—and the last one this morning at a place called Island Mack's. A quick Google search on that place—a local restaurant and bar—confirmed it.

Svetlana was still here.

Relieved, Finn searched his photos for a good one and locked it onto his screen. Then he grabbed his bag and ducked to keep his head from hitting the roof as he headed toward the front of the plane. The cabin door was open and the humid air thickened as he reached the exit. Just like the web pages had said, low eighties and humid all year round.

The others stood in a semi-circle on the tarmac, waiting with their bags. Jon had collected his purple suitcase from under the wing, where a few other passengers milled, looking for their luggage.

Nikki had both hands on her hips. "Should we alert a medic?"

Finn descended the stairs. "Just wanted to be sure she's still here. After crossing the world and all."

"She buy a house?" Nikki asked. "Maybe an estate?"

"Not yet."

Standing there, Finn noticed two large men that had been seated up front on the plane. They were entering the airport with a third, much smaller man, who Finn hadn't noticed until now. The small one wore a Yankees baseball hat and a black jacket. When he turned to adjust his bag, his profile came into view. And it was unmistakeable.

Dillon West.

Dillon said, "I told you, I don't know where she'll be. And I don't want to be with you when you kill her."

One of the larger men slapped the Yankees cap off his head and said in a Russian accent, "Shut up or it will be you first."

Perfect.

Glancing around, Finn spotted an exit at the other end of the short tarmac and said to the others, "Follow me."

Nikki peered at Finn. "Seriously boss, you okay? Look like you saw a ghost."

"Just...let's keep moving." Finn walked straight through the building and to the taxi stand. There were two cabs waiting—both facing left, as Australians used the same road rules as the UK—and no sign of Dillon or the Russian thugs.

Jon said to no one in particular, "Do I need powder? I feel all... shiny."

A man with a sharp black widow's peak asked, "Where to, mates?" He stood poised with a pad of taxi slips.

Finn unlocked his phone and handed it to the man. "My friend arrived two days ago. Can you tell me where she's staying?"

"The Russian." He smiled big. "Oh yeah, she's in the shack on the hill." He pointed.

Shack. That didn't sound like Svetlana, but then again she was on the lam. "That's where we're headed then."

As taxi operator filled out the form on his pad for the driver, Finn slipped him a fifty dollar bill and said, "Her ex-husband and brothers are behind me. Make sure they get lost, okay?"

"You got it, mate." The operator took the bill and winked, as the driver moved a pile of paperback books off the seat for Finn to sit up front.

"You found Svet in less a minute. That was like private detective genius," Jon said from the back.

Nikki being the smallest was seated in the middle. She said, "How were you so certain that they would know where she was?"

Finn glanced at the rear view mirror and spotted the trio headed to the taxi stand, as he said, "Fifteen hundred people live on this island, and only two types of visitors ever come. Refugees and wildlife enthusiasts. Svetlana breaks the mold."

The cab driver pulled away, and Finn watched as the two men and Dillon slipped into the taxi behind them.

"So, these refugees are like, what, defectors?" Nikki asked.

The second cab did a u-turn and headed in the opposite direction, and Finn relaxed a bit.

"Mostly Afghanis and Iranians, I think," Lindsay said from directly behind him. "There're what, over two thousand housed in the detention centers here?"

The cab driver slowed to the stop sign and said with a strong Australian accent, "Almost five thousand now, they're crammed in like olives in a jar."

"Why here?" Jon asked, peering out the window.

"Who knows. They get shipped off to the mainland, eventually. But the boats, they keep a coming."

"So...what the fuck do—I mean, what do people do here for fun?" Nikki asked.

The driver turned up a steep hill and shifted gears. "Most visitors come to see the rainforest. I figured that's what you're here for, yeah?"

"We came to see the crab migration," Lindsay called from the back.

The cab driver looked into the rear-view. "Aye, you're from a nature channel, then? I didn't see any cameras."

"Just to witness, not film," Lindsay said.

"Crab migration?" Nikki asked.

"If you're lucky, you'll see for yourself," Finn said. "According to Wikipedia, it should start any day now."

"Yep. And you can't miss it, once it starts." The cab driver took another hard turn and they ascended an even steeper hill.

Jon said, "What's the nightlife like here? Any clubs?"

The driver glanced back at Jon. "We've some good pubs, if that's what you fancy."

"We're only here for a day or so," Finn said. "No time for nightlife."

"Right then, here we are." The driver shifted the gears one more time and they came to a clearing in the trees, where an enormous contemporary style home came into view.

Constructed of white limestone and steel framing, and maybe ten thousand square feet of living space, the shack turned out to be a mansion worthy of a Pacific view off a cliff in Malibu. They rounded the circle drive in front and the plates of glass allowed a direct view through the house and into the backyard. There, on a white lounger, cocktail in hand, lay Svetlana.

Topless.

A tanned skinny guy in a banana hammock swimsuit emerged from the infinity pool and toweled off, then took the lounger next to her. A laptop sat open on the table to his left, and music was echoing through the house. It looked like a scene from a James Bond movie.

"Party time," Jon called from the back.

"That Svetlana," Nikki said. "She knows how to get a bang for her buck." She leaned forward and said to Finn, "Or, as in this case, your buck."

After paying the driver, Finn led them up to the house and

rang the doorbell.

Nikki crossed her arms. "If it were me, I'd break down the fuckin' door, march through the house, take that bitch by the hair, and drag her back to the United States."

"That's why I'm the one doing the retrieving here," Finn said as Svetlana turned, saw them, and waved. She wore mirrored sunglasses the size of flying saucer snow sleds.

"Maybe break bugnut's neck too." Nikki nodded toward the skinny dude, who was peering over his laptop as Svetlana made her way through the house. Still half-naked.

"Your attitude is something to behold, truly," Finn said.

"What? I'm in a good mood."

Lindsay moved to the other side of Finn, away from Nikki.

"I'll be your girlfriend, don't you worry." Jon reached for Nikki's hand.

"Oh for fuck's sake." Nikki slapped it away.

Svetlana unbolted the door, swung it open, and immediately hugged Jon.

He pushed away, saying, "Eww, don't press those against me, you know I'm allergic!"

Svetlana turned, took Finn's hand, stood on her tip-toes and gave him a kiss on the cheek. "You have come for me, I thank you so much. I have been so scared. So worrisome."

Finn glanced at Nikki who still stood with her arms crossed, and was now giving him a look of, *hope you aren't really buying this shit, 'cause I'm not.*

Lindsay said, "Maybe we should let them talk. You know, after Svetlana puts some clothes on."

Svetlana looked down. "Oh, so embarrassing. I am forgetting I have been tanning of the sun."

Lindsay reached into her bag and pulled out a silk pashmina, handed it to Svetlana. "Here, darling."

Svetlana kissed Lindsay on the cheek, then wrapped the scarf over her shoulders, leaving her breasts still half-exposed. "Please.

You all go into the back and relax. Have a cocktail with Vlad. He is making very good mojito."

Jon said, "He looks cute, is he…"

Svetlana said, "I'm sorry Jon, he is very busy with the work. And…he likes the women."

"A challenge, then." Jon giggled and took Lindsay's hand. They stepped past Svetlana and walked toward the back.

"It's okay," Finn nodded to Nikki. "Go ahead, chill out for a bit. Svetlana and I need to have a heart to heart."

"We could make it more than that, if you like." She let the silk wrap fall off one shoulder.

As Nikki turned to enter the house, she whispered to Finn, "Why not? Either way, she's fucking you."

CHAPTER FOUR

SIR JAMES CHADWICK HAD EXITED THE FLIGHT and watched from behind a pillar near the tall window in the minuscule airport with a large amount of disbelief. How could it possibly be? Was fortune finally on Chadwick's side? Could this be pure coincidence? Or was it something more sinister? Last year, Finn and his pals had made off with over seven million dollars, or was it euros? Either way, it was his and Vanessa's money, and now they could get it back.

The sheer luck of it all was amazing.

Perhaps they were here for Vanessa. That must be it, why else would they come all the way out to a place like this?

In any case, they had no idea Chadwick was here, too. Otherwise, they would have confronted him. But they hadn't as much as glanced in his direction the entire flight. And the nice man they were with, Jon something or other, had been seated right across the aisle from him but had not as much as looked at Chadwick either. It was as if none of them had any idea that Chadwick was on the flight at all.

Chadwick considered that he was mistaken, just seeing things. But that was not true either. This was the sports agent named Patrick Finn and that girl, Nikki, was his assistant. How could one miss a pair like that? The two of them looked like a kitten and a moose walking together. Well, a very angry kitten, anyway.

Even angrier than Vanessa.

On that, Chadwick wondered how she was making on. She had been on Christmas Island for over seven months now, a long time in a detention center, no matter how nice they were. At least she got three square meals per day, more than Chadwick could say for himself. Working at a pet shop turned out to be an all-consuming profession.

It had all been a big accident. First, the tranquilizer gun had fired in a mishap and one of the darts had accidentally hit Vanessa in the bum. Then the smuggler was entering the shop at the exact moment that Chadwick had realized the error. He had no choice but to hide her inside the crate and get the smuggler out of the shop. That gave Chadwick time to clean up the mess and also allowed him to assume the identity of the shop owner who he had —also accidentally—shot earlier. Except that was with Vanessa's SIG.

The shop owner had died.

In any case, Vanessa would be rightly cross with him for the action, having been stuck in a crate with a teenage bobcat for a two week journey across the ocean. Then it had taken Chadwick over half a year to embezzle enough money from playing pet shop owner in order to buy a plane ticket out to Christmas Island to collect her. Well. He could've gone sooner, but all those puppies needed selling first.

In any case, he hoped Vanessa wasn't too angry. He'd done his very best and she should recognize that.

After all, here he was to help her, as promised. She should be happy to see him. But first, he had to let that Finn and the others leave the airport without seeing him. Chadwick would follow, see where they went. Then he would sign Vanessa out of the center and they would ambush Finn.

Of course she would have to wait a bit longer in her cell. But the result would be even better than finding that boy named Relay who had taken the smaller amount of money.

Yes, not only would Vanessa be happy with Chadwick, he

decided that she would be downright thrilled with him.

After telling Finn about the attack and the Russians, Svetlana pouted her lips and said, "You are mad, I can see."

Finn looked down at her and concentrated to keep his eyes above shoulder level. "You chartered a jet. A Gulfstream. On my credit card."

Svetlana said, "What? I needed to go. Why are you being upset with this?"

"That was like, a seventy-five thousand dollar flight."

"I had need for the privacy."

"So wear a ball cap and sunglasses. Fly first class."

"I don't like the ball cap. This is not a good look for me."

"Svetlana."

"And first class. What is this? They don't even serve in proper champagne glass. And you call this food? This isn't fit for the dog."

Finn wanted to answer that she came from a glorified third world country, barely out of a communist state, where they used to beg for toilet paper and milk, how could she suddenly turn her nose up to first class? But he collected himself and said, "You're digging quite a financial hole for yourself. For me."

"I will make it up to you. I promise." Svetlana made another perfect little pout as she said this. Lips that had no-doubt enabled her to get away with countless mini-crimes against the men in her life.

"Why Christmas Island?" he said.

She shrugged. "Vlad is my friend from the childhood. I knew I could trust him."

"You could've called me. That may have been easier. And cheaper."

She nodded once. "You are right. Next time, I will do this."

"Next time?"

"I mean this won't happen again. None of this." She touched his arm.

Finn thought of Dillon and the two Russians getting off the flight today, right in front of him. He said, "What are you not telling me about Dillon?"

"Nothing. I am saying the truth!"

Finn stared at her as he contemplated the tripod and its possible significance in all of this. He said, "So...tell me about the sex tape."

Svetlana scrunched her face up, paused, and said, "This was Dillon's idea. He talked me into this."

"And is there any possibility that the tape shows something you aren't telling me?"

"It would show a lot of things I am not telling you." She leaned close and put a hand on his leg. The inside of his leg. "And maybe you would like some of what you saw, yes? Maybe you would want to do some of these things to me."

Just in time for Nikki to see as she returned from the backyard party. "Am I interrupting?"

"Maybe." Svetlana peered down at Nikki through her giant sunglasses.

"Of course not." Finn stepped back.

Svetlana shrugged at Finn, as if to say, *what?* as Nikki gave him a look that said, *WTF?*

Finn said, "Svetlana was just explaining how there is no need to worry about video evidence of any wrong doing on her part."

"You can see the video, please. Watch for yourself." Svetlana gave a quick shrug and turned to Nikki. "You can watch too, if you like. Maybe learn some things."

Readying himself to break up a tiger fight, Finn was pleased that Nikki didn't pounce. Instead she said, "How about we make a new fuckin' video? You know, one of me shoving your head up your own ass?"

"Okay, Okay." Finn stepped between them and whispered to Nikki, "Our client is in trouble and so let's focus on helping her, yes?"

"Sure, boss," Nikki said, then, "So shouldn't we be headed back to the airport then?"

Finn said, "No flights until tomorrow."

"We could charter the flight. I have the phone number." Svetlana pointed to the door.

"No!" Finn and Nikki yelled it together.

"Then we stay here for tonight. Vlad will make us the cocktails and Nikki can cook the dinner."

Before Nikki could respond to that, Finn said, "I don't think that's such a good idea."

But Svetlana kept digging. "What? She is not a good cook?"

Feeling Nikki bow up behind him, Finn said, "Nikki makes the best baked ziti I've ever had. But that's not what I'm taking about. I mean we shouldn't stay here."

"Why not?" Svetlana gave a pout.

"Because…" Finn glanced at Nikki and said, "as we were getting off the flight, I saw Dillon."

"Shit." Nikki turned away.

"For real?"

"Not only that, but he was with two men. Two very big men. Like, almost my size."

"Jesus," Nikki said.

"And…"

"Don't say it." Nikki raised her chin.

Finn finished, "They had Russian accents."

Jak stood at the edge of the cliff, leaning back slightly to keep his weight balanced, but looked to be having difficulty while holding the ankles of the taxi driver. Dangling a good hundred feet above the next ledge, you would think the man would hang still, make it easier for Jak to hold him. But he just kept wiggling around.

Milo said, "Tell us again this address."

The driver said, "They call it *The Shack* around here." And he rattled off the street and number again, which Milo memorized this time.

Dillon called from the backseat of the cab, a Subaru Impreza, about ten feet away, "There's probably only four or five taxi drivers on this whole island. If you kill him, they'll notice."

"Is this true?" Milo said to the driver.

The man wriggled again, knocking his head against the stones on the ledge below Jak's feet. "He's right. They'll notice straight away."

Milo said, "But then we will have a car."

Dillon said, "Aw man, we have to drive around in this POS? Can't we rent like a Hummer or a Jag or something? This one smells like Aborigine ass."

"They rent Hummers here?" Jak peered down as he asked the driver.

The man said, "You can get a truck, I bet. Maybe with a nice cab and air conditioning." Then he said, "Please. Pull me back up and I'll show you. Or you can take my taxi. I don't mind one bit. Just let me up, okay?"

A pack of cigarettes slid out of the man's pocket and floated. Down. Down.

Down.

Milo leaned to see as the pack skittered against the rock cliff and finally bounced off the rocks below, sending cigarettes in all directions.

The man whimpered.

"You are positive she's staying at this shack? It doesn't sound like the Svetlana we know," Milo said.

"It's not really a shack. It's bigger. I promise, she's there."

Jak raised his eyebrows at Milo. "So?"

Milo nodded. "Let him go. We need to go see."

And Jak released him.

The man screamed all the way down, as Milo spun back and said, "I meant let him free. Not to kill him."

"Oh," Jak said, as the man landed with a thud.

"Jesus." Dillon pushed all the way back against the far door of the back seat. "You killed him!"

"He fell," Jak said.

"You dropped him! I saw it!" Dillon yelled.

Jak shrugged. "Hard to prove."

Dillon shook his head rapidly. "Don't you feel bad about it? Anything?"

Jak stopped tilted his eyes up and said, "Yes...and so I should write a poem."

Milo climbed into the front seat. "We don't have time for poems, get in."

"But it is already forming in my mind's eye. I must write it now or it will be lost forever."

"Write it on the way."

"The creative process requires solitude, brother."

Dillon pointed a shaky bony finger. "Solitary confinement is what you need. Both of you."

"Shut up," Milo said as he started the car.

Jak put both palms together and held then them to his chest. "I have it. But I must write it down. It goes like this,

We are lost little lambs,

Our guide has fallen.

The winter rocks catch us all."

Milo said, "Get in now, or you will join the lamb on the rocks."

"I will write it on the way."

CHAPTER FIVE

"I HOPE YOU DON'T BELIEVE HER, I sure-ass don't," Nikki said to Finn as they walked to the front of a black Hummer pickup parked in front of a faded-orange Jeep. With a total of six passengers, they had to take both vehicles.

"I'll find out what she's hiding, trust me," Finn said, opening the driver's door of the Hummer. "You going to be okay driving that thing?" Finn nodded to the Jeep. With no doors or rear-windshield, it was basically a roll-cage on wheels.

Nikki nodded with a frown. "I've owned worse."

The rest of the crew entered the garage and Jon fussed with fitting his suitcase in the rear of the Jeep as Vlad climbed in the backseat, headphones on, laptop open, and working the whole time. Svetlana's host and the cars' owner, Vlad had not said as many as four words in the past thirty minutes, and two of those were *mojito*.

Nikki said to Svetlana, "Does he talk?"

Svetlana, still wearing the giant sunglasses, smiled. "He is genius."

"Yeah, well, so was Rain Man."

Svetlana ignored that as she climbed into the front seat of the Hummer, pulled out a small bag, and took out a bottle of gold nail polish. She shook the bottle and handed it across to Finn. He glanced at Nikki, who rolled her eyes at him.

After twisting it open, he handed the bottle back to Svetlana, and she said to Nikki, "You need to let him be. He likes the quiet."

"What is he working on?" Nikki asked.

"I heard moaning," Jon called from far side of the Jeep. "I think he's watching pornography."

"Nothing you need to be concerned of," Svetlana called back. Then she turned to Nikki, held up a hand, spread her fingers wide, and painted her nails. "And who is this raining man you speak of."

Nikki looked at Finn. "She's a tit-wit."

Lindsay climbed into the seat behind Finn. He said to Nikki, "Just follow closely, and if you see anything suspicious, call my cell."

"Got it." Nikki took a step away, then leaned back and nodded toward Svetlana as she whispered, "And try not to have sex with that."

"I'll do my best." Finn climbed up and into the Hummer.

A souped-up model, the floor of the vehicle was about three feet off the ground and had a command station to rival NASA—complete with rear-view and side-view cameras, as well as touchscreen GPS. It reminded Finn of the cockpit of a military helicopter. Well, except this one had a custom red and black leather interior.

God-awful, by the way.

With Nikki, Jon, and Vlad ready in the Jeep behind them, they were set to head to the other side of the island. Someplace that Vlad insisted would be safe and the closest to Svetlana's standard of luxury of any hotel around.

After getting the lay of the controls—opposite side from US—Finn started the Hummer and steered them down the long drive and out onto the main road. Built like a civilian tank, literally, the vehicle had so much torque it felt like it could climb a damned tree.

Not a bad little unit for the day's mission.

First, Finn had to get the truth from Svetlana, know what the hell they were dealing with. Then he had to formulate an exit plan off this island and back to the States. But with a single flight in and one flight out per day, their choices would be limited. Especially if they were being watched by the Russian underground.

He said, "Look, Svetlana, I understand you want to avoid reality here, but you are in some serious shit and if you don't tell me what the hell is going on, I have no way to help you."

"I am telling you what is going on. Nothing. I have defensed myself of an attack, and I ran away before anyone else could hurt me."

Finn steered the Hummer around a tight bend—the roads were small and difficult to navigate with so much car. He said, "Have you seen the news?"

Svetlana finished painting one hand and moved to the nails of the next. She stroked the paint onto a nail as she said, "No, what news do you speak of?"

Lindsay leaned forward and put a hand on Svetlana's arm. "Do you remember us discussing you keeping a low profile until you qualify for another tournament? To help protect your brand, maybe enhance your image?"

"Yes, but I think my branding needs the upgrade. More excitement." She held her hand high as she inspected her nail work.

"Because of that, now everyone wants to find you."

"Why me? I was a visitor of the condom. Not even the owner. They should be looking for this Dillon."

"You mean, condominium?" Finn asked.

"Yes. It is what I just said."

Lindsay explained the nuance and Svetlana shrugged, *whatever*.

"They are looking for Dillon, trust me," Finn said. "But they also want to know about a possible video. I think we should consider handing whatever tape you may have made over to authorities. Assuming it helps prove your innocence."

Svetlana looked away. "This will prove nothing."

"Did it show you acting in self defense? Throwing the racket? It sounds like it was all an accident from your end."

Svetlana lifted a cheek and peered at her ass. "This end is no accident."

Finn continued, "Okay, look. Let's say the men were after Dillon. What did they want? And how could you be involved?"

"I am not involved. I am telling you this thing."

And just as Finn was about to dig deeper, a Subaru hatchback taxi approached from around the bend ahead of them. The driver was one of the Russians Finn had seen with Dillon.

"Get down," Finn said to Svetlana.

"Why? What are you meaning?"

"I said…" Finn reached to push her lower in the seat, but it was too late. The driver had already spotted them and was slamming on the brakes and turning around.

Jak spun around and yelled at Dillon as he watched the black Hummer speed past them, "Who is this driving the car?"

"The big dude? No idea, man."

"And who is behind them? In the Jeep."

"I didn't even see them!"

Milo jerked the taxi in a three-point turn and slammed his foot on the accelerator. He said to Jak, "Look in the glove box. See if there is a gun in there, something."

"Jesus, you're going to kill someone else?" Dillon slid low in his seat.

"Shut up, or it will be you." Jak rifled through the glovebox but came up with a box of soggy tissues, an old lighter, and a broken pen.

"Check the back," Milo said, swerving as he overcorrected on the turn.

"Good thinking." Dillon put his hand on the door handle. "I

bet there's a tire iron back there. But we'll have to stop quick and open up the wheel well."

Milo glanced at him in the rear-view. "Do not get ideas of running. Jak will catch you and you will wind up in a poem."

Dillon looked away. "You two need help."

Jak climbed to the back and peered over into the hatchback space behind the seats. "Here, a box of fishing tackle."

"What, are you going to hook him in the mouth? Reel him in?" Dillon laughed.

Jak pulled the box into his lap and flipped it open. Then he drew out a thick revolver of some sort.

"That will work," Milo said.

"Yeah, give it to me. I can send an SOS flare for someone to save me from the psycho twins." Dillon held out a hand.

Jak slapped him in the head. "We are not twins."

"Asshole," Dillon muttered.

Meanwhile, Milo slammed the accelerator and steered the Subaru to the rear side of the Jeep. There was a young woman driving and a man in the passenger seat wearing a purple suit. He looked like a character from Alice in Wonderland. Behind them, a man worked on a laptop. He was wearing headphones.

"Do you know them?" Milo yelled at Dillon.

"No, they're probably from the outback."

Milo said, "They don't look like outbackers."

"And they are in our way," Jak said

"Not for long," Milo said, and he jammed on the accelerator again.

Having caught a glimpse of Dillon West riding in the backseat, Nikki noticed the Subaru taxi way before the driver slammed on his brakes, spun, and began to chase them.

"Heavens, glory. Someone's in a hurry!" Jon said, staring at the side-view mirror.

"It's not just someone,"Nikki said, shifting into fifth and pressing the accelerator to the floor. "That's Dillon and the Roo-skis."

"Ooh, I like that. It sounds like a groovy jazz band." Jon leaned over and peered at the gauges on the dash. "Think you can speed it up a bit, honey? They're gaining on us."

"This is it, fast as she goes."

"Oh God." Jon looked from one mirror to another. "They look like meat-eaters."

Vlad hadn't as much as looked up from the laptop yet. Headphones still on, he just typed away amid the confusion.

Nikki fought to control the Jeep, but driving on the left side was unnatural to her and she overcorrected on a hard bend of the road.

The Russians sped though the turn and bumped the rear of the Jeep.

"Ahhh!" Jon screamed and braced himself, pressing one hand to the dash and the other on the roll cage.

Nikki said, "Fuck you, if you think I'm just getting out of your way, Roo-skis."

Vlad looked up and peered at the Subaru behind them. "Who are they?"

"They're terrorists!" Jon yelled.

The road dipped and then steepened, allowing Nikki to pull away again, but then a sign appeared that showed a hair-pin turn approaching. Finn's Hummer had disappeared up and around the bend already.

One of the Russians leaned out of the Jeep.

"He's got a gun!" Jon ducked his head between his legs.

Vlad typed furiously on his laptop.

"Hold on, everyone!" Nikki jerked the car right and then slammed on the brakes.

The Russian driver spun the Subaru and with the force of the turn, the man with the gun fell back into the car just as he fired a shot. But what came out was not a bullet.

It was a ball of flame.

And it never exited the vehicle.

A bright orange fireball now, the Subaru taxi slammed into the rear of the Jeep and the two cars spun out of control. Nikki's Jeep shot to the left, straight toward the edge of the cliff, and the Russians' Subaru rocketed off the road to the right, straight toward a tangle of rainforest trees and the middle of a waterfall.

Jon yelled from between his knees, "Don't crash Nikki, I haven't even met Lady Gaga!"

And Nikki said, "Well, shit," as the Jeep struck the center of a boulder and vaulted, like a hapless glider.

Right off the cliff.

After rocketing forward like a dying star, the Subaru taxi and the Russians soared—roof ablaze—off the road, over a giant fallen oak, and straight through the stream of a waterfall as wide as an Olympic sized pool and into a massive bed of jungle fauna. Now, enveloped in a thicket of ferns and vines and nestled below and behind the waterfall, Milo, Jak, and Dillon sat in the Subaru, drenched, their feet swimming in a solid foot of water at the bottom of the car.

Not one of them said a word until Dillon called from the back seat, "Christ, you just killed a whole carload of innocent aborigines and then you almost killed us!"

"They were in the way." Milo still had both hands on the wheel.

"Don't worry, brother. I will write the poem to cleanse our guilt." Jak nodded.

"I am not guilty," Milo said, as he released the wheel and opened the driver side door. Water sloshed out of the car in a steady stream.

"You should be," Dillon said. "You kill everybody you meet."

"We never met them," Jak said. "We only drove past."

"Jesus, you two really are psycho-twins."

Jak reached back and gripped Dillon by the collar and twisted until the boy's face reddened. "I told you. We are not twins."

Dillon said something, but it came out about as loud as a hamster fart.

Milo said, "Let go of him and the both of you get out. We need to find another vehicle." He stepped from the car and finished, "And then we need to find that man and Svetlana."

Finn slowed the Hummer down and glanced between the road ahead and the rear-view mirror. "Any sign of either of them?"

"Nothing," Lindsay said. "But I see some smoke."

"Really?" Finn slowed down further.

Lindsay peered through the window out the back of the Hummer pickup. "And what looks like police lights."

"Damn." Finn pulled off the road and to a complete stop.

"Why are you stopping?" Svetlana asked.

"Because we have three friends in a car back there that may have been in an accident?"

"If that is so, then there is nothing you can do about it now. We must keep going." Svetlana pointed to the road ahead. "You said this yourself. I am being looked for and we need to stay low of the profile."

"She's right, Patrick. We can't go back there. We could all be deported on the spot."

Finn thought about the prospect of fumbling right into Australian police custody. That would result in them handing Svetlana to the US authorities. They needed to get her story straight first. Not to mention they'd be dumped into some detention center—those sounded like a mere-star-above-prison rating—in the meantime.

He retrieved his cell phone and held it up to find a signal. Managing to find a single bar of reception, Finn pressed speed-dial for Nikki's phone. It rang five times—meaning she had a signal, too—but no answer.

"Well, we're not leaving them. I'll walk back and see what I can figure out from a distance."

"I'll go with you." Lindsay unstrapped her seatbelt.

"No, you better stay with Svetlana."

"I am a large girl. I can take the care of myself." Svetlana held up her hand and checked her finished nails.

"Yeah, maybe you're right." Lindsay nodded. "Just…keep out of view, okay?"

"Relax. I used to do this for a living, remember?" Finn slipped out of the car and had taken a total of four steps when his phone rang.

Nikki's number.

"Thank God," he said, as he answered.

"Yeah?" Nikki sounded uncharacteristically frazzled. "You got that right."

"Where are you? And where are the Russians?"

Nikki told him about the chase, the flare gun misfiring into the Russians' car, and then all of them flying off the road in separate directions.

"Shit, you okay?"

"I'm fine. Jon's, well…he's a bit shaken up. He's already kissed his ass goodbye twice. And he says he needs a stiff drink."

"I said stiff *one*, not drink," Jon called in the background.

Finn smiled. "We can see some smoke from here, that you?"

"No smoke from our car, but…we are stranded, that's for sure."

"How so?" Finn asked.

Nikki sighed, then she said, "Let's just say that my non-fear of heights is being tested right now."

"We're like a hundred feet in the air. Maybe higher," Jon said, looking over the side of the Jeep.

Nikki parted the palm leaves and peered over the other side. Jon was exaggerating, they were only about forty or fifty feet above the sand below. She said, "I can't believe this tree can hold us."

"Sweetheart, it's huge! Look at the size of those coconuts!"

Vlad had yet to utter another word since asking who the other Russians were. He was busy with his headphones back on, working on his laptop again.

"We need to figure out how we're getting out of this little tree house." Nikki looked over the hood of the Jeep. At that angle, though, all she could see was the Indian Ocean.

"Well maybe Mr. Talkative has an idea." Jon glanced at Vlad.

"Except he's about as social as a hermit crab."

"You think he's one of those people who has a disorder?"

"No. I think he's like a Russian hacker and he's stealing credit cards from about a billion people right now."

"For real?" Jon peeked back at him again. He whispered, "You think he can hear any of this?"

"Doesn't appear so." Nikki glanced back at Vlad, who was bent over the laptop, typing away again.

Jon said, "He's supposedly a genius."

"According to Svetlana. Though she's just a self-proclaimed sex-pert."

"She's not that bad, really. She just plays the part. Know what I mean?"

"Yeah? She fooled the shit out of me. I could've sworn she slept with the entire Miami Heat last fall."

"No, honey. Maybe a few of the substitute players, but even

then, not all at the same time." Jon fanned himself at the thought. "Who could?"

"Oh good. I had her pegged as easy."

"The key to Svetlana is designer goods. Get her a Chanel bag or a pair of Louboutins and she'll stick around for breakfast." Jon winked.

"I see. She has standards, then. And to think...I had her all wrong."

"I hear sirens!" Jon said, turning and twisting.

Impressive. Nikki said, "How the hell did they even know we crashed?"

"Because..." Vlad peeled off the headphones, looked at Nikki, then Jon, and back to Nikki, then held up the laptop as he said, "I was not busy stealing credit cards. I was alerting the police."

"Well fuck me," Nikki said.

Jon leaned over, patted her leg, and said, "Not in a million years, sweet cheeks. Maybe longer."

CHAPTER SIX

VANESSA HOLMES SHUFFLED TO THE END OF the exterior corridor and handed the torn-but-completed half-page form to the attendant behind the waist-high counter. The same exact action she'd performed at the exact same moment, exactly one week earlier.

The attendant took the form, read it, made a note on the clipboard beside her, and placed the form in a metal box to her right. The same response as the week before, and the week before that, and the week before that.

And so on.

And then the attendant turned, located the key on a ring beside her, and inserted it into the padlock that secured the cage of items that—once Vanessa had become stranded and held captive in Christmas Island Detention Center Number Three—had become priceless to her.

The attendant gave Vanessa a wide, toothy grin, making her look like that character from Lilo and Stitch. A cartoon that Vanessa had witnessed no fewer than four dozen times in the past month in the telly room. These people and their cartoons. And they wondered why they were all turning starkers.

The attendant said, "There we are then, your weekly ration. Smoke wisely." She handed her the envelope that Vanessa knew to contain precisely fourteen cigarettes and a book of sixteen matches.

Vanessa took the packet without a word, without a smile.

Then she shuffled back down the corridor and turned left, halfway down, turned right, three quarters down, another right, ten and one half steps, a right, and seven more steps, stop.

The smoking area. It was empty of exiles and imbeciles for a change.

A jolly miracle.

Vanessa carefully removed a single cigarette and the packet of matches from the envelope, extracted a single match, struck the match, and cupped her hand over the flame to shield it from the wind as she sucked air through the ciggie.

Ahhh, she thought, a moment of Heaven while she wasted away in Hell.

Savoring each inhalation and holding it to the maximum of her capacity, Vanessa stared out at the Indian Ocean in the distance. She tried to think of something, anything, but with less mental stimulation than a Congressional filibuster in the past two hundred and seventeen days, her mind had become nothing more than a sack of porridge.

She needed to take up crosswords or something. Maybe that numbers game, what was it called, Sidoko? Sudiki? Sooki?

Fuck it.

She extracted another cigarette from the pack and lit it. Her day's ration.

Looked like she'd have to trade tonight's mashies for someone else's ciggie ration again. Lamb and Potatoes, Chicken and Rice, Mystery Meat and Mashies. The three staples of dinner in this institution.

She had to find a way out. She had to find a way off this blasted island and get back to the United States. She had to find Chadwick.

Because she had to kill him.

The bastard who had betrayed her. Stuffed her inside a box. A box that contained a live animal. And not just any animal, one with claws. And then shipped her halfway across the world in it.

She felt her face.

Razor, fucking, sharp claws.

A bloody bobcat, for God's sake.

She was lucky she'd used the helmet and the gloves wisely, knocking the damned beast out by striking it in the skull. But that had made such a ruckus that she'd been discovered by the ship-hand. He'd promptly taken her into custody and handed her over to the authorities here at Christmas Island Detention Center Number Three.

She'd been imprisoned as a stowaway ever since.

Chadwick would pay. He would. He would fucking pay.

She thought this over and over as she smoked the second cigarette to the very nub, so small that she singed her fingers for the umpteenth time. She stubbed the nub out and kicked it through the metal fencing and onto the threadbare grass on the other side. Then she turned and gave the CCTV surveillance camera the finger.

Vanessa trekked back to her dormer. Seventy-nine steps in one long row.

She opened the door to find her roommate, Chakra or Chankrara, whatever, sitting at the center of her bed and watching Dr. Phil.

'My Spouse Acts Like a Child' was the name of this episode.

She didn't know how the small Iranian woman could stand to watch any show on that ten inch telly, no less Dr. Phil. Senseless dribble, it was.

Vanessa peered at the digital alarm clock in the corner. One hour and seven minutes until dinner. Sixty-seven minutes of nothing.

She couldn't stand it anymore. She was going to burst. She was going to be like one of those people you read about who is walking down the street in the middle of Puerto Rico or Rio de Janeiro or something—why was it always a Latin country that this happened in, anyway?—and then out of nowhere, no warning, no hint, nothing. Just a sudden and immediate event, no different than being struck by lighting or a runaway car. You're just walking along and *WAMMO*.

Spontaneous combustion.

Vanessa was sure of it. She was on the edge, the very precipice of finality. And it would happen soon.

She shuffled to the tall chest against the wall and slid open the top drawer, then drew out the pill bottle.

One sorry excuse for a generic version of Xanax left.

She'd already taken twice as many this week as last, and knew they wouldn't give her another medical ration for at least ten more days. It would take another trade to make up the difference. So, there goes the Mystery Meat. She'd have to wait until tomorrow for her next meal.

Fuck it.

She popped the pill in her mouth and exited the dormer. Down the hall to the left, sixteen steps, a right turn, eleven steps, a left, nineteen steps. She stopped at the water fountain and waited in a line of four people.

The pill began to dissolve between her gums and her lip.

The second one in line drank a veritable lake from the fountain. For God's sake.

The next one was apparently trying to drown herself.

The bitter pill continued to dissolve until it was nothing more than a tiny pile of grainy wash in her mouth. No sense having any water now, she thought.

Fuck it.

Foregoing the drink of water, she turned and walked back to the dormer. But just as she arrived at the door, a man in dark blue shorts and a light blue shirt approached her. He carried a clipboard in one hand and a walkie talkie in the other. A Christmas Island Detention Center Number Three Guard. Lovely.

The guard clicked the button on the radio and said, "I think I found her."

Vanessa stopped before him and wondered what it would be this time. Last week, she'd been placed in isolation for what had been deemed *antagonistic behavior toward other detainees.* She'd explained that if the other prisoners wanted to retain their vision, that they would be wise to keep their sticky mitts off of Vanessa's belongings.

To which, that guard had responded with some false sense of superiority, the magazines were for the general population, not any one individual's to retain as their own.

And then Vanessa had challenged him to try and take them from her himself.

She'd spent five days in solitary-containment for her response to that one.

And the guard—she'd heard from the other prisoners—had spent three days in the infirmary only to emerge with a patch over one eye.

She smiled at the thought.

The guard before her now nodded. "Vanessa Holmes?"

"Maybe."

"If you are, you'd be smart to answer yes."

"Why's that?" Vanessa swayed a bit, as the fake Xanax had begun to take effect, having gone straight into her bloodstream and all.

"Because this is your lucky day. Your time here has come to an end."

Vanessa stared at him, dead-panned. "If you are toying with me, you are hereby advised that you may lose vision in one eye."

He rolled his tongue inside a cheek. He held the radio to his mouth and clicked the button. "It's her."

She smiled.

"Follow me." The guard half-turned and said, "Better yet. Go ahead, I'll follow you."

"Brilliant," she said. "Let me get my belongings first." She entered the room, grabbed the annual issue of Vogue Australia from under her pillow and exited without saying goodbye to *what's-her-face*.

It had taken them a total of nine-hundred and forty-four steps to reach the exit vestibule, where they then were identified and cleared through three separate electronic steel gates. The same sort they'd used in the basement of that MI6 interrogation cell in Poland. The place could hold a T-Rex captive, for God's sake, why we're they so intent on calling this a detention center and not a maximum security prison?

In any case, without a trace of ceremony or pomp, the guard held the clipboard out to Vanessa, pointed out the line for her to sign, mumbling all the while, then called security central or whatever to have the final doors unlocked.

And with a single smile and a nod, he freed her to exit to the dirt road.

Vanessa glanced back, swayed—the Xanax was really in full effect now—and wondered where the hell she was supposed to go and how on earth she'd get there in her condition.

But just as she'd had the thought, she vaguely remembered the guard saying something about a man to collect her as she signed that last set of papers. And so she looked up, surveyed the street, and paused her gaze upon a small red hatchback vehicle. Inside, sitting behind the wheel and grinning like a full-blown wanker, was the man she'd been dreaming of all these days out here. It was him, truly and undoubtedly him.

Sir James Chadwick.

The dead man walking.

He exited the car, saying something no doubt idiotic that the blood boiling in her ears thankfully drowned out completely. Then he walked over to Vanessa and, all the while waving, he bent to give her a hug.

And in that moment, the effects of the Xanax all but evaporated as every ounce of energy that Vanessa had saved for all those months, every drop of adrenaline, every atom of anger, returned.

The door behind her clicked twice, indicating that her release from Christmas Island Detention Center Number Three was now final.

Chadwick said, "...missed you so much, Vanny!"

Vanessa held one hand in a tight fist, the other gripping the rolled up Vogue. With her strength coiled like a rattlesnake's, her mind and soul separated from her physicality, like an out of body experience. Then, without a word, she leapt forward, swiped the magazine like a pipe across his skull, knocking him to the ground.

And she beat the living shit out of him.

With five police cars surrounding them, seventeen policemen in total, it was like they'd sent the Aussie militia to stop some sort of terrorist threat that Milo and Jak somehow posed. They even arrested the dopey kid Dillon along with them. Then they'd shoved them into a police van, hands zip-tied behind them, and driven straight to a facility that housed thousands of other prisoners. Something called Christmas Island Detention Center Number Two. Constructed of concrete and metal and having a thick wire fencing that ran from ground to roof, it looked like a giant chicken coupe. One that a mountain lion couldn't break out of.

In fact, there was even a bobcat roaming the space in a long pen, just outside the sleeping facilities.

As the guard left them in their room, Jak said of the bobcat, "He is...how you say...adorable, yes?"

"It's a fucking predator," Dillon said. "Not a house-pet."

"I will name him Feliks."

"Oh rich, like Felix the Cat."

"Not like the cartoon. It is named after the famous Russian anti-hero of The Man From St. Petersburg. F-E-L-I-K-S."

"Do you know how psychotic you sound?"

"My voice is steady and even. I do not sound psychotic."

"Yeah, so is Charles Manson's."

"He is singer, yes? The Mansons. I like his voice."

"No, the mass murderer, you imbecile."

Jak turned and whispered, "You are lucky there is a guard here, or I would crush your skull like rasping berry."

Dillon drew back and said under his breath, "Raspberry, moron."

The guard opened the door to their room, glanced at Dillon and Jak, shook his head, and left.

Entering their room, Milo took stock. With a desk and a chair, two sets of bunk beds, and chest of drawers, it was something between a Gulag holding cell and a first floor room at a Detroit EconSuites.

"This will not hold us." Milo tapped on the wall with the back of his fist. Then he circled the room and looked at the ceiling. "We will not be staying."

Dillon climbed to the top of one of the bunk beds, and Jak sat on the bunk below him.

Dillon placed his hands on his knees, palms up, like a yoga student. "I think we'll be headed back to the United States in about an hour. That's my guess. Especially when they figure out who I am. Speaking of, they better upgrade us, since I'm a celebrity and everything. This room smells like peasants."

Jak said, "You are an idiot."

"Yeah? You think it's easy memorizing all those lines for movies and shit? Not just anybody could do it. Especially not an idiot."

"Lindsay Lohan does it."

"She's just a little messed up from doing drugs every once in a while."

"Drugs or no drugs, anyone who passes out on a street, the legs open and with no underwear is an idiot in my book."

"Like that book you fill with retarded poems?"

To that, Jak reached up and hooked a hand around Dillon's leg. Then he yanked him off the bed so hard that the boy swung into the bottom bunk and hit the wall.

"My head, you hit my head again!" Dillon rubbed the back of his skull with both hands.

"I will tear the head off if it keeps talking."

"Enough." Milo walked over and pulled Dillon off the bed and shoved him to the other bunk. "Sit there and shut your mouth."

Milo sat next to Jak. "And you. Calm down. We need to be thinking about escape. Not fighting."

Jak shrugged. "I am not fighting. I am disciplining."

"Jesus, I'd hate to see your dog." Dillon crossed his arms and slid against the far wall.

"I do not have the dog. But if I did, I would feed him each day. I would love him."

"Sure. Like a hyena loves a pet rabbit."

"Hyenas do not keep pets."

"Christ, are you brain-damaged?" Dillon looked at Milo. "Tell me, are you his father and his brother?"

"Shut up, or it is you who will be damaged of the brain."

"I'm going to tell the cops here, or whatever they are, that you guys are holding me ransom, that I've been kidnapped."

Milo walked over, leaned down, and stared at the boy. "333 West 72nd Street, remember?"

"Shit."

"Now be quiet and listen. You are going to help, and we are going to get out of this place."

"How are we going to break out, brother?" Jak asked.

"Easy." Milo smiled at Dillon. "He is going to do it for us."

"Me? Ha! I'm an actor, not a psycho villain, remember?" he said the word in a mocking voice. "How exactly do you Kielbasa-heads expect me to break us out?"

"Easy." Milo shrugged. "You are going to start a fight."

CHAPTER SEVEN

IT TOOK A HEFTY DOSE OF INSISTENCE peppered with a colorful menagerie of profanities, but Nikki had convinced Finn that she was safe and that he did not need to *prove macho chivalry and risk being caught by the Christmas Island police by coming to her rescue.*
Nikki then further informed Finn that Vlad had a lineup of Vespas back at The Shack and the three of them would meet up with Finn by sundown.

No worry.

Reluctantly, Finn, Svetlana, and Lindsay pushed on toward the other side of the island, where Vlad's suggested sanctuary was located.

They drove through the main town on the island, someplace called Flyfish Cove, along the coast, and then through a smaller settlement called Poon Saan, which appeared to be Chinese and maybe Singaporean. Then, as they entered the rain forest area, they passed one of Christmas Island's infamous detention centers —basically a cluster of steel buildings with steel roofs, like airplane hangars or giant hockey rinks. Droves of detainees wandered the grounds, and some even sat perched on the roofs of the buildings. It was clear, by the way some of them sat against the fences, that the women were separated from the men by ground-to-ceiling fenced enclosures. All in all, the place looked more or less like a medium security prison.

Not where Finn wanted to spend the night.

And certainly not a place he wanted Nikki to be dumped into. Talk about multiplying your troubles.

After that, it took exact GPS coordinates to reach the destination known as Winifred's Bluff. Hidden deep under rainforest flora, the access road appeared to have been unused for the last decade as the lack of footing caused the Hummer's All Wheel Drive to kick in. Svetlana assured Finn that this was okay, as she herself had been there once already. Finn contemplated this, but said nothing as the Hummer ripped through branches and knocked over small trees that had grown into and onto the path.

After twenty minutes of jungle driving, the vehicle poked through a veil of umbrella-sized leaves to reach a clearing that opened to a cove that displayed a magnificent view of the Indian Ocean beyond.

Finn slowed to a stop at the edge of a cliff that dropped about seventy feet.

Svetlana directed him to drive along the bluff and toward a single palm tree that reached a good thirty feet higher than any other tree in the area.

"I'm not so sure that's a good idea," Finn said, eyeing the uneven rocks and the coral reef below.

"Vlad has done this many times. I assure you."

"Uh huh. And Vlad is Russian. I've seen those daredevils in Moscow on Youtube."

"They are just kids. Not the same as Vlad."

Lindsay said, "Are you talking about the guys who hang off bridges and do handstands on tops of icy buildings? They're nuts."

"They are not crazy. They just have the boredom." Svetlana tapped Finn's shoulder and pointed ahead. "Trust me."

Finn put the car back into gear and a drop of water about the size of a mango hit the windshield.

"Son of bitch." Svetlana peeked out the windshield and up at the sky.

"What?" Finn asked.

Lindsay said, "Don't tell me this is a monsoon coming."

"We will have to hurry. There will be no vision, soon. Go!" Svetlana said.

Finn hit the gas, careful to stay between the wall of flora and the emptiness of the drop-off.

"I bet it's beautiful after the storm." Lindsay leaned forward as she spoke, close enough that Finn felt her hot breath on his neck. "A great setting for afternoon yoga."

He shivered.

Svetlana shrugged. "It is just very wet."

The drops fell faster and smacked the SUV like paintballs. Finn struggled to see through the furious movement of the wipers.

"Shit. Shit. Shit." Svetlana sat back and folded her arms across her chest.

"What now?" Finn asked, squinting at the road and stealing a glance at her.

"I did not finish my tanning today." She pouted her lips and held up an arm.

"We'll find you some spray-on," Lindsay said. "Besides, too much sun exposure gives you cancer."

"This is not true. It is a lie told by the sunscreening lotion companies."

"Svetlana, that's absurd," Lindsay said.

"I am right. My plastic surgeon told me this."

"The one you dated?" Finn asked.

"We never dated, we just had sex. But why does this matter?"

Lindsay said, "It may explain his interest in your tan lines over your health."

"Hey! I do not have the tan lines."

"Then maybe we should start thinking about a Coppertone promo," Lindsay said.

"Not sexy enough for me." Svetlana tapped the dash with her

palm. "Here it is! Slow down!"

Finn eased off the accelerator and turned the car onto a small dirt path leading back into the rainforest. After less than fifty feet, the path turned back toward the ocean and abruptly stopped at the edge of a row of villas. With teak wood decking and meticulous care of the thatched roofs, they could have been part of a Four Seasons resort.

"We will have to hurry to not be drenched." Svetlana pushed her sunglasses up the bridge of her nose and patted Finn's leg. "Will you please bring my suitcases inside?" And she stepped out and strode to the safety of a thatched overhang of the closest villa.

"I've got mine," Lindsay said, as she popped open her door and avoided puddles as she trotted to the villa, her bag slung over a shoulder.

Finn climbed out of the front, into the back, and hauled his duffel and Svetlana's suitcases out. Then he trudged through the sheets of rain and shin-deep puddles up to the villa. Svetlana was busy checking her lipstick, and Lindsay announced she was going to find the ladies room.

Setting the luggage down and kicking off his waterlogged running shoes, Finn peered around the corner. "See the owner anywhere?"

Svetlana was too engrossed with inspecting her nails now to answer.

Finn walked around to the back, where the u-shaped veranda looked out onto the expanse of the ocean. With the monsoon, he could only see about twenty yards out, but still, the bright white coral and neon colored sea anemones radiated from the teal-blue water below.

"Almost paradise, isn't it?" A man seated at the corner of the deck, bare feet extended before him, said. With a tangle of dirty-blond hair and a deep tan, he held a large seashell in one hand and a knife in the other, and was shaving the pale grey, horn-shaped shell into some sort of likeness.

"Almost?" Finn said, glancing around.

"What do you think?" He held the shell up and rotated it. "Not finished yet, but can you guess who?"

Finn studied the carving, but couldn't make anything distinctive out of it. He said, "A dolphin?"

"Ha, ha! The man laughed. "Not exactly, but close. This is Alan Dershowitz, you know, OJ Simpson's lawyer?" The man's accent was not Australian or English. In fact, it was soundly American. New England, perhaps. He turned the shell in his hands and said, "Though it's beginning to look a bit like his pal Shapiro, isn't it?"

Finn smiled. "Those ears cry Dershowitz." He extended a hand to the man. "I'm Patrick Finn."

"Chart Westcott, pleasure." The man shook Finn's hand without getting up. "Go ahead and give yourself the tour, then grab a cold one. May be here a while." He nodded out at the rain.

Finn took him up on the offer, finding the fridge in a gourmet kitchen, and two racks full of beer bottles with names like Hop Hog, White Rabbit, and Four Wives. Grabbing a bottle, Finn popped it open and took a look around. No sand, no dust, no clutter. Place was spotless. And for a villa, it was huge.

Six, maybe seven bedrooms—one door was locked—a semi-formal dining room that looked out to the ocean, an office that looked out to the jungle, and a game room with theatre seating before a big-screen LCD television, along with a pool table and a whole wall of carved shells. Finn could make out Ronald Reagan, Mike Tyson—facial tattoos included—Mick Jagger, Stephen King, Bill and Hillary Clinton, Pelé, and Madonna—singer not saint—to name a few.

Impressive.

He returned to the deck to find Svetlana topless and sprawled out, arms above her head on one of the loungers. Sunglasses still on. A live track of Grateful Dead was playing through hidden speakers.

Chart glanced up at the bottle in Finn's hand. "Hop Hog, a

local brew. Good choice."

"Thanks." Finn took the seat next to Chart and tilted his head to Svetlana. "She does that, sorry."

Chart winked. "I'm not exactly offended."

Right.

Finn nodded at the overhang, as if the sound was coming from above them, and said, "Fillmore East, New York, 1970?"

"Close! Yale Bowl, seventy-one...my first live concert!"

"You were there?" Finn looked him over. He didn't appear to be more than a few years older than Finn. Maybe early forties. Being at the concert even in his teens would make him well over sixty.

"Sure, man." Chart glanced back up at Finn. "It's where my mom and dad hooked up." He danced his eyebrows a few times for emphasis.

Finn smiled. "So, you were conceived at the concert."

"On the backseat of a VW Beetle. It'd be a cliché, except the seat had been removed and was wedged between a Live Oak and a pile of old bongs." He looked reminiscent for a minute and said, "I figure I was a single cell by Act II."

Svetlana added, "The Grateful Death did not play in Siberia."

Before Finn could respond to that, Chart said, "So, what're you running from?"

"Excuse me?"

"Who's looking for you, is what I mean." He studied the shell and shaved a bit off of one ear.

Svetlana turned her head a bit and said, "I told him of the men with the machine gun."

Finn said, "First, it was a flare gun."

"It made a lot of fire." She turned her head back.

Finn said, "You see there's no sun out here, right?"

She shrugged. "My plastic surgeon also told me of the sun coming through the clouds."

Maybe this was all a language barrier issue, Finn thought,

trying to make sense of whatever Svetlana had learned from her so-called medical expert. He said, "I think he was talking about the UV rays, the bad ones. The ones that burn you?" He pointed out to the rainforest downpour. "Besides, nuclear radiation couldn't pass through this."

She smiled and licked her lips. "Then I'll be ready when it does. And you can have something pretty to look at while we all wait." She traced a finger from her neck, straight down between her breasts, over her bellybutton, and to the inside of one thigh.

"Grateful Dead's loss, not playing Siberia." Chart toasted Finn's bottle and took a big drink.

Finn said, "To answer your question, I'm not exactly sure who is trying to find us or what they want. I hope you don't mind us parking it here for a night while we figure it out."

"Glad to have you. I don't get many visitors, and there's not a chance anyone will find us all the way out here."

"So, why *are* you all the way out here?" Finn asked, taking a long drink. Cold and with a hint of pine, it also had the mild taste of meat. Finn's kind of beer.

"Tell you what. You and your friends can stay here as long as you like, but don't ask that again." Chart got up and went inside.

Svetlana said, "He doesn't like this question."

"I see," Finn said, wondering if this was yet another alligator pit they'd crawled into. Drawing out his cell phone, he checked for a signal. Nothing.

He needed to talk to Nikki. There was no way she, Jon, and Vlad could drive all the way out here on Vespas in this drenching rain. Getting up, he raised the phone high and walked around the other side of the villa until he found a spot where a single bar lit up on the phone. He dialed Nikki's number and the signal disconnected as he put the device to his ear.

Damn.

He tried again, holding the phone up and then easing it down to his ear as it connected, but lost the signal again.

Climbing up on a small bench outside the front door, he found the spot again and kept it at that level as he dialed and then leaned his ear out to the phone. With one hand on the thatched roof, a foot on the bench, and another on the railing of the deck, Finn looked like a black bear balancing in a fig tree.

"Fucking torrential," Nikki said, answering without a hello.

"Where are you?" Finn strained to keep his arm still as he leaned out.

"Some hole of diner called Island Mack's. Place smells like fried fish and stale beer, worse than Frankie's in the Boston Market. I'm gonna smell like a fish's ass after this."

"Maybe I should come get you." Finn's leg began to shake as he held the pose.

"Nah, we're fine. Vlad knows the owner and says we can stay. Wait out the storm." The line cut out for a second and came back to Nikki saying, "...some fish and chips and a couple brewskis and my mood will change. Promise."

"OK, listen." Finn glanced around, but he was still alone. He said, "I've been thinking about all this, and I'm not so sure Svetlana is innocent here."

"Fuckin' revelation, boss."

"Yeah, yeah, I know. What I'm saying is, there's got to be some sort of connection from home, these Russians. Maybe they're mobsters and they've been extorting her all along, like they did with Pavel Bure and the NHL players who paid millions to keep these guys away from their families back home." He shifted his leg and continued, "It would explain why she has no money left."

"Her Hollywood lifestyle explains that, Patrick."

"Maybe, but, I still think that may be the connection."

"So, what're you suggesting we do about it? She's not exactly forthcoming, if you know what I mean. And she owes you a shit-ton of dough now."

"So..." he lowered his voice and said, "I'm going to make a few phone calls and I'll let you know what I find out. In the meantime, just stay smart and safe. And get your ass here first thing in the morning. I'm getting us off this island as soon as I can."

Nikki agreed to that and they hung up.

Finn shifted again, switching legs and turning to trade hands. Then he dialed the number to the Beran twins and waited. Billy and Bobby Beran were twin bail bondsmen in Boston who Finn used to work with in his past life as a high-stakes bounty hunter. They were connected in the police world, and they had a line to just about every state and federal database in the nation. They were Finn's go-to guys in situations like this, and their fee for helping Finn was simple.

Playoff tickets.

The phone rang four times and someone answered, dropping the phone twice before getting on the line. "Finn? You better need me to post bail or identify a body calling at this hour."

Finn calculated the time difference. He was pretty sure it was twelve hours back, making it about five am in Boston. "Yeah, look Billy—"

"It's Bobby."

"Right, sorry Bobby."

"So? Fuck you want?"

"I'm kinda out of the country...and I need a little help researching something."

"This have to do with that Russian broad of yours and that actor? It's all over the fuckin' news here. Like every paper and ESPN, twenty-four seven." Finn smiled at the familiarity of the Beran's accent. Not one *r* or regular *o* in any of the words. Hard Boston. Southie-hard.

"Actually, it has to do with that, yes. Remember that night club that burned down? It was called Red Eye, the one that Dillon—"

"Yeah, that dead guy they found in Dillon's condo—the Russian? Supposedly he was the head of security of that nightclub."

"Supposedly?"

"Records are sealed, brother. Whatever compensation settlement they came to, that shit's tighter than a frog's anus. Not even Matt Drudge has been able to crack it."

"Damn."

"What does that have to do with all this, anyway?"

"I'm not sure, but I was hoping you could get me a line on the guys who owned that club. It connects them to Dillon and then maybe will help us connect to Svetlana. I'm thinking they're Russian mob. I need anything you can find out about them. Maybe she was even there that night the club burned down."

"Okay, listen." Bobby said, "Billy and I played hockey with a guy who just moved down there. He's an Assistant DA in the Miami district. You know, Miami-Dade. Of course, that shit's gonna cost you."

"More than the usual?" Finn's ankle had begun to cramp and his back was arched like he was wearing a cinderblock necklace.

"We're talking me calling in a major favor here, Finn. Like this guy could get disbarred or whatever for this shit."

"You just said it's Miami-Dade. That place couldn't keep a recipe secret."

"Still risky, brother."

"So, it's too early for NHL playoff tickets. What're we talking about here?"

"Were talking…" his voice trailed off and Finn could hear him whispering with someone, probably Billy. After a few moments he came back on and said, "Fenway. Game six, World Series. Four seats, touching the Red Sox dugout."

"Serious? Last I heard, they were down two games to one. There may not be a game six."

"Where's your fuckin' loyalty? Of course there's gonna be a game six, cause these guys are gonna' win the next two games. They're gonna' bring it back to Fenway, and then they're gonna' win a third in a row for the championship. That's what's gonna' fuckin' happen next."

"Fuck an A'," Billy said in the background.

"If you say so," Finn said, contemplating where the hell he would scrounge up four dugout seats for what would be the biggest game in modern Fenway history. A game that may or may not even happen.

"Don't you doubt the Sox now, Finn. They need you, brother!"

"Right. I'm on it. They're on a roll, got it."

"One hell of a fuckin' roll. That's for sure."

"Fuck an A'!" Billy said again.

"One more thing," Finn said.

"Fenway for the championship? You name it."

And as Finn's left calf curled into a tight spasm and a sharp pain shot up from his lower back all the way to his shoulder blade, he imagined his house swarming with reporters and news vans. He grimaced as he said, "Do me a favor and take a drive to Saquish. I need you to check on Lobster and Hobey."

"Done deal," Billy said just as Finn's grip gave, the phone fell to the deck, and his body followed in one gigantic heap and thud, shaking the entire villa as he landed on his back and knocked himself out.

CHAPTER EIGHT

MILO STOOD AT ONE BACK CORNER OF the common room and Jak stood in the other corner, both monitoring Dillon. The rest of the hundred or so occupants—almost exclusively Iranian men—were either seated cross-legged, knees touching, or standing shoulder to shoulder and staring at the single large television screen at the front. Dillon had the perfect position for his job, seated in the front corner, closest to the sensor at the bottom of the screen. In his lap, he was hiding a remote control that Milo had somehow swiped from a guard desk outside the cafeteria.

The place smelled like a mixture of boiled sausage and armpits, Milo thought. Not unlike the hockey locker rooms of his youth. He nodded at Jak, who nodded at Dillon, who looked like he was about to shit a cinderblock.

The soccer game featured Iran vs. Uzbekistan, and was a critical match for Iran, as they had to win in order to qualify for the next World Cup. To say that the television crowd was on edge would have been a massive understatement. These people's stares were literally glued to the action before them. It was as if they had nothing left to live for, but this very moment. A silly soccer game that determined their qualifying fate for a tournament they would never win in a million of years. Maybe longer.

Dumb fucking dish-towel heads, Milo thought, waiting for the opportune moment to begin the fun.

Letting the pressure and the enthusiasm build, Milo stood and watched, quietly, from the corner. Jak glanced at him every so often, but he also watched intently from his own corner, arms crossed and ready.

By the twentieth minute, the men were yelling at the television, complaining about the referee, while Dillon had begun to fidget like a ferret with a rash.

By the thirtieth minute, they were shouting at each other, arguing over what was going wrong, why they hadn't scored yet, and the damned kid Dillon looked like he'd broken out in hives.

At the thirty-fifth minute, Uzbekistan took a shot that hit the goalpost, Iran counterattacked and almost scored. Twice. The men were now all yelling, and a few more had erupted in anger. Dillon looked he was about to have a coronary.

Jak nodded his head at Milo, indicating that they needed to get this underway.

Agreeing, Milo closed his eyes and nodded back.

Jak took the signal and waited for Dillon to glance back at him, then did the same.

Dillon took a deep breath, shifted his weight to give a line of site for the remote under his bent knee.

And then he changed the channel.

When Dr. Phil's face came onto the screen, the room momentarily fell silent. As Dr. Phil talked about anger management and temper control, a man charged the television and pounded at the buttons to change the channel back to the game. All the while, swearing in a language that Milo did not understand.

A few of them shouted and cursed in the same and what sounded to be other languages, maybe blaming the television or the guards. They found the channel and stared intently again.

Milo nodded again. So did Jak.

And Dillon changed the channel back to Dr. Phil.

A shoe was launched from the back and hit the screen so hard that it cracked the upper corner. Another man hurried to the television and switched the channel again, as the men began to yell and shout, and curse even louder. They closed in on the television and stayed there, watching the game from tip-toes and the balls of their feet. Dillon was forced to stand and hold the remote under a hand at his side.

Iran took the ball up the sideline.

Milo nodded a third time.

Iran centered the ball to their star striker.

Jak nodded to Dillon.

The striker swiveled and leapt up in the air, scissoring his legs for an overhead bicycle kick.

The men in the crowd sucked in their breaths.

Dillon changed the channel.

And in the next few seconds, the television was ripped from the wall, smashed to the ground, and a full-fledged riot—fists, feet, heads, anything that could be used to strike another man—had begun.

"I think you broke my nose." Chadwick sat pressed against the vehicle's door, hand to his face, as Vanessa steered up the narrow road. It sounded as though he were speaking into a conch shell.

She said, "You're fortunate that's all I broke. Considering…"

"But I saved you!" he said.

"Saved me? It was you who got me into that mess in the first place." Vanessa jerked the car, causing Chadwick's head to bump the window.

"Ow! Slow down!"

Vanessa made a face at him. "Now where?"

He pointed to the windshield. "Just keep going straight. I'll tell you when to turn."

"Where are we going, anyway? It better not be some rodent infested, flea bag motel."

"I have a mind not to even tell you now."

She swerved for no reason, as she said, "You better find a mind to do it, if you don't want a broken arm to go with that nose of yours."

With a hand pressed to the dash, Chadwick said, "You should've listened then, instead of hitting me over and over with that bloody magazine."

"What, so you could give me more reason to strangle you? Dump your body in the ocean?"

"You would rather hear…" Chadwick tapped the dash with a finger, and continued, "that I have news."

"I've a mind to flee this sorry excuse for an island and leave you on it."

"You won't want to leave when you hear this." Chadwick nodded his donkey head.

"Oh this ought to be rich." Vanessa swerved to avoid a family of bright red crabs this time. The stupid critters were crawling across the road as if they owned the damned place. "What, are you going to tell me that you've found us a job? Something that will actually bring us an income?"

"No."

"What then?"

Chadwick raised his chin and said, "You won't believe who is here, on this island, with us. Right now."

"Won't I?"

"Patrick Finn and that little lady terrier of his."

"Nikki?"

"Yes."

"What on earth?"

"I've no idea, but it looked like they had that Swedish actress with them. Svetlana Titova. The blonde one."

"You mean Takitov?"

"Yeah, that's it. In all the gossip mags."

"She's not Swedish, she's Russian. And she's a tennis star, you simpleton. Not an actress."

"She looks Swedish." He scrunched up his face so tight, he looked like a goat trying to pass a melon.

"Well she's not."

"She could be of Swedish heritage, how do you know?"

"Because. She is from Russia. She speaks Russian. She acts Russian. Her last name ends in 'ov. That's Russian."

"But you just said yourself...she's an actor. Maybe she's a Swedish actress playing a Russian tennis star."

"Oh for God's sake."

"Anyway, that's where we're headed now."

"And how is that?"

"I followed them from the airport."

"Followed? As in undetected?"

"Precisely."

"Chadwick, that's brilliant! I didn't know you had it in you!"

"Well, I do." He nodded once.

And Vanessa had a vision of the sack full of euros. Millions and millions of them. They could take it back now. All they had to do was locate that Finn and pry it from him. If he hadn't spent it all already, of course. But he didn't seem to be the type to do that. Surely, he would squirrel it away instead.

Wondering, she said, "What was he wearing? An expensive watch, maybe? Or designer clothes?"

Chadwick sat there, blank-faced, as if he were giving thought to it. "I don't remember the watch, really."

"Was it metal? Gold, perhaps?"

"I think it was hard rubber. Like a diving watch, maybe."

"That's good." As her excitement grew, she fought to stay focused. "And what was he wearing for clothes?"

Vanessa slowed the car, searching for a good spot to park for a bit. Talk this through.

"A pair of shorts. Cargo, I think. With a stain of mustard on one thigh."

Seeing a small clearing ahead, she steered toward it while trying to hide the sudden flush she felt in her face. Her whole body had begun to tingle. She said, "What sort of shirt? Was it collared? Did it look shiny and silky? Expensive?"

"Not at all. It said *Phish* on it. But spelled all wrong, with a P-H, not an F."

"Phish? P-H-I-S-H?"

"That's it."

"That's a rock band."

"Never heard of him."

"It's a *them*."

"Well if he gets popular someday, I may give him a listen. I only listen to popular music, you know, Pop."

"I'll give you a pop, you—" and Vanessa stopped herself. Refocused her thoughts on the matter at hand. The clothing. She stopped the vehicle next to a bushel of jungle plants and under a towering palm tree. "Plain cotton, you say?" She engaged the emergency brake, just for good measure.

"I'd say, yeah." Chadwick looked around. "But this is not the place, we need to keep going. It's up ahead."

"That's right. We're taking a moment, to...strategize."

"We are?"

"Sure." She leaned forward, letting herself feel the excitement, letting all the images flow back into her mind. The ones she'd banished, burned, executed from her mind when she'd been stuffed into that detention center months ago. She had vowed to never ever touch Sir James again.

But that was then. Before she'd heard about Chadwick's brilliant find.

And so the image of Chadwick's treasure came to her mind. As long as a table leg and as thick as a policeman's baton, it was simply glorious. She'd missed Sir James. And after all this time of solidarity, she deserved to see him again.

"Chadwick?"

"Yes?" He peered at her with his purple nose and bloodied lip.

Vanessa didn't mind, though. She'd never see those with her eyes closed. And she always closed her eyes with Chadwick. She said, "I take it all back. You are wonderful." She leaned over, placed her hand on Chadwick's leg. Moved it a few inches. "So very wonderful."

"Vanny!" He slid back. Eyed her. "What are your intentions?"

"I think you know."

He glanced around. "I think you're crazy. Or you are just toying with me. So you can hurt me again."

"Oh, I may play with you a bit, and…it may hurt." She traced a finger along the growing python in Chadwick's trousers. "But in a good way."

"Vanessa, I don't—"

"Shhh. Sit back." She unbuckled his belt, lowered his zipper.

"I don't—"

"You don't, what?" She took hold of the magnificent member. Stroked it.

Chadwick's eyes fluttered. "Trust you."

"Oh, and you shouldn't." The python was now as rigid as a steel cell tower, and almost as tall. Vanessa's mouth watered as she studied it. She whispered, "Oh, how I missed you."

"I…I missed you too, Vanny."

"Shhh. Not you." She pressed a finger to his lips. Then she slipped off her panties and climbed aboard.

And she rode Sir James Chadwick with a vicious purpose and ferocity, reaching climax in seconds. Then another. And a third. And she kept going. Orgasming over and over again. She didn't stop. She wouldn't. She couldn't.

She just kept going and going and going. All but ignoring the gasps and pleas beneath her, Vanessa rode Sir James like it would be the very last time of her natural life.

CHAPTER NINE

HOBEY HAD TWO MAIN objectives for the moment: avoid Cranky Old Man, and find a meal. Shouldn't be too hard. After lifting his leg on Cranky's bitchy cat this morning, Cranky had booted Hobey out the back door and hadn't let him back inside. The escape was as simple as that.

And people assumed bulldogs were dopey.

Hobey had no idea why The Big Guy had asked Cranky to take care of him in the first place. It wasn't as if the two of them were best buds or anything. And the old fella was so sleepy that Hobey had run of the place anyway. With the dog door back at The Big Guy's place, Hobey could have just stayed there, slipped out and found crabs any time of the day. Why did he have to put up with Cranky?

Besides, from the looks of it, the old geezer could slip into a coma before lunch.

So, Hobey trotted past Loud Lady with the big truck that had what looked like a giant cone collar on top—like the one The Big Guy had put on Hobey when he'd kept trying to chew that itch from between his toes. Loud Lady had been there all night and again today, and a few more trucks just like hers had shown up, too. Hobey stopped and let her pet him for a few minutes, and why not? She smelled like Cranky's rose garden. The one Hobey liked to "be a good boy" in, as The Big Guy called it.

Though, it was really just a pile of poop.

Taking one more good sniff between her legs—smelled even better up there—Hobey wiggled away from Loud Lady and squeezed between the slats of The Big Guy's picket fence, then trotted across the small yard and over the dunes. He made his way down toward the water to find himself a crab to kill. About halfway there, though, Hobey caught the distinctive scent of The Long Nap.

Yummy.

The smell became stronger and stronger and almost unbearably good as Hobey reached the water. And there, wedged between two large rocks, belly up, sat the biggest crab Hobey ever did see. In one claw, he held a red, white, and blue can of sorts— looked like the kind Cranky Old Man always drank out of—and in his mouth, a long sleeve of crumpled up rubber. The kind the humans always used when they injected each other with their bodily substances.

It was clear this crab had died a life of excess.

Didn't matter to Hobey, he wasn't one for judgement. All he knew was that this long bodied crab was the kind that tasted damned good for one whole week after The Long Nap. So he took hold of the claw that was empty, and as he dragged the stiffened beast back to the dunes, he heard Cranky calling his name.

Dangit.

Disappointed, Hobey muscled the giant crab up over the dunes and deposited him under The Big Guy's back porch. Then he kicked a good pile of sand up and over the catch to keep the poachers aways. Then, just in case he forgot where he'd made the deposit, Hobey waddled up onto the porch and took one of The Big Guy's smelly sneakers—still wet from yesterday—in his mouth. Yummy. Hurrying, Hobie waddled back and pushed the sneaker into the sand. Snug. Then he hurried toward Cranky, who had called his name yet again. Because for now, Hobey had to go make nice.

And this pending feast would just have to wait for tomorrow.

"You took quite a spill." Lindsay smoothed a cold, wet cloth across Finn's forehead as he fluttered open his eyes. Wearing a plush robe, no makeup, and with her hair tied up into a knot, she looked nothing short of delectable.

Finn moved to sit up, but she placed an open palm against his chest, preventing him. "Shh. Give yourself a minute to catch up."

"Where am I?" Finn glanced around to find that he was in one of Chart's bedrooms. Then he noticed Lindsay's floral bag at the foot of the bed.

Lindsay's bedroom.

"How did I get here?"

She smiled, tipped her chin up and said, "You somehow managed to get this far, and then said you were dizzy and passed back out again." She moved her hand to the back of his head. "Gave yourself a bump the size of an apple. What were you doing?"

Finn explained the cell phone troubles and she said, "Did you think of asking Chart if he had a landline?"

Finn smiled sheepishly.

"Of course you didn't." She took a bag of ice from the side table and placed it against the wound. "Hold this."

"Yes ma'am." Finn watched her get up, walk across the room. With long and graceful, open-footed strides, she had obviously done a fair amount of ballet in her lifetime.

She listened at the doorway for a few moments, then eased the door closed. Then she turned and leaned against the closed door, crossed her arms, and said, "Tell me about you and Svetlana."

Finn eased himself up on an elbow as he held the bag of ice to the back of his head. She wasn't kidding, the bump was huge.

"Not much to tell, why?"

"I mean, are you fucking her?"

Finn laughed.

"I'm serious."

"So am I."

"She's a gorgeous girl. With a rock hard body."

"Right. She reminds me of that poisonous flower...what's it called?"

"She's Russian. Aggressive, she seems to get what she wants."

"Autumn Crocus, that's it. I hear there's no antidote."

She eyed him from across the room.

He said, "Give me a little bit of credit here, would you?"

She smiled, then said, "I believe you." She pushed off the door, took two long strides toward him, and said, "Feeling better?"

"Much." He rubbed the back of his neck. "But I'm sore. My neck."

Lindsay nodded. "You probably gave yourself a muscle spasm, all that weight falling on your head like that."

"You think?" Finn asked, blatantly rolling his head with the hopes that she would come over and rub it.

"So. Bottom line." Lindsay licked her lips and said, "You've never had sex with Svetlana." It came out as a confirming statement, not a question.

"Correct." Finn nodded. All systems go, now. "Why the sudden interest?"

"Because..." she took hold of the robe's belt and tugged it, letting the robe fall open just enough to show the crease above her breasts.

Finn gulped, and Lindsay continued, "I have a special... remedy for muscle spasms." She tilted her head and, holding the robe closed with a hand now, she took one long, slow step toward the bed. "But I need to know how...experienced you are in the practice."

Finn nodded. "I have just enough experience, I would say." He held up a hand. "But not too much, of course."

"Yoga?" she asked.

Finn eyed her. "Is that what we're talking about?"

"Of course." She opened the robe fully, revealing a slender and creamy white figure, with freckles and Brazilian trim, causing Finn to drop the bag of ice to the floor and almost pass out again as she said, "but have you ever practiced naked?"

After moving through a vigorous round of poses that Lindsay described as the stretching phase, she then led Finn through an aerobic phase. Here, Finn performed what he thought to be a near-laughable *Warrior Three* pose, his leg sticking not-so-straight out behind him, and then the *Tree Pose*, where Finn wobbled as he stood on one leg, his other bent inward like he was an enormous, injured flamingo.

And naked as one, too.

They finished with a series of *Vinyasas* and *Downward Dogs* and then moved into *Savasana*—otherwise known as the corpse pose—where they lay flat on their towels, eyes closed, hands to their sides, in silence.

Sweating like a grizzly trapped in a steam room, it took Finn a good five minutes to regulate his exhales and relax enough to fall into a near-slumber.

Lindsay said, "You were better than you're giving yourself credit for."

"You mean that part where I almost crushed you in *Reverse Warrior*?"

"I scrambled free."

"Yeah like avoiding Kong inside a Starbucks."

She laughed. "Please. I noticed exactly how big you are."

"Oh."

And as he thought of something witty to say, he heard a grunt and a bang from the other side of the house.

"What the—"

"Shh. Listen." Lindsay moved to sit up.

Another grunt and then a moan.

"Is that...?" Lindsay crept to her feet.

"I think it is."

And the grunting and moaning became rhythmic. A clinking sound, like wind-chimes joined the medley, and Lindsay giggled. "Well. I suppose it was only a matter of time."

Then she grabbed her robe from the floor and slipped it on. She took a second robe from a hook on the back of the door and tossed it to Finn. "Put this on. Hurry."

"I think they're busy and won't be coming back—"

"C'mon." And she opened the door and tiptoed out.

Seriously?

Finn shrugged into the robe and followed Lindsay who had tiptoed all the way down the hall to the end, where the master bedroom door stood open a few inches. She waved Finn down the hall to her.

An *ouch* came from inside the room. Then a slap and another *ouch*.

Finn crept down the hall and stopped right behind Lindsay. He whispered, "What are you—"

She held a finger to her lips and then whispered, "Isn't that the most wonderful sound in the world? It's invigorating." Her eyes lit up.

"I guess it's—"

And before Finn could finish that thought, she put an open palm on the door and eased it open.

Oh boy.

Then she tiptoed into the room and down the short hallway before her.

The grunts grew louder—along with the wind-chimes—and though the slapping had stopped, the *ouch*es hadn't.

Lindsay stopped at the end of the hallway and hid behind a tall bench that stood pressed to the wall.

Finn rolled his eyes to himself and followed. The warped floorboards creaked and cracked with each of his steps, and he now sounded like a grizzly trying to sneak into a confessional.

It didn't seem to phase any of the others, though.

Finn stopped behind Lindsay again, and this time she reached behind her and placed a hand on the inside of Finn's leg.

Finn stiffened as the noisemakers came into view. It was not exactly what he had pictured.

There, both wrists bound with marine rope fixed to the finials atop a canopy bed, Svetlana stood facing away and prone. Blocking the money shot, Chart stood directly behind Svetlana, both hands on her hips. He was wearing a leather fighter pilot helmet with goggles, while Svetlana wore a large necklace of seashells that clinked with each thrust.

The shells of celebrities.

Finn was about to pull Lindsay back down the hallway when she moved her hand up and up Finn's leg until she reached the goods. Then she stopped, peered back at Finn and stroked him.

Finn eyed her and shook his head.

She nodded back to him, eyes wide. *Yes*. She stroked him.

Finn wavered. *Maybe*. Then he motioned his head to the doorway and gave her a look. *But not here*.

And she nodded again. *Yes, here*.

Finn gave her his own wide-eyed look back. And he glanced around him. Surely not.

And she stroked and nodded, stroked and nodded. Until she brought him to full rigidity. Then she shrugged off her robe.

Svetlana squealed. The shells clinked and clinked.

Chart grunted.

Lindsay took hold of the bench back and bent over before Finn. She widened her stance and wiggled back toward him. And she gave him a look that said, *now*.

Finn hesitated.

Lindsay took hold of him again.

Ouch.

Groan.

Clinkle, clinkle, clinkle.

And Lindsay pulled Finn forward. *Ouch.*

And pressed him to her. *Groan.*

Until Finn had no power left to overcome the utter insanity around him.

CHAPTER TEN

Vanessa had swapped driving duties with Chadwick, figuring the man could watch their surroundings better while she drove. Perhaps he'd recall some small bit of direction or a landmark that would guide them to this so-called residence that Finn and company had taken up. But her hope faded with each minute they drove on.

"You've no idea where we're going, do you?" Vanessa peered out the windshield and up at the towering leaves above her.

"Do so."

"Do not. Look, we've passed that same shanty three times already. And I remember that sign there. The one with the crab on it."

"It's not my fault they have signs with pictures of creatures and none with street names around here."

"For heaven's sake, it's like we're in the bloody Amazon."

"It is humid."

"I'm not talking of that, Chaddy. I mean the fauna. It's as tall as trees."

Chadwick glanced up. "I believe those are trees, mum."

She waved a hand. "It can't be a tree if there's no trunk."

"You're right at that."

"Of course I am." Then she thought of it, the thick oak that Chadwick had stored back away in his own trousers. And she shuddered. They'd done it two more...well, three if you count the last bit, which was more of a fumbling than a fucking...but Vanessa could barely see straight she'd had so many orgasms.

So many, splendid, leg-shaking, toe-splitting, eyes-crossing orgasms.

She shuddered again and flushed just thinking of it.

"Watch it!" Chadwick called out.

"Christ!" Vanessa swerved to avoid a cluster of crabs trotting across the road. All tangled together, there must have been twenty or thirty of the little buggers. "Where did they come from?"

"They look tasty."

"Eww. They remind me of insects."

"Good with butter. And a squeeze of lemon."

"I'll squeeze your lemon."

"You'd better not."

She patted him on the leg. "Don't you worry. I'll take good care of Sir James. Just choke him a bit here and there."

"Vanny!"

"Besides. Those don't look like the kind of crabs for eating. They look like giant dung beetles."

"I'd still eat one. I'm starving. Could eat a whole chicken."

"You'd eat the ass out of a warthog."

"You're so mean to me."

She glanced at Chadwick who had crossed his arms and was staring out the passenger window. She said, "There, there. I was just playing. I'll be nice now."

"Watch it!"

And she swerved to avoid another family of crabs. This one was moving like a pile together, almost rolling across the road. "It's unbelievable. Like an infestation."

"I believe their number are growing." Chadwick studied the road ahead.

Fuck it, Vanessa thought. And as the next patch of crabs walked into the middle of the road, she drove straight over them with a crunch and a wobble.

"You killer!"

"You're one to talk." She gave him a sidelong glance. "Besides, I can't keep trying to avoid them. We'll likely have a wreck."

"You're pure evil, destroying helpless little creatures like that."

"They're not helpless, they have claws. Remember?" Vanessa reached over and pinched Chadwick's bloody nose.

"Ouch!" Chadwick swatted her away. "Those claws do nothing for defense against the large vehicle we're in."

Vanessa swerved this time to purposefully hit the next cluster of crabs. "If they're smart, they'll time their death right and hold up a claw to poke the tire."

Crunch.

"Do you reckon they could really pierce one of these tires? I believe they're made for off-roading and the like." Chadwick tilted his head to the window as if he could actually see the tires from his vantage.

Crunch, crunch.

"Why not? The claws look big enough." Vanessa stared into the rear-view mirror to admire the trail of road kill she was leaving behind.

"Look out!" Chadwick yelled, covering his face.

"Good God!" She hadn't noticed the old man who had suddenly stepped into the middle of the road ahead. Vanessa swerved and the car spun all the way around, a full one-hundred and eighty degrees, as she slammed on the brakes and braced herself for impact.

But the car just stopped. No crash.

Vanessa dropped her head to the wheel. "Bloody, bloody hell."

Chadwick leaned to her. "Are you alright, Vanny?"

And then she heard a loud *pop*. Then another.

And by the time they heard the third one, Vanessa realized what was happening. The old man was vandalizing their vehicle with the sharpened end of his cane.

Chadwick rolled down his window and leaned all the way out.

"Just what do you think—"

Bap! The old man rapped him on the head with the club end of the cane before Chadwick could finish.

"OW!" Chadwick said. "What are you—"

The old man said, "Dem crabs, you hit them, yeah? No kill the crab. No hit the crab." He knocked Chadwick's head again and finished with a finger pointed to his nose, "No even touch the crab!"

And he hobbled back to the same damned shanty that they'd passed four times already. He turned, gave them the international symbol of *fuck off* with a single middle finger, and slammed the door closed.

"What's his problem?" Chadwick asked.

"Maybe they're his pets," Vanessa said.

"He has a lot of them, then."

Vanessa ignored that as she got out to inspect the damage.

Sure enough, their tires had been destroyed.

"Now what?" Chadwick climbed out.

"Well, we can't drive this anymore."

"I say we take the old man's car. It's his fault we can't use ours now."

Vanessa turned to Chadwick, who stood there, arms crossed, all self-righteous, staring at the shanty which consisted of no more than a few rickety boards and a crumpled tin roof. The yard, if you could even call it that, was a thin stretch of stones and dirt. A few straggles of crab weed. Nothing more.

"Chadwick?"

"Yes, mum?"

"Look hard, at the dwelling."

"Yes?"

"What do you see?"

"I can't see the old bugger, if that's what you mean."

She crossed her arms and turned, stared at him. "No. That's not what I mean."

"Then what?"

"Do you think that old man, even if he could drive...all half-crippled as he is...do you reckon he owns an automobile?"

Chadwick peered around as if he was searching for a clue. Vanessa wished he found one.

She said, "As far as I can tell, he can't even afford glass for windows of that lean-to. "

Chadwick shrugged. "Perhaps his vehicle doesn't have glass. Maybe it's a Jeep. You know, a soft top."

"You're the one with a soft top."

Chadwick waved her off. "Maybe we can find a service station, one that repairs flat tires. I heard they can fix those in five minutes these days."

"Five minutes?"

"So I hear."

"Hear this. We need to get moving and find this blasted house you claim you saw Finn drive to. Before he leaves." Then Vanessa reached up and with two open palms, she boxed both his ears.

"Ouch!"

And then she turned and started up the road.

Nikki pushed open the door, peeled the shirt from her back, wrung it out on the concrete, and pulled it back over her head as she stepped inside.

Jon said, "If I was straight I would've thought that was hot."

"And because you're not?"

"Your nipples were all hard." Jon scrunched up his face. "Eww."

The front door popped open and Vlad walked between Nikki and Jon without a word.

As he sloshed upstairs, Nikki thought of the inedible pile of fried fish fodder that pub had tried to serve her. She said, "So, you have food here? I'm still starving."

"Kitchen." He pointed down the hall and continued up.

Jon said, "What's with him?"

"Who knows? Who cares?"

Jon said, "How about a cocktail?"

"Or maybe something without ice? I'm still shivering here."

"I make a mean Irish coffee. That'd fit you."

"Sounds great."

"Let's hope he has whipped cream." Jon stood on his tip-toes and clapped softly as he rolled his suitcase into the half-bathroom under the stairs.

Nikki turned toward the living area and stopped at the tall set of bookshelves in the foyer. An eclectic mix of vases, clay pots, and nesting dolls lined the shelves and nothing seemed to come from Australia, no less this island. On the opposite wall, an array of vintage Russian items hung, including a red and black retro-looking Stalin poster, a large red-washed map of Moscow, and a black iron, five-foot long harpoon large enough to kill a sperm whale. Though it too had a Russian inscription, it was the only item that remotely belonged in the island setting.

Still, she wondered how tech-boy Vlad could afford all of this, and figured he was probably one of those hackers who stole people's online identities and credit cards and resold them to other thieves. Would make sense why he operated all the way out here on this remote, desolate island outside of Australia. Or maybe he had been caught by the Kremlin doing something else and had fled here.

Heading into the living area, Nikki switched on the television and turned it to a weather channel. After being pounded by that storm on the way back to the house, she wanted to be sure there weren't any more headed their way before they tried to cross the island on Vlad's Vespas. She discovered that, indeed, the storms were gone for now, but in their place, a different kind of disruption had begun.

The great annual crab migration.

Screen shot after screenshot showed the critters crawling all over the place. Across roads, under cars, over cars, through open houses, into and through restaurants and places of work. They were everywhere. And, according to the weatherman, they would continue to be everywhere until every last one of them either made it to the beach to lay their eggs and returned to the depths of the island's rainforest or died in their journey.

Either way, the great migration would last for about a week.

Jesus.

She was about to head to the kitchen in search of some food, when a loud bang sounded upstairs, like a heavy door closing.

She yelled, "Hey Vlad, we need to get moving soon. Before your brethren show up here."

No answer.

She flicked off the television and tossed the remote onto a leather lounger. Then she walked down the hall to find Jon in the kitchen, arranging a cheese tray. Two glass mugs were full of what looked to be Irish coffee. One had a tower of whipped cream that had begun to lean toward the counter.

Taking some bread and a few slices of cheddar, Nikki said, "Fuck is he doing up there anyway?"

"Maybe he fell off the bed, watching his porno."

"Nasty."

"Good news is that he has everything here! See?" Jon held up a jar of mixed nuts and one of Greek olives. "But we're out of cornichons. A travesty." He held up the empty pickle jar.

Nikki nodded. "Devastating."

"Whipped cream?" Jon pointed at the second coffee.

Nikki made a *no thanks* gesture, and took a sip. "This is good."

"I told you."

She said, "Right, but tell me this. How do you expect to fit your suitcase on a Vespa?"

He looked perplexed for a few moments, then pointed his

finger straight up. "I'll just sit on it."

"Brilliant."

Another bang sounded, this time from the garage. Then the buzz of an engine.

"Shit."

Nikki put down the coffee, ran back down the hallway, and flung open the front door to see Vlad rumbling down the driveway on a bright red Vespa, a backpack slung over his shoulders.

"Vlad! Stop, Dammit!" Nikki ran after him, but he kept going, quickly disappearing around the bend.

"What the fuck?" Nikki said to Jon, who had run outside with a long loaf of French bread in one hand and an empty jar in the other.

"Maybe he's gone out for more cornichons."

Having first stopped to rescue Feliks the bobcat from its cage across the hallway, Milo and Jak fitted a rope around its neck and hustled him and Dillon into the backseat of their newly stolen vehicle.

A green and white *Supagas* propane delivery truck.

Attaining the vehicle had been easy. While all the guards were preoccupied with the ensuing riot inside the detention center, Milo, Jak, and Dillon strolled straight out the side gate and to the propane delivery man. He was too busy refilling the detention center's tanks to notice the riot that had broken out around him. Startled by the bobcat, the man originally threatened to spray them with the gas hose. But then, after Jak explained to the young and quite thin Australian driver that he could either give them the truck or become Feliks' dinner, the man promptly handed over the keys and stepped aside for the Russians.

"They are so polite here on this Island of the Christmas," Jak said.

"You mean Christmas Island." Dillon was once again scrunched to the edge of the backseat of the vehicle, heels up in case he had to fend off a bobcat attack this time. "And they're just scared, not polite."

"What is the difference?"

"Has it eaten today?" Dillon watched the bobcat lick its paws, avoiding the huge, hooked claws with its tongue.

"He is a cat, he can wait." Milo drove the winding path of the detention center and out to the main road.

"No, I believe what Dillon says is of the truth. Feliks must eat."

"He can gnaw on the boy's foot." Milo turned onto *N South Baseline Road*. The direction of The Shack.

"Ha ha." Dillon hugged his feet to his chest and stared at the animal.

"How can this road be named North and South at the same time?" Jak said. "It is making no sense."

Milo drove over a wide bump and the tanker car jostled with a splashy sway.

"Be careful, brother. This vehicle. It is highly flammable. The stickers say so." Jak pointed to the back.

"Yeah, don't hit anything," Dillon glanced back at the large pill-shaped tank at the back. "That's like natural gas and really explosive."

"Shut up." Milo glared at the boy in the rear-view mirror and then heard a crunching sound. Turning his attention back to the front of the vehicle, he realized they were driving over a family of crabs. There must have been dozens of them littering the road.

"What the—" He stopped short.

"It is the great Red Crab migration. I have read of this." Jak pushed open his door and exited the vehicle. When he returned, he was holding two large red crabs, their claws reaching out and snapping at the air.

"I hope it clips off your finger," Dillon said

"For Feliks. Feed him." He tossed the crabs back into Dillon's lap.

"Ah!" Dillon wiggled and flicked at the crabs. One had begun crawling up his shirt. "AHH!"

Milo shook his head as Jak howled at the imbecile boy.

"Help!" Dillon pried the crab from his shirt and threw it at the bobcat, hitting him in the face and earning a screech.

The bobcat then reached down and pinned the crab to the seat with a paw and sniffed it. Seemingly satisfied, he then bit the crab's head off and began to chew.

"Gross!" Dillon whined as he moved to peel the second crab from his leg.

"There. Now he is no longer hungering." Jak nodded once and pointed ahead. "We can go to The Shack now. Find this Svetlana."

Milo, with the mind to shove both his brother and the idiot boy out of the car, go find Svetlana and make the riches himself, decided in the end that Jak was too valuable in the quest. The boy though, he may have to just kill and leave roadside somewhere.

He shifted the vehicle back into Drive and was about to go forward when he heard a whimper from behind. Glancing back, he saw Dillon, arms up, as if trying to back away from something.

"It's in my lap, it's in my…"

"Don't move. It will pinch you," Jak said with a smile.

"It's right on my…oh shit." And Dillon slowly reached down toward the crab as it moved between his legs.

"Easy now, fella," he said.

The crab looked up at him. Raised a long arm and claw.

"Just gonna move you over. I promise you won't get eaten or anything."

The bobcat looked up at Dillon. Chewed the catch in his mouth, then tore another piece of crab off with a *crunch*.

"Not like your buddy there." Dillon eased his hand down and opened his fingers to grab the creature. "You'll be fine, I promise."

Jak said, "I am having another haiku coming to me."

Dillon whimpered.

The crab opened its claw.

Dillon grabbed its back. "Gotcha!" but then he froze, as the crab darted its claw straight into Dillon's crotch.

And he pinched.

"Well there goes our tour guide." Nikki stomped back to the house.

"Why would he leave?" Jon hurried inside behind her and shut the door.

"He's Russian. Who the fuck knows." She continued upstairs and found the door that led to a back stairway. "Son of a bitch."

Jon, still following, said, "Now what?"

She hurried down the stairs. "I say we hightail it out of here. Get to wherever Finn is and get the fuck off this tropical landfill."

"I agree. It's so humid." Jon fanned himself with a hand.

Nikki pushed open the door that led to the garage and flicked on the light to find that there were three Vespas, as Vlad had claimed back at the wreck. The only problem now was that the other two matching cycles he'd left behind were sitting on flat tires.

"No! No! NO!" Nikki walked over to the bikes and inspected the flats. A short, stab wound extended just below the thread of each tire.

"That's sabotage!" Jon slapped his leg.

"I'll make that little bastard pay."

"Think we can fix it?"

"Not unless you have a canister of Fix-A-Flat in your pocket."

"Darling, that's no canister." Jon posed.

Nikki stood up. Put a hand on her forehead and closed her eyes. "Jon?"

"Yes?" Still posing.

"Give it a fucking rest."

He tightened his lips, waved a hand and started toward the house but then stopped. "Do you hear something?"

A rumbling sounded. Like a diesel truck coming up the drive.

Nikki said, "I sure hope it's the garbage men."

Jon smiled. "Or the mailman."

Nikki ignored that and hurried to the house, jogged through the kitchen to see out the front.

Jon followed and when she stopped short, he almost knocked her over.

Nikki made a face and pushed him off her back.

The truck was some sort of delivery vehicle. Natural gas or something. She was no Australian expert, but she was pretty sure that there was no such thing as residential delivery of natural gas. Unless the driver was a friend of Vlad's or lost, it didn't add up. Which meant...

Jon said, "It can't be the Russians. They're in a detention center somewhere."

"Unless," Nikki said, then exhaled hard when she saw the face of the driver. "Shit."

"Uh oh." Jon backed up and put a hand to his mouth. "Looks like the naughty boys escaped the pokey."

The Russians had been smart, one entering the house from the front, the other through the back, eliminating any chance of Nikki and Jon escaping. Then the whiz-kid actor, Dillon, came through the garage limping like he'd been kicked in the nuts. He had a medium-sized bobcat with him.

On a fucking rope.

Now, as the smaller Russian—obviously the leader—searched the house, and the rest of them corralled in the kitchen, the one named Jak held Nikki by the hair with one hand and pointed the antique harpoon at Jon with the other. He said, "Where is Svetlana?"

"I told you, she's not here. Probably out shopping for an Australian Rules Football player or something."

"You are not funny." Jak twisted her hair and Nikki winced.

"Keep doing that and you'll lose a hand."

"Not likely."

Jon, who stood as stiff as a surfboard against the refrigerator, stared at the large cat. He said, "What is that, a baby leopard?"

"A bobcat, you moron." Dillon struggled with one hand on his groin and the other on the rope to keep the animal from jumping up to eat the cheese.

"Just let him eat." Jak slapped Dillon across the back of the head.

"Whatever." Dillon dropped the rope and the bobcat leaped up onto the counter and attacked the tray of cheese and bread like it was a family of baby squirrels.

"My God." Jon half-turned away. "He's vicious."

"Yes, and he will be eating you next if you do not have the cooperation," Jak said.

The smaller Russian stormed down the stairs and into the kitchen. "Where are they? Tell us now, or one of you dies."

"I can shoot them." Jack swung the harpoon toward Nikki and then back to Jon.

Nikki could give two shits if the thugs took *Slutlana*, but she wanted to keep them from finding Finn. And Lindsay. She was nice enough. Now Vlad, that was another story. That asshat had it coming two ways and then some.

"Tell you what, why don't you take a piece of Vlad's clothing and use that nifty bobcat of yours to sniff him out?"

"This will not work. The island is too big." Jak made a grand gesture with an open palm.

Milo stood, arms crossed, staring at Nikki. "Perhaps we could kill you and wait until they return for your bodies instead."

"I don't like that idea as much," Jon said.

"Milo, there is a pool in the backyard, see? I can hold them under the top of the water until they drown. Then there will not even be blood to clean up this time."

"Can I take a dip first? I'm all hot and don't want to swim in a pool with dead people." Dillon fanned himself.

"Listen, bugnuts, nobody is dying here." Nikki wrenched herself free of Jak's grip.

"We will see about that." Milo strode across the kitchen, pushed the bobcat off the counter as it screeched, and then grabbed handfuls of cheese."

"What are you—" Jon backed away as Milo approached him.

And Milo stuffed hunks of cheese and bread into Jon's pockets and down his shirt. The bobcat circled the counter, took one good sniff, and approached Jon. Then he moved to swipe a claw at Jon's leg and Milo stomped on the rope, saving Jon's jewels by an inch. The bobcat snarled and snapped its jaws.

Jon screeched.

The bobcat lunged, its neck snapping back with the rope.

Jon squealed. "Please no! Please!"

"You sick son of a—" Nikki lunged at Milo, but Jak jerked her back by her hair and pressed the harpoon arrow into the soft flesh under her jaw.

Milo loosened his foot's grip on the rope and the bobcat swiped a tear straight through Jon's pant leg, blood seeped through the slits in the fabric of his thigh.

"Dear God!"

"Felix will eat his balls and I will shoot this through your brain." He moved the tip of the harpoon to her temple.

"OK, OK!" Nikki yelled, hands up.

They all turned to her.

"I'll take you to them."

CHAPTER ELEVEN

AFTER THEIR VOYEUR INTERLUDE, FINN AND LINDSAY snuck back to the guest quarters, where they showered and completed round two—Lindsay's back pressed to the marble wall and her feet pressed flat to the glass door, Finn's hips locked between her knees.

But Lindsay wasn't finished.

She led him back to the bedroom, where she lay Finn on the yoga mat and straddled him for round three. Finn, not exactly a passive participant in the activity, guided Lindsay by her hips with one hand, and—to keep her from crying out like she did in the shower—let her bite the fleshy part of his other hand as she climaxed for the fifth or maybe sixth time.

He'd stopped counting when he lost his footing and stepped on the bottle of shampoo back in the shower, causing the bottle to explode a blu-ish green goo all over the glass and reminding him of a scene from Men in Black. He regained his concentration soon enough, though, and was back in the groove again.

Now, she chomped down, arched her back, and said, "Namaste, namaste!"

Then she collapsed on his chest.

Thank god, he whispered to himself, but Lindsay didn't answer.

She was snoring.

He left her there, sleeping on him like that, for a solid half-hour. Until he heard a rustling in the kitchen and then smelled something along the lines of lobster and steak.

"Lindsay," he whispered.

She didn't budge.

"Psst."

She reached up and put a hand over his mouth. Then a long moment later, she said, "Don't wake a sleeping tigress."

"I'm hungry," he said in a muffled voice.

She blinked her eyes open and said, "That does smell good. Too bad I'm vegan."

He peeled her hand off his mouth. "You're what?"

"I only eat leaves."

"That sucks."

She smiled. "Tell me, how's my ass?"

He feigned looking down her backside, frowned, and said, "Spectacular."

She winked. "Leaves."

"I thought you said it was from yoga."

"From not eating meat."

"Not even fish?"

"Nope."

"Shit, if I tried that, I'd have to eat the bark and tree trunk, too. Maybe the roots."

With that, Lindsay pushed up and said, "C'mon, let's get you fed, big fella'. You earned it." She patted his chest, kissed him, and stood.

He had to admit, her ass was spectacular.

A few minutes later, they were properly dressed and entering the kitchen, where Svetlana stood on one side of the granite island, shaking a cocktail shaker with both hands. A huge bottle of Grey Goose vodka stood open before her, along with four chilled martini glasses.

"Just in time," Chart said, entering the kitchen with a platter of lobster tails and steaks.

Svetlana was wearing what appeared to be one of Chart's white linen shirts. With the first three buttons undone and all that shaking, it was apparent that she was wearing nothing beneath.

"Do you ever wear, like, a full outfit of clothing?" Finn asked.

Svetlana stopped shaking, looked down between her breasts, and shrugged. "I am fully dressed now."

Then she poured two drinks, handed one to Chart. "The host of the party." Then the other to Lindsay. "One for a lady." And she went to work on the next two.

"How about we dine outside?" Chart said, and Lindsay offered to help set the table.

As Svetlana strained the next two drinks, she eyed Finn and said, "That leaves only us."

Then she made a big show of puckering her lips, blowing Finn a kiss, and saying, "You are a bad boy, Mr. Finn." She took a sip of her martini.

"How so?" Finn sipped the vodka. It was smooth as an icy mountain stream, just what he needed after the day.

She winked. "You know of what I am speaking."

Before they could get any further into that, a clap sounded behind Finn, and Chart said, "Let's eat!"

Turned out Svetlana had some sous chef skills, as she'd made mango and pomegranate with chopped radicchio salad, steamed plantains, and sautéed spinach for sides. All ready and arranged on long cutting boards and clay bowls and set on the veranda table that overlooked the Indian Ocean.

After Finn had eaten four lobster tails—his two plus the ones that Svetlana and Lindsay gave him—two flank steaks, two baked potatoes, a heaping of the sautéed spinach, and a plate of plantains, he looked up to see all three of the others looking at him.

"Something wrong?" he asked, fork heaping with spinach and halfway to his mouth.

"Astounding," Lindsay said.

"You eat too much. You are going to die of the heart attack." Svetlana pursed her lips and took a healthy drink of her martini.

"I could tell you what's going to kill you," Finn began, and was going to finish with a list of known STDs, but stopped when Lindsay kicked him under the table.

Chart laughed, "I have to say, you do eat a heck of a lot, but..." he chewed a cut of steak and continued, "you worked up the appetite for it all." Then he winked at Lindsay. "Surprised you're only having salad."

So much for his silencing tactics, Finn thought.

He was about to change the subject, when Lindsay downed the rest of her martini and turned to Svetlana. "Speaking of interludes, I think it's about time we discuss how we're going to deal with yours."

Svetlana held her martini with a stiff arm and a limp hand, so the vodka tipped right to the lip of the glass. "I have nothing to hide." She smiled at Chart.

Lindsay said, "Right, but...I'm speaking about the reason we're here. All the way out in the middle of the Indian Ocean, running from Russian thugs. And I'm thinking it has to do with your little movie making project with that actor, Dillon West."

Finn sat stone-still, waiting to see whether he needed to protect Lindsay from Svetlana lashing out or call Lindsay off. Let Svetlana come to grips with everything that was going on before drilling her into a confession.

Svetlana glanced at Chart and said, "This is not appropriate timing for discussing of these things."

Chart laughed. "Not going to surprise me, honey. Or make me blush." He stuck his fork with a bite of lobster, dipped it in butter, pointed it at Lindsay, and said, "fire away, counselor." Then he chomped the lobster and sat back.

Svetlana shrugged and said, "I came because of Vlad. He is the expert movie maker. From Moscow, he is the genius. And I want him to make the perfect motion feature."

Finn put down the fork. "You're not kidding. You really did make a sex tape?"

"And Vlad is going to make it the best ever. This will be like the Hollywood. But better, see?" Svetlana pushed back from the table and lifted her foot to the edge of the table. Then she ran a finger all the way down to and across her pointed toes. "Perfect for the movie."

Lindsay made a *not bad* face and whispered to Finn, "She likes leaves, too."

Finn said, "Where is this movie?"

"It was in the condo of Dillon. You know, his bedding room."

"I meant where is the tape now? The recording?" Finn said.

Svetlana drew her foot from the table, took a swig of vodka, then eased back into her seat. "With Vlad, of course."

Then Lindsay shook her head. "I can see this turning into a publicity nightmare."

Chart said, "Hey, maybe it goes viral. You know, like that Paris Hilton tape. Nothing bad there."

"I am better than this Paris Hilton. My ass and my moves."

"Amen!" Chart cheered to that.

"The video, Svetlana," Finn said. "Did Vlad make copies?"

"I am hoping so."

"No, no no," Lindsay said. "We need to get it from him before he does."

"Speak of the devil," Finn said, holding up his buzzing cell phone. Nikki's number appeared on the screen. "Let's make sure he brings all the copies with him."

But when he answered, it wasn't Nikki on the line.

Finn stood at the table and held the phone close to his ear as the man with a Russian accent said, "If you ever want to see your pitting bull of a girlfriend again, you will do what I say."

In the background, Dillon said, "It's pit bull, not pitting."

Then another Russian man said, "Shut up." And a slap

sounded.

Dillon mumbled something inaudible.

"Okay…" Finn walked a few steps away from the table. He stared out at the setting sun as he said, "What do you want?"

"Svetlana, of course."

Finn glanced back at the table, where Svetlana was polishing one of her rings with a napkin and Lindsay was giving Finn a *what the hell is going on* look.

Finn put up his index finger and turned back to the water. "I want to hear that Nikki and Jon are okay."

"Fine."

A moment later, Nikki yelled in the background. Something about shoving a man's hand up his own ass if he did it again.

Good 'ol Nikki was in fine spirits.

And Jon said, "Thanks to you Russian retards, my suit now smells like Limburger."

Finn asked, "What do you want with Svetlana?"

"This is not of your concern, Mr. Sporting Agent. Just bring her to us and you can see your friends again."

"And where's Vlad? You haven't…done anything to him, have you?"

"He is not with you?"

"No, but…" thinking fast, Finn said, "He must be on his way here."

"Where are you?"

"On the other side of the island, where Svetlana and Vlad will be together, so maybe you should come here."

"Da. Then perhaps you, being Mr. Sporting Agent, are willing to make a trade. Svet and Vlad for your Nikki and Jon."

"Two for two, then."

"You are good at the counting. Yes, a fair trade I think. Just don't try any of the funny things."

Finn said, "I wouldn't dream of it. Just make sure Nikki and Jon are okay and you can have Svetlana and Vlad. Fair trade, like you said."

"We will be there in thirty minutes." Milo hung up.

Finn turned back to the table as Svetlana said, "who am I being the traded for, and where is Vlad?"

"Nobody. I'm not trading." Finn slipped the phone in his pocket and looked at Chart. "Got any weapons here?"

"No weapons." Chart held out two empty palms. "But I may have something just as good."

CHAPTER TWELVE

"As good a spot to sleep as any," Chadwick said, pointing ahead of them. "Look, the tree will shelter us from rain, and the sand is soft. Also, I don't see any crabs about. You can rest your feet and we can be back on our way by morning."

"Thank god for that." Vanessa rubbed the bottom of a foot as she studied the tree. Something strange about the leaves. A dark and quite large item was wedged up top. "What is that up there?"

"It appears to be a canopy of sorts." Chadwick stood with both hands on his hips, as if he were now an expert on the outdoors. Where to sleep, how to stay dry and all that. Next thing you know, he'd be telling her how he can make a camp fire with nothing more than two twigs.

"It's not a canopy. It looks like a car. Hard to say with the sun setting, but maybe a Jeep."

"Well, I don't know how that would be possible."

"Nor do I, but I see it up there. That's what it is."

"Maybe not."

"And what on earth do you think it is?"

"Maybe a sleeping tent. Someone already took our idea."

"Rubbish. First off, we aren't thinking of sleeping up in the tree, just under it. And besides. Even if it were a tent—and it's not, it's clearly an automobile of sorts—how would the occupants even get to it?"

Chadwick stood tall, studying the tree and then the cliff about ten feet from the top. "Perhaps they leap to it. From there." He pointed at a spot on the cliff face that jutted out a meter.

She let out a long, exasperated sigh. "Chadwick?"

"Yes?"

"You're a bloody idiot."

Then she moved off to find some larger palms in order to fashion a bit of bedding on the sand. Soon enough, Chadwick was at her side and helping. The least he could do.

He said, "Where do you reckon they've escaped to?"

"Finn and company?" Vanessa shook a few bugs off the largest of the palms and set them aside. "They can't have gone far. And if I overheard the other detainees correctly, there won't be a flight from here until at least tomorrow morning."

"So what, we do them right there at the airport?"

Vanessa dropped a few palms into the growing pile and looked at Chadwick. "We're not going kill them, Chadwick. We need them, remember?"

"Right."

"We're going to find this blasted house you claim to have seen them in. Before first light. We'll get it out of them there."

"And for the record, I meant take them. Kidnap and the like."

"At the airport?"

"Where else?"

"And what, be thrown straight away into that hellish hole of a detention center again? Sounds brilliant."

"Well alright, then perhaps we could have a bit of talking to them there on the flight, then. Rough them up a bit, make them tell us where they've put our money."

"And then we'll be arrested by American police when we land on US soil. Your ideas are getting worse by the second."

"We could kill them on the flight. This way they can't talk to the authorities."

"Kill them?"

"Don't see much choice in the matter, actually."

She placed a cold hand on her forehead, took a deep breath. "Chadwick?"

"Yes Vanny?"

"Here's what I want you to do." She pointed at the pile of palm leaves and said, "Take these over to the tree. Lay them down as if they were a mattress."

"I can do that."

"I wouldn't bet on it."

"You're so mean to me."

"Chadwick?"

"Yes."

"I don't want to hear another word from your lips. Not until you've thought long and hard and actually figured out something intelligent to say. Something that can help us. Because other than that lug wrench you have stowed away in those trousers, you are of no use to me, do you understand?"

Chadwick stood there, pondering all that while holding a pile of palms he'd gathered in his arms. Then, after a good fifteen seconds, he said, "I know how to make a fire."

CHAPTER THIRTEEN

"Not the smartest of Russian mobsters, are they?" Chart said, moving a lamp off a small side table and then moving the table to the edge of the living area.

Finn said, "Not exactly Rhodes scholars, no."

"Usually these men are not the educated ones. They skip the school and murder and steal instead. It is the one ugly truth of Russia." Svetlana nodded once.

"The?" Lindsay said. "As in the only one?"

"Yes. The rest of the Mother Land is beautiful. It is almost perfect."

Lindsay crossed her arms and said, "Then why do you live in the United States?"

"Good question." Chart winked at Lindsay.

"Because, I like the Miami and the sun. It helps my tan, see?" And she made a move to pull up her dress again.

"Okay, okay, we've seen enough of that for today," Lindsay said.

"A man can never see enough of that." Svetlana raised her eyebrows and chin.

"She does have a point," Chart said, eyeing Svetlana's legs and then ass.

"How about we prep for the so-called, not-so-brilliant, killer Russians arrival now?" Finn said.

"Good idea," Lindsay said, "Now where exactly is this trap

door you were describing?"

"Right." Chart plugged the lamp into the far wall and placed it atop the moved table. He said, "Help me with this." He motioned toward Finn and pointed at the sofa.

Finn and Chart each took an end of the long sofa and moved it to the edge of the room where the table and lamp now sat. Then Chart rolled the antique rug back, revealing a square about the size of a pickup's flatbed cut out in the wood flooring.

"Where does it lead?" Lindsay said, as Svetlana made herself comfortable on the resettled sofa.

"See for yourself," Chart said, then motioned to Finn to help him.

The two of them grabbed the corners of the cutout and hauled it up. A light spray of saltwater wafted up into the room, and as Lindsay approached the opening, Chart held an arm out to stop her. "Careful, honey."

Then she saw why.

The opening dropped clear down the cliff that the edge of the house sat on, and into a small pool bordered by huge boulders. It was about fifty or sixty feet down to the pool.

"Jesus." Finn peered over the edge.

"Why exactly do you—"

And before Lindsay could finish her question, Chart said, "Was supposed to be for a killer wine cellar. Damp, cool, hidden. But then the whole ship of wine that I'd ordered for delivery sank, and I didn't have the heart to finish the cellar. Or the money, really."

"So you left it open?" Lindsay said.

Chart shrugged. "I may finish it out someday."

"So what, we lure them here and push them in?" Finn glanced back at Chart.

Chart said, "Actually, I'm thinking we put one of these rugs over the hole. When they enter the house, we'll manipulate them to walk forward and...*poof*. They're gone."

"Poof?" Lindsay said, "We're talking murder here. "

"Self defense, actually." Chart nodded.

"And...what if that clown actor falls through?" Finn said. "He's some sort of pawn in all this, I'm sure. He's too naive to be involved."

"This is true," Svetlana said from the sofa behind them. "And his balls are too small, for real."

"Way too much information," Finn said.

Lindsay put a hand over her eyes and stared through the opening. "And what about Jon and Nikki?"

"That'll be your job." The waves crashed below as Finn said, "To make damned sure they stay back."

With both wrists bound by thick rope that was strung over the top of the natural gas tank and bound to Jon's wrists, Nikki struggled to keep footing on the slim metal rail as the truck bounced over each crab a tire pummeled.

Nikki shook her mud-soaked hair free from her face and called over the top of the tanker to Jon, "Happy now that you insisted you wouldn't ride in the same car as the goddamned cat?"

"It's safer out here, trust me honey," Jon's sentence was punctuated by a crunch and the spatter of crab-goo on Nikki's ankle.

"Nasty," she muttered to herself. Then she yelled, "One more crab splats on my leg and I'm going ballistic."

"Please don't, we're attached, remember?"

"How could I forget?" She yanked a wrist, eliciting an *ouch* at the other end.

"Stop that, I have fragile arms!"

The passenger side window rolled down and the one named Jak leaned his head out. "Stop with the yelling as we go through the town. We don't want to attract extra attention."

"Right," Nikki called back. "Having two people strapped to

the sides of a gas tank is perfectly normal, as long as they're not yelling."

"Don't forget the bobcat on a rope! That can't be legal!" Jon yelled.

Jak yelled, "Shut up or we will pull over the truck, and I will hold you down as I feed you to the bobcat, one limb at a time."

"You're not human!" Jon said.

The truck screeched to a halt.

Nikki said, "Jon, shut it."

Jon said, "Okay, okay! I'll be quiet!"

Three minutes later, as they drove through town, Nikki spotted two children on the front step of a small house waving to her.

She gave them her best fake smile.

Then one of the children threw a piece of fruit of some kind at her. It hit her in the boob.

"Little bastard, I'm coming back for you," she said.

"What?" Jon called in a loud whisper.

"Nothing."

A symphony of crackling and splattering sounded and a trail of crab roadkill was left in the wake of the truck. A villager yelled, another threw a piece of fruit. This one hit Jon and he gave a muffled *oof*.

"No hit the crab!" A woman yelled. She threw a papaya and it smacked the tank above Nikki's head.

"Son of a bitch!" Nikki said.

Another villager hurled a rotten mango and it thumped the side of the truck, leaving a crescent-shaped orange slush. Then one hit the window, cracking it.

The Russians sped up, crunching and crackling over the crabs, bouncing as they swerved, not to avoid the creatures, but the villagers who were now in the road, chasing and yelling at them. Still throwing fruit.

"Ouch!" Jon yelled. "I think I was just hit by a jackfruit!"

"What the hell is that?" Nikki said.

'It's green and hard, kind of looks like the Hulk's boner!"

"How would you know what—"

"It's the Hulk, Nikki! Who hasn't imagined it?"

The truck bounced hard over a mound of soil at the edge of the road, and the rope attached to Nikki's right wrist scraped against a bolt on the frame of the tank. The rope frayed and split.

"Well well," Nikki said. "Hang on, Jon-boy, I may have a way out for us after all."

With all the lights extinguished, Finn kneeling on one side of the front entrance, Chart kneeling on the other side, and the girls safely tucked behind the sofa at the far side of the room, Finn and company were all ready to pounce on the Russians the moment they entered Chart's house.

Finn gripped the antique cricket bat with one hand and steadied himself against the door frame with the other. He couldn't see across the doorway just five feet from him, it was so pitch black inside, but Finn knew Chart was gripping his chosen weapon, a wooden field hockey stick that had looked to be about a hundred years old. Finn hoped the weapons wouldn't just crumble on first strike.

Even so, the weapons were just in case, as the plan was to allow the Russians to enter through the front door, see Svetlana stand up across the room, and go after her. If they strayed from the path of the trap, then Finn and Chart could nudge them in the right direction.

Simple as that.

Waiting quietly, as the Russians should arrive at any minute, a strange clucking noise broke the silence. Then a thump sounded and more clucking, then scraping.

"What is that?" Finn asked.

"That there is a *birgus latro*, also known as the coconut crab or the robber crab. They like to clip coconuts off the palm trees and eat them."

"They can eat coconuts? How big are these things?" Lindsay whispered loudly across the room.

Finn leaned back and peered between the shutters of the front window through the muted moonlight. At the base of the largest of the palm trees out front, he made out a black creature about the size of Hobie and with claws as large as catchers' mitts tearing open a jumbo coconut. "Is that really—" he stopped himself, figuring it might freak out the ladies if he described the scene, but then Chart plowed ahead.

"Oh, they grow up to three feet claw to claw. Sometimes larger," Chart said.

"*Uhwhwh.*" Lindsay audibly shuddered. "Do we have to be in the dark here? Can't we turn on a little nightlight or something?"

"Trust me, it'll help entice the Russians to come through the front," Finn said. "Then they'll walk right over the trap."

"Don't worry. The crabs never come inside," Chart said.

Damn good thing, Finn thought, they looked like damned aliens.

And just after Chart said that, Finn felt a presence directly behind him. A warm, floral-smelling presence. Then a whisper. She must have taken off her shoes.

"You could come inside," Svetlana said into Finn's ear, so close that her tongue flicked his lobe. "If you like." Then she reached down and put a palm on the inside of Finn's leg and moved it up to his groin.

Finn steeled himself against the offensive. "You should be on the other side of the room. Away from the door. Remember?" he whispered back.

She licked his ear. "Let's sneak away for a minute, yes? We have the time. I will make you satisfied very fast. I am good at this." She began to knead his groin.

Finn took her hand and moved it away. "Svetlana. This is not the time. And I am not the man."

"I will make you the man. I don't mind if the others hear us." She pushed her hand back onto his groin. "And it will stop the men in their entering, they will be so surprised seeing us in our love position. Then the others can capture them."

He moved her hand away again. "I don't like that plan."

She huffed and stood, said out loud, "Fine. This is the choice of your own." She made a big deal about stomping back into her heels.

"Everything okay over there?" Lindsay called from behind the sofa.

"Just fine. Svetlana was confused about the plan." Finn repositioned himself.

Svetlana said, "Not confused, just giving alternative ideas." She strode very close to the rug and across the room, her heels clicking in tune to the clucking of the crabs eating coconuts outside.

"Lights approaching." Chart said.

"Everyone quiet," Finn said. "Remember the plan."

"What is this plan?" Svetlana said.

"The one where you are supposed to stay right there and not say a word," Lindsay said.

"I cannot guarantee I will not talk. But I have idea how these boys could make me shut up."

"Soon as this is over, I'm in line for that," Chart said.

"Oh boy," Lindsay said. "Don't you think you've had enough exhibition for the week?"

"You haven't even seen the film as of yet. You cannot judge this then." Svetlana stopped walking and presumably settled behind the sofa again.

"Shh!" Finn said. "Please, Svetlana."

"You can shush me," she said.

A rumbling sounded as the lights cut back across the fauna outside and onto the house. A moment later, the truck's growl silenced and lights cut off. Peeking through the shudders again, Finn made out just what kind of mental stability they were up against.

Because in the muted moonlight, Finn could make out the two figures emerging from the truck. The smaller one approached empty handed, but the larger one was holding what looked to be a huge, black iron harpoon of some kind. And then Finn saw what the driver pulled out of the backseat on a leash.

Was that a bobcat?

"Jesus," Finn whispered. "These guys look two bottles short of a six-pack."

CHAPTER FOURTEEN

MILO EXITED THE CAR AND OPENED THE back door, then yanked the little shit actor out by his collar.

Dillon yelped and hit the ground with both arms outstretched. His puny arms didn't help break his fall much though, and he bit the mud face first. "Fucking terrorist!" He wiped the mud from his mouth with the inside of an elbow.

"Shut up." Jak poked the back of the boy's head with the tip of the harpoon.

"Ouch!"

Jak then tugged the bobcat out of the car by the leash. The bobcat snarled and reared up, taking a swipe at Dillon who skittered backwards like a water bug.

Jak stretched the leash taught. "Now what?"

Milo studied the bungalow. With no lights on and no movement, he was pretty sure they were being set up for an ambush. But unless Svetlana's friends were crack shots or suicidal, Milo and Jak were probably safe from gunfire.

For the moment, anyway.

Milo nodded at Jak. "Get the hostages. We'll use them as cover."

"Good idea." Jak made a move for the truck but then stopped. "Son of bitch."

"What?" Milo turned to see the gas tank and no Nikki or Jon. "Shit."

Jak spun around in search of them, but they weren't in sight.

"What did you expect? You geniuses tied them to the back of a truck," Dillon said as he stood up.

Jak waved him off. "Should I find them?"

"No time. Let's go." Milo tugged the bobcat and headed toward the door.

Jak said, "This is reminding me of the nursing rhyme, Handsome and Grumble."

Dillon said, "It's Hansel and Gretel. And it's a nursery rhyme, not nursing. Big difference there, Mr. Literary."

"Either way, they are both eaten by the big wolf," Jak said.

"No they're not, you moron. They—"

"Maybe you want to be eaten by a wolf." Jak poked the bobcat and it spun, giving a high-pitched, throaty scream.

"It's a cat." Dillon held up both muddy hands in a feeble display of self-defense.

"Not much difference in the teeth."

"Enough!" Milo slapped Jak on the shoulder. "Let's find this Svetlana!"

"Good luck with that," Dillon said, flopping down and leaning against the back wheel.

"Get up." Jak reached down, took hold of Dillon's scrawny neck, and yanked him back to his feet. Then he pushed him forward. "You are the distraction."

"Ouch!" Jon yelped.

"Shh!" Nikki slapped one hand over his mouth and pressed the other to back of his head.

"It's not my fault," he whispered through her fingers. "I twisted my ankle on one of those little crabs!"

"Gross." Nikki glanced down at the mangled creature. Jon's wide-heeled shoe had torn the thing's arm off. The crab spun in a circle and then picked up its severed arm with the good claw and scampered off like some demented sea-creature version of Platoon.

"These are Jimmy Choos!" Jon shook the slime from his sole as Nikki grabbed his cuff, dragging him with her behind a palm tree.

"Look." Nikki glanced around and said, "These fucktards are out here with a harpoon and a bobcat. I suggest you keep it down."

"Right. Sorry." He placed a finger to his lips and made wide eyes. Then he whispered, "What's the plan?"

"I say we hightail it out of here. We can meet up with Patrick and the others later."

"Shouldn't we be helping them?"

"Nah. These dopes have exactly zero chance against Finn. He's way too street savvy to be taken by inbreds."

"Good God, do you think it's like…their mother is their sister sort of thing?"

"Have you listened to Jak speak? There's not a whole lot of light shining in the attic, if you know what I mean." And as Nikki turned to walk, she heard a scrabbling noise above them and then a crackle and thunk.

A coconut landed on the leafy floor at their feet.

"What the—" Jon looked around, as if somebody had thrown it at them.

Nikki followed his gaze, then turned to look up.

There, up at the top of the tree, barely visible in the moonlight, an enormous inky black spindly creature hung between the palms, one claw outstretched, snipping a coconut from the branch.

"Jesus," she said. "That crab looks like a fucking alien."

Snip.

"Where?" Jon turned his face up to follow her gaze.

"Jon, look out, it's headed right—"

But she was too late.

Because the coconut struck Jon between the eyes, knocking him out cold, and sending him in a crumpled heap to the ground.

"Right at you," she said.

Eyes adjusted to the dark now, and with the moonlight peeking in the windows, Finn could make out the happenings in front of the bungalow.

First, The bobcat leapt up onto the deck, jerking the leash tight in the larger Russian's hand. Then the Russian shoved the actor boy, Dillon, ahead. Taking hold of Dillon again, he then climbed the steps, leaned the harpoon against the railing. Then he pulled a notebook from his pocket and began to write something.

"What are you doing?" the smaller Russian asked.

"I will write a poem of this moment. It is one for remembering," the large man said, and then he began to mouth words to himself.

"Jak, this is not the time for poetry."

Poetry?

Finn used a single finger to ease the window open a few inches and cupped his ear to hear them.

Jak said, "Milo, listen..." he scribbled something else, paused a moment, and then stood up straight. "In the darkness the little whore hides. The pitting bull woman and fairy man flee. As dead as hunted rabbits they will be."

"Brilliant," Milo said, stepping up to the door with a look of exasperation.

"Do you really think so?"

"No. I think you are an imbecile. Now let's go."

"What do you know of art anyway?"

Finn pulled back and fought to refocus his mind. These guys were stark-naked crazy. Not a thread of sanity or rational thought anywhere in sight. Or at least earshot.

Chart, seemingly unaware of the proceedings, gave Finn the

thumbs-up. *Ready?*

Sure. Finn nodded, waiting for the knob to turn and the door to swing open.

But neither of those things happened. Instead, a loud *thwack* sounded. Then a *thud.* The door vibrated and shook. Two more *thwacks* and *thuds* and it split, the large black arrow of the harpoon penetrating the wood.

Lindsay screamed and scrambled to the back of the house.

Svetlana stood. "What are they doing? I thought you left the door unlocked."

"I did!" yelled Chart. "They're destroying the house!"

Thwack.

Thwack.

Thwack.

And then a boot came through and a pair of forearms worthy of a heavyweight prize-fighter.

"Damn," Finn said, standing and taking a step back.

The next thing he knew, all hell—the entirety of chaos and insanity—broke loose.

First, Dillon came stumbling through the broken door and into the small hallway, as if shoved from behind.

Then Svetlana screeched, "You!" as she hurdled over Finn's back and tackled Dillon like some sort of vicious animal, screaming, "You traitor! You should go to the Gulag!" Legs and arms flailing and wrapping around him like an octopus, as if she was trying to beat and suffocate him at the same time.

Dillon screeched and fell and then he rolled, Svetlana choking him.

They rolled forward. Toward the rug.

The two Russians entered the house.

They stared at the melee.

"Svetlana!" Finn leaped forward and took hold of her arm.

"Get off!" Dillon rolled to the soft spot of the rug as Chart took hold of his leg.

Lindsay dived forward and grabbed Finn's back foot with both hands.

Finn peeled Svetlana off Dillon with one solid tug, and pulled her backwards, clear of the danger. But as he did this, his front foot planted squarely on a spot of the rug with nothing below.

He flung Svetlana to the floor behind him.

Chart yelled as the rug gave.

Dillon made a large *O* with his mouth and face.

"Shit," Finn bellowed.

The rug collapsed inward.

And the four of them were swallowed by the emptiness below.

"What just happened?" Jak said, a bewildered look on his face, the harpoon held loosely at his side.

Milo stared into the hole. The large man hung, gripping the rug that was swaying back and forth as it had snagged on the rafters. The spray of seawater splashed against the rocks below. "I don't know. Grab the crazy bitch."

Jak took hold of Svetlana by the wrist, twisting it to her back and pushing her across the room. She yelped and he said, "Stand there."

Rubbing her shoulder and wrist, she looked him up and down. "You like this? Playing rough?"

"If I want to play with you, I will do it."

Placing a finger in her mouth, Svetlana had suddenly returned to her sultry persona. "You want to try? We could play right here, on the floor." She turned to Milo. "You can watch if you like, I don't mind."

"I am not interested." Milo walked over to Svetlana and stared straight into her eyes.

"You made me chip a nail." Svetlana held up her hand for him to see. "You will pay for this."

"Let's go." Milo grabbed Svetlana and headed for the door.

"Wait, I need to get Feliks," Jak said.

"We are not taking the animal."

"We must. I have named him and he is family now."

"We don't have room or time. Tie him up outside."

"You make me sad. He is the only pet I have ever had."

"Well now you have this one." He nodded at Svetlana. "She is as feisty as that cat."

"I can be as feisty as you wish," Svetlana said.

"Whatever." Milo walked through the broken doorway.

"Wait!" Svetlana said, tapping a toe on the hardwood floor. "Why are you taking me?"

"To find Vlad."

"Why him?"

"To get the video." Jak wrapped the rope-leash around a post on the porch and patted the bobcat. "Good kitty."

The bobcat growled and bit at the air.

"Of course." Svetlana smiled. "Everyone will want to see this video. I am beautiful in it."

"Yes I am sure. It will be worth a lot of money." He grinned. "This is why we are taking it from you."

Finn swayed back and forth, clinging to the rug with one hand, as Lindsay clutched his leg for dear life. After falling into the hole with Finn, she had been desperate enough to keep a tight hold of his ankle. The rug had torn and slumped lower as they swayed, though, and she now dangled only about ten feet from the water.

"Let go!" Chart said from the darkness below.

"No!" Lindsay yelled. "I should jump first, he'll crush me!"

"I'm not letting go yet," Finn said.

"You're right over the middle of the water."

Finn could make out the silhouette of Chart who sat on the

rocks to one side, and a skinnier one of Dillon who sat across from him.

Dillon said, "She's right. The big guy will flatten her like a skate fish."

"Relax, nobody is flattening anyone," Finn said. Then to Lindsay, "Ready?"

"No."

"Okay, how's this for motivation? I can't keep holding on here. I maybe have another five or ten seconds until—"

And Lindsay let go of his leg. She splashed into the water as Chart yelled, "Geronimo!"

Dillon clapped in sarcasm. "I give that a two-point-seven."

Lindsay, not one to be a wallflower, waded across the water that sparkled with moonlight. She glanced up and then said to Dillon. "If you let go now, Patrick, this human pillow will break your fall."

"Wait! No!" Dillon pushed backwards and fell into a pile of rocks. "OW!"

"Okay." Lindsay hefted herself up. "Pool's all clear now!"

"How deep is it?" Finn called down. His hand had begun to burn and his grip was slipping.

"About four maybe five feet," Chart said. "So no cannonballs."

"Wasn't planning on it." Finn studied the glittering inky scene below. With about fifteen feet to the water, he figured feet first, flat footed, would be best. But then what? Would they all be stranded down there? Have to wade in the ocean to get back to the land?

Though climbing this rug and somehow getting back through the hole seemed like a task from Mission Impossible.

He said, "Chart, let's say I let go and we're all down there. You have a way for us to get back up to the house?"

"Sure, just going to take a little while."

"Why's that?" Lindsay said, glancing out toward the ocean. "Can't we just swim over to the beach and head up the rainforest hill?"

"Not unless you want to be shark food. Nope." He nodded behind her. "We'll have to climb the cliffs from here."

"That's going to take a while in this dark," she said.

"Which is why the big guy needs to let go. So we can get a move-on."

"All right, all right." Finn steadied himself and took a breath. Then without warning, he let go of the rug.

One-one thousand, he said to himself as his feet hit the water and drove right through to the bottom of the pool, slamming into the sandy surface, and causing his knees to buckle under him so hard that his entire body submerged under water for a moment. He sat up and his face was out of the water again.

"So much for the natural pool," Chart said. "You just drained it."

A moment later they heard, "Christ on a cracker."

It was good ol' Nikki, who stood in the now lighted living room above, both hands on her hips. She said, "Fuck are you all doing down there?"

CHAPTER FIFTEEN

VANESSA HAD TOSSED AND TURNED ON THE uneven bed of palm leaves and sand, unable to get comfortable, unable to get warm, as the wind had picked up considerably in the last hour, and there was a scratching noise coming from every direction. Must have been little shells blowing all over the sand, tumbling over the rocks about them.

Meanwhile, Chadwick snored away seemingly oblivious to both temperature and noise. As if he were a walrus or the like, made for sleeping in the elements.

Vanessa turned away from him, clapped her hands over her ears.

Throggle...glop.

Her back vibrated with the racket.

She squeezed her eyes shut, willed herself not the strike the man.

Throg...gurgle...glop.

She twisted and pulled her knees to her chest. Buried her head between her legs. Clamped her thighs over her ears. *Please God. Make it stop. Please let me sleep.*

And eventually she began to relax. Though it was a bit uncomfortable, she was now warm and it was silent. All she could hear was the sound of blood rushing through her skull. Perfect.

Vanessa began to drift off, as her breathing steadied, her muscles untensed. The darkness became soothing and quiet and

…

Shnoggle…goggle…GLOOP.

"Chadwick!" Vanessa spun and slapped him on the back of the head and punched him in the shoulder.

"AH!" Chadwick bolted to his feet, swinging his arms around, flailing like an injured crane. "What are you—?"

"Stop snoring!"

He ceased swinging his arms and rubbed his eyes. "I'm not snoring."

"I assure you." She kicked his leg. "You most certainly are!"

"Ouch! You are a bully!"

"What I am, is a saint for not strangling you."

"You are no saint." He stood there, wagging a finger at her, standing upright.

And that's when she noticed.

Staring at the behemoth form nearly busting from his trousers, she said, "Chadwick, were you having a wet dream?"

"A what?"

"Well look, you're all excited." She reached up and flicked the staff.

"Ow! Stop that!"

"Does it hurt?"

"It does when you do that!"

"And what about when I do this?" She reached back up and stroked it.

"No."

"No…what?" She kept stroking, her mouth now hanging open. She wanted to drool on it.

"No way you're going to talk me into anything lurid."

"Lurid?" Vanessa eased herself onto her knees. She placed both hands on the bulge and rubbed.

Chadwick's head dropped back. He moaned.

"And would you call this lurid?" She eased down the zipper and took hold of the beast. The magnificence of Chadwick. The essence of all his worth in one not-so-little package. His perfection.

"What are you…" he moaned again, "doing?"

"This." And she licked it.

"Vanny?"

"Yes, Chadwick?" He'd better ask his questions now, because once this monster filled her mouth, there'd be no talking for it.

"Don't."

"Don't what?" She tickled the bulb with another lick.

"Stop."

"Don't?" She flicked her tongue. "Or do…" Flick. "Stop?"

"I mean…"

And she sucked the tip.

"Yes. Don't ever stop."

But this tool of perfection was too good to be wasted with an oral exercise. No she needed to use this to all its potential. She needed to take this for herself.

And so she yanked down his trousers, wiggled out of her jeans, pulled Sir James lower, and wrapped her legs around him. "Push."

And he did.

He pushed and thrust and pressed and filled her with his magnificence. She pulled him forward, deep, as deep as she could take him into her. Sir James was splitting her with his sword, breaking her in two.

She kicked her heels out wide, yelled in beautiful agony, "Oh God!"

And he stopped. "Are you okay, Vanny?"

She blinked her eyes open. "Yes, yes! Don't stop now! Keep going!" She pulled him back into her, bucking her hips up to meet his.

"Go!" she yelled.

And Chadwick pounded forward again. He drove his mighty joust straight up through Vanessa, all the way up to her very being. The knight slaying his dragon.

He thrust and thrust and thrust.

Her arms shook and then her legs. She tightened and she came. And then she came again. And again. One orgasm after another. A steady, endless stream of them.

She kept coming and she couldn't stop. She had all she wanted. All she hoped. All she'd ever needed. Right here. Right now. "Yes. Yes! YES!"

Chadwick gave one brutal and unforgiving thrust and collapsed on top of Vanessa as her vision faded from star-bright to blackness.

She moaned, "Vivat Rex!"

And then she lost all consciousness.

CHAPTER SIXTEEN

"YOU KNOW WHERE HE IS AND YOU are going to tell us." Milo jerked the wheel of the tanker vehicle and Svetlana slid across the backseat, thumped against the door.

"You are driving too fast." She pulled up the hem of her dress, inspected her hip. "You have bruised me. See?"

"Put down the dress. We are not interested." Jak sat up front, arms folded across his chest.

"Why are you not interested? I am beautiful woman. I have the great legs." And she hoisted up and straightened her leg, placing her heel on Milo's shoulder as he drove.

"What are you—?" He swerved.

"See? Perfect." She smoothed her fingers all the way to her toes. "Do you want to touch for yourself?" She took hold of Jak's hand. "It is very smooth, the skin."

He jerked it away. "We told you. We are not interested in sex now."

"Wait." She folded her leg and pulled her dress back down. "Are you into the men?"

"Don't be ridiculous," Milo said.

"And him? Is he?" She lifted her chin to Jak.

"I am into poetry," Jak said. "I write Haiku."

"Writers don't have to be homosexual," Svetlana said.

"I am not homosexual."

"Then what are you?" Svetlana eyed him under her sunglasses.

"I told you. I am a poet."

"He is a poet," Milo confirmed.

"If you are lucky, I will write some poems of you."

"And if I am not lucky?" She dropped her sunglasses back to the bridge of her nose.

"We will kill you."

"Where are you from?" She stared out the back window.

Milo avoided a villager on the shoulder of the road and ran over a family of crabs. He was rewarded with the thump of a jackfruit on the truck's rooftop.

He said, "We are from Miami."

"I mean where did you grow up?"

Jak said, "We were born in Chernobyl."

"This is not a good place to be from." Svetlana made a face.

"No, The Federation gave us a new house, a new life after the accident. In Siberia."

"Yes The Federation is good to our people." Svetlana nodded once.

Milo said, "It was too cold. We moved to Miami and started a nightclub."

"You owned a nightclub? I love the Miami nightclubs. So many beautiful women and men and stars. It is where I belong. What one is yours?"

"It was called Red Eye, but it is no longer."

"Red Eye?" Svetlana asked. "This club had a fire, yes? It is burned down?"

"That is the one," Jak said, glancing back at her.

"What happened? Did you have a bad heater? Cigarette accident?"

"Your friend, the actor. This Dillon?" Milo stared at Svetlana in the mirror.

"What about him?" she asked.

Milo gripped the wheel. "He caused the fire. In the men's room."

"The whole club burned down. All our money and investment is gone!" Jak pounded a fist against the dash, rattling the whole car. "And this is why he owes us. And now it is why you are owing us. He traded his life for your money!"

"This is not fair!" Svetlana protested. "I have nothing to do with this!"

"You do now." Milo nodded and swerved. "Tell us where the Vlad and the video of pornography is, and we will let you live."

"I am a businesswoman too. I want the profits."

"If we kill you, there will be more profits for us," Milo said.

"If you let me live, I can make more tapings," Svetlana answered. "I will share with you for fifty percent of profit."

"She makes a good point," Jak said.

"Okay. We let you live. But we share the profits eighty-twenty. Eighty percent for us. And we decide how the film is to be distributed. We are the producers. We will never split these profits for fifty percent."

"No." Svetlana crossed her arms. "Eighty-twenty. Eighty for me!"

"Sixty-forty," Milo said. "Forty for you."

"Forty for you."

"Not a chance. We will take fifty percent. That is our final offer. Nothing less."

"Fine." Svetlana opened her purse and drew out her lipstick. "We have a deal then."

"Fine." Milo stopped the car at a fork in the road. One way to the village of the island, the other to the airport. "Now, where can we find Vlad?"

"Take a right," Svetlana said. "We will need an airplane."

"Where is he?" Jak said.

"He is in the mainland Australia. At the Tennis Open."

"We cannot afford the jet. We will steal a boat."

"No," Svetlana said. "By then it will be too late."

"We have no choice." Milo moved to turn left, toward the

village, where they could find a boat. But Svetlana placed a hand on his shoulder. "Don't worry. I have a way to get a ride for us.

"How? We cannot steal an airplane," Jak said.

"Steal one? No." Svetlana held up a Platinum American Express card. "We will charter one."

After Nikki had sent Jon to retrieve the rope they'd been secured to the back of the truck with, she tied it to the sofa and dropped an end down to Finn and the others. Dillon, being the smallest of the group, climbed the rope first, then Lindsay, then Chart. Then, with all of them sitting on the sofa, they yelled down to Finn to go ahead and climb.

He wrapped the rope around one leg and one arm and hoisted himself up. With each hoist, he gained maybe six inches and lost about ten percent of his energy.

Nikki said, "I'm serious about that diet, boss."

"Me too," he called back up.

Twenty minutes later and with no oxygen left, Finn hauled himself over the lip of the wood floor and collapsed.

Lindsay patted his heaving chest. "Tomorrow we start you on a healthy diet of leaves."

"Okay, okay," Finn said. "But first, I need a steak or something. I'm spent here."

"I have some ham steaks, how's that?" Chart said.

"That'll do."

"Christ boss." Nikki hid her eyes with a hand.

"Great I'll whip a few up. Anyone else?" Chart asked.

"No!" the rest of them said in unison.

Chart nodded and ducked into the kitchen.

"Where're we headed, Clark Gable?" Finn pushed up on an elbow.

"Who's that?" Dillon asked.

"The actor?" Nikki said, then rolled her eyes. "You are truly an empty condom aren't you?"

"What, am I supposed to know every single actor who has ever been in a movie before me? I'm busy like memorizing lines, you know."

"He was in Gone with the Wind. And Mutiny on the Bounty, bugnuts," Nikki snorted.

"Yeah? And like nobody from my generation has ever even heard of those films. What are they, Indies?"

"What are you, brain-damaged?" Nikki asked.

"I think it's the drugs," Lindsay said.

"No. The drug rumors aren't true." Dillon glanced away. "Sure, maybe I popped a few Xanax and some Oxy-cotton, but that's all. I was going through a rough patch!"

"It's Oxy-*con*-tin, dopey." Nikki shook her head.

"Whatever. You don't know what it's like, all the pressure from the fans. Demanding you give all of yourself to the screen and whatever is left over to them."

Maybe you need a better publicist," Lindsay said.

"Like, duh." Dillon made a face at her. "I'm gold to someone who has any idea what they're doing."

"Okay, Goldfinger." Finn sat upright, feeling almost sprite now with the prospect of food coming soon. "Let's get back to the issue at hand. Finding Vlad. Any idea where he went?"

"Maybe." Dillon shrugged. "Maybe the drugs screwed up my memory and I don't recall."

Nikki stepped forward, pinched Dillon by the ear, and twisted him to the hole still open next to Finn. "How about I jog your memory by dropping you and your forgetful skull on those rocks down there?"

"Okay! Okay! Jesus, Finn, call her off!"

"I can't control what she does."

"Doesn't she, like, work for you?" Dillon grimaced.

"She's terribly insubordinate," Finn said. "So if I were you, I'd start talking."

"They're headed to Australia, okay? The Tennis Open."

"I thought that was in January," Lindsay said.

"They pushed it up this year. Something about the Australian Rules Football final in Melbourne taking precedence."

"Why are they going to the Tennis Open?" Nikki torqued his ear. "If I recall correctly, Svetlana failed to get seeded for the tournament, because she was too busy being seeded by little punks like you."

"Ow! Shit, that hurts!" Dillon yelped.

"That's a disgusting image that I'll never be able to erase from my memory now, thank you," Lindsay said, pushing up off the sofa.

Dillon whined, "I don't know, I think Svetlana is meeting someone, going to sell the porno to him there. Some big deal for a lot of money."

"Which means we'd better beat them to the meeting." Finn pushed himself up to his feet just as Chart entered the room with a plateful of ham and two Hop Hog brews.

"No problem. You can eat this on the way," he said.

They all turned to Chart as he continued, "Did I tell you I have a boat?"

Plymouth, Massachusetts

Patrolman Tony Flood had just stepped into the shower when his cell phone began to ring. Ignoring it at first, he realized it wasn't his cell phone after all. It was his home phone. And only one person in this world still used that number. Rossi the Bossy.

Plymouth's Chief of Police.

Damn.

Shaking the glop of shampoo from his hand, Flood switched

off the water, grabbed his towel, and answered, "Yeah Chief?"

"Tony, am I interrupting something?"

"No, why?" He wiped the rest of the shampoo off.

"It rang three times. I figured maybe you and the missus, you know…"

Flood shook his head to himself. Having a hot girlfriend was like a curse to a police officer. The endless stream of sexual innuendos and outright suggestions were borderline ridiculous. But he took it all in good stride, saying, "Want me to take some photos? You and the boys can send 'em around?"

"Always edging for a promotion, aren't you, Tony?"

"You know me, boss."

"Anyway, since you're not at the station yet, I got a drive-by for you."

"Don't tell me Mrs. Pinkle is shooting at her neighbors' squirrels again."

"No, no. Nothing like that. This is serious and…" He coughed and continued, "could be political. I need someone I can trust."

"How so?"

"Getting reports of a body out on Saquish."

Flood sighed to himself. A trip out the peninsula would waste half—maybe the whole—morning in the car. He said, "A body? Why not send in a dick, then?"

"That's the thing, we haven't seen it yet. Just getting reports of a *foul odor* from a neighbor."

"Probably the college kids pulling a prank out here. Dead possum in the old man's mailbox again."

"Tony, I'm not asking here."

"Alright, alright. What's the addy?"

Rossi read off the address and Flood said, "Wait, that sports agent Patrick Finn lives out there, right? He's got that Svetlana babe who's all over the news about some Miami murder."

"Now you're getting the picture. Place is a circus, enough media to cover a goddamned Royal wedding."

"Perfect. I'll bring my roach spray."

"You may want to bring the salts."

"That bad?"

"Neighbor who called it in is three houses down. Good thing the media trucks are all parked upwind."

"Noted. Thanks, boss." Flood moved to end the call and Rossi cut back on.

"Hey, Tony!"

"Yeah?"

"Bring Martin with you to help. Like I said, this could turn political. I don't want to see a bunch of photos of some dead Russian model all over the news, got it? Keep the scene clean."

Easier said than done, Flood thought, especially with Martin, but he responded, "I'll keep it as tight as your wallet, boss."

"Not possible," he said and hung up.

So after a real quick shower, Flood grabbed a packet of smelling salts and headed out to Martin's house.

Martin, it seemed, was not quite ready though.

Flood pulled out a package of Slim Jims, opened one, and then dialed the number to Martin's cell phone.

After about five rings, he answered, "Hold on Tony."

A loud bang sounded, like the phone had been dropped. Then a scuffling noise and Martin came back on, "Hear me?"

"Sounds like you're in a prison cell, but yeah, I hear you." Flood unsheathed a long Slim Jim and took a bite.

"Sorry, man. Dropped you into the sink and you're on speakerphone."

"Uh, okay." Flood hoped the guy was dressed and ready. "You coming out or what?"

"Look, Tony, I already told the Chief. My kids, they all got lice."

Lovely. Flood took another bite of Slim Jim meaty goodness. "Okay…so what, are you babysitting?"

"Nah, man. I sent them back to school. Spread the wealth you know?"

"Your ethics are astounding, Martin."

"Yeah well, anyway, I'm trying to check myself here, but it's not so easy. These little bastards are tiny. Gotta wait for 'em to jump a round a bit, then I get 'em."

Flood forced the next swallow of meaty glory down. "Did you think of using that medicine? Nix or whatever?"

"Used it all up on the kids." The phone rattled around and Martin said, "Ah screw it. I'll be right out."

"Martin."

"Yeah?"

"Tell you what. Why don't you take your Chevy? I'll text you the address."

"Yeah, maybe that's better."

Flood hung up, texted the addy, and then drove up through Kingston and Duxbury to cross the bridge to Saquish. After winding his way through the tangle of media trucks, he parked as close to Patrick Finn's entry path as he could. Most of the reporters were either sleeping or enjoying their morning cup of coffee—too tired yet to make a fuss over the arrival of a policeman.

Or so he thought.

Because it wasn't ten seconds after he'd exited his vehicle that about a dozen reporters, paired with their respective cameramen, piled out of their trucks then scrambled to form a half moon of a crowd behind Flood.

Their sleepy murmurs quickly turned into rapid-fire questions.

Are you here with a subpoena?

Is Patrick Finn under arrest for the Miami murder?

Is Svetlana hiding in there with Mr. Finn?

Who killed that bodyguard in Miami?

Where is Patrick Finn?

Where is Svetlana?

Are they here?

Flood ignored them, and as he made a move to open the gate,

he heard a low rumbling growl on the other side. Flood peeked over the fencing to find a short, squat, formidable looking English Bulldog.

"Hey there, buddy," Flood said.

A cameraman leaned over and said, "Yeah, he's been keeping us from getting into that yard for the past two days. Little tyrant."

"That'd be trespassing anyway," Flood said. "Good job, little buddy." Then he uncurled a long Slim Jim from his pocket and unwrapped it.

The bulldog woofed once.

"We got a deal?" Flood said.

Woof.

"Okay, then." Flood unlatched the gate, opened it, and kneeled down. "Here you go." He held out the Slim Jim and the bulldog—apparently named Hobey, according to his neck tag—grabbed the stick and made a hell of a mess trying to get it in his mouth.

Flood wiped the slobber that Hobey'd slung onto his hand on a pant leg and walked the down the path.

Hobey followed.

A reporter yelled, "That mean we can—?"

"Still trespassing," Flood yelled behind him.

And that's when the smell just about knocked Flood over.

As if a whole cow had been rotting inside the house.

Flood walked to the front door and peered inside. No lights, no movement. He knocked. No answer. Then he peered inside one of the windows.

A reporter yelled from behind, "Not a sign of movement in two days! If they're in there, they're in the basement!"

Hobey, apparently finished with the Slim Jim already, barked loudly.

Flood turned to him. "What is it, pal?"

Hobey barked and took off around the side of the house, over a sand dune and through some tall weeds poking from the sand.

Flood followed, noticing the scent was getting stronger. He

hadn't smelled anything this bad since that time they'd found that whole rock band called Mushroom Anatomy in the lead guitarist's basement. Apparently the band—not as knowledgable as their name would suggest—had ingested a heap of bum psychedelic mushrooms, as the stems left on the coffee table had been identified as *Amanita phalloides*. Easily mistaken for the common *Amanita 'puffball'* variety, the *phalloides* is one of the deadliest mushrooms known to man. A simple case of mistaken identity.

And the smell from that basement. Well...

It was just about as bad here, but with the wind whipping down from the North, it would have never reached the front of the house. Good thing.

Flood kept following Hobey around the side of the yard.

As he turned the corner, his name was called out from the front of the house.

Flood turned back to see Officer Martin approaching, hat in hand. "Hell is going on here?"

Flood stared at the man. Dressed impeccably in his uniform, shoes shined, belt buckle sparkling, his badge nice and straight. Perfectly groomed, and not a single detail out of place. Except for the man's hair, which was now glowing bright, the color of nuclear lemonade.

"What about up there?" Flood said, nodding toward the man's head.

"Yeah, that. I couldn't take it anymore. It was like they were multiplying faster than I could kill 'em."

"So what, you dipped your head in plutonium?"

"Nah, man, bleach. You know, Clorox."

"Martin, I'm not so sure that's safe for your skin."

"Yeah." He held up his hat. "It burns a bit."

"It's a good look for you."

"Serious?"

"Sure."

Flood turned back to the side of the house and said, "Tell you what, you keep the media rats out behind us, and I'll go check out the stiff."

Holding his nose, Martin said, "Deal."

So Flood made his way around the house and stopped when he saw Hobey sitting at the edge of a short row of bushes and next him, a leg protruding from the leaves.

Hobey barked.

Flood drew one of smelling salts from his pocket and broke it. He took a good sniff of the ammonia and edged closer, all the while thinking about how he had just a few more years of this nonsense. No more Mrs. Pinkle, no more raucous teenage parties to break up on the beach, no more drunk, texting drivers, parking their cars in their own living rooms. Nope. Just Tony Flood and a fishing boat. He'd soon watch every sunrise with his coffee and every sunset with a cold brew. And when not playing hide the lure with his girl, he'd be dropping a line in the water.

Every man's Heaven.

But for now, he had a body to identify. And from the looks of the shoe, it was no Russian supermodel, and it was no giant super sports agent.

Woof. Hobey seemed to agree.

Screw it, Flood thought, and took one more breath of ammonia and then four long strides, eyes closed. And he opened them to see something that he never could have imagined.

Because there, at the edge of the house, lay what looked to have been a man in his late seventies or early eighties. He wore an old, tattered Red Sox ball cap, now crumpled to the side of his head, and a tan Members Only jacket with tan khaki pants. His mouth was wide open, showing off a full set of teeth and his face was frozen with a look that held equal parts of sheer terror and unbearable grief.

But the strangest part of the scene was that the old man was gripping with both arms, tightly to his chest, as if he would never let go, he would hold on for all eternity, the enormous—no, gigantic—black lobster. Its eyes were clouded and its claws hung limp down the old man's ribs. Clearly dead.

But then the lobster twitched.

Flood leaned forward, hand over his nose. "What the—"

The tail flickered, and he jumped back. How could it possibly be...Then he saw it. A smaller tail, poking from beneath the larger one. And then another.

Flood leaned forward again and eased the huge tail upward. And there, all nestled together in a tangle of tails and claws and tiny antennae, were about two dozen baby lobsters. Flood took hold of them, cradling the stinky little guys in his arms. He had to get them to water, and fast.

"Who the hell is that?" Martin said, startling Flood as he turned.

And then a blaze of flash bulbs and cameras lit the scene like the red carpet at the Oscars.

"Uh, oh," Martin said.

So much for discretion, Flood thought.

CHAPTER SEVENTEEN

When Chart said he had a boat, Finn pictured a deep-sea fishing type of rig, complete with trawling wires and a captain's deck. Maybe a large ice cooler built into the deck. But what he never expected to see was the gleaming silver and blue specimen that rocked back and forth before him.

"A power yacht?" Finn asked. "For real?"

"You got it." Chart slapped the side of the hull with an open palm. "Meet Sweet Judy Blue Eyes."

"Who's Judy?" Dillon asked.

"A tribute to Crosby, Stills, and Nash," Finn said. "You know, the song?"

Dillon just stared back like a dazed walleye.

"What are you some kind of drug runner?" Nikki asked Chart.

Good old Nikki, she knows how to be circumspect and lead up to a difficult or confrontational line of questioning.

Chart laughed it off. "Not exactly, no."

"That's a shame." Dillon climbed aboard and almost slipped on the polished wood deck. "I could use a pick-me-up."

Nikki turned back to Chart. "So what, then, trust fund, baby? Lucky sperm club?"

"Nik, go easy." Finn placed a hand on her shoulder.

"Simple questions," she said.

Finn stepped forward. "What she's trying to say is, we can't climb aboard a boat that may or may not attract the attention of the authorities and get us all arrested. That's all."

"Understood and no offense taken," Chart said.

"So...it's not stolen either?" Lindsay winced as she asked.

Jon said, "Good Lord, I think we should ease up on Mr. Chart here. He looks legitimate to me. When you're cute like him, people tend to give you things. Right, Mr. Chart?" Jon tilted his head.

Chart laughed and slapped Jon on the shoulder. "The way of the world, my man."

Jon beamed.

Nikki said, "Some schmuck gave this to you?"

"No, no. I earned it fair and square." Chart laughed and then untied the boat from the short dock's mooring hitch and jumped aboard. "Won it in a poker game last year from some crazy Kiwi!"

A poker game. Finn didn't know a ton about boats, but after the little adventure with his NHL All-Star hockey goalie client, Lew Kunkle, last year—the one who'd bought a yacht to live on in South Florida—Finn had learned a few things. For one, this sleek little silver model was an Italian designed and manufactured Pershing 88. The outside looked like a boat version of a Maserati and the inside was as nice as any designer apartment in Milan. He was pretty sure he'd seen it in more than one Bond film.

"Jesus, what was the game's buy-in?" Finn asked.

"A hundred bucks, but..." Chart squeezed his chin and said, "Fella was into me for a good three or four K by five am."

"Correct me if I'm wrong, but this boat has a street value a little higher than that," Finn said.

Chart nodded. "Oh yeah, I think it's five-hundred or so."

"Thousand?" Nikki said. "Fuck me."

Chart looked her up and down and raised an eyebrow as he smiled.

Nikki shook her head. "Tell you what, Romeo, when we find Svetlana she can do the honors."

"Suit yourself, but there's a fantastic stateroom downstairs if you change your mind. Fine Italian leather benches, full kitchen, and a flatscreen overlooking the silk-sheeted bed." He glanced around and continued, "No worry, there're a couple sets of bunk beds down there, too." He winked.

"I don't see what you guys are making such a big deal about. These are like a dollar a dozen in Miami." Dillon crossed his arms and shrugged.

"It's *dime* a dozen, you fucktard," Nikki said.

"Whatever, everything's more expensive in SoBe." Dillon made an idiotic face.

"Including intelligence, obviously." Lindsay slid down onto a long leather bench that was covered by the boat's half-roof.

"I don't even know what that means," Dillon said.

Finn turned to Chart. "So, how long is it going to take to get up to mainland?"

Chart said, "Settle in and make yourselves comfortable, gonna be two days to Melbourne."

"Seriously?" Nikki ran a hand through her hair. "That's the fastest way?"

"Direct route," Chart said. "Hey, you're lucky I juiced this baby up. It can go 70 knots now. Twice as fast as OEM."

Jon sighed. "Well I for one am going to see how soft those silk sheets are then."

Dillon said, "I'm laying up front so I wake up to the rays. Need to work on my tan for the babes when we get back to civilization."

"Not sure that's safe while we're going that fast." Lindsay peered around Finn and up at the small flat white deck at the front of the boat.

"The motors are in the back, genius," Dillon said and walked away, climbing up on the deck.

Nobody took the time to explain that if he fell out that the motors would go right over him.

"So…" Finn peered down the stairs to the stateroom. "You said there's a pantry down there?"

"Jesus, boss, you just ate two pounds of ham steak," Nikki

said.

Finn shrugged. "What?"

"Fully stocked," Chart said. "Help yourself."

"Say," Lindsay leaned over and whispered, "Why don't we go stake a claim to the master bed?" She nodded to Chart. "He'll be busy playing captain, and you could be my deck mate."

Finn felt like he'd split open Pandora's box with Lindsay. No way to put the sex kitten back in the bag…so to speak.

He said, "Aren't you concerned?" And glanced at the people around them.

"Not really," she said, "I need a good stretch, if you know what I mean."

And so there you go.

"On second thought," Finn said. "Maybe I'll eat something later."

At such a late hour, the airport terminal was empty, except for the lone attendant at the check-in desk waiting on a lone customer. Milo, Jak, and Svetlana hadn't needed plane tickets to get into the building, and nobody even noticed the large, simple man carrying a harpoon inside. Milo wondered how early the flights took off each day as he he racked his brain for a new plan.

Meanwhile, Svetlana stood by the shitty little window that faced the shitty little runway while speaking to American Express on her cell phone. Her English became more broken the angrier she became.

Of course her agent had cancelled the credit card, Milo mused. He was amazed the man had given one to Svetlana in the first place. That was like putting a rat in charge of the cheese factory. Milo looked her up and down as she continued her cell phone tirade. *Albeit a very sexy and persuasive rat,* he thought.

She yelled, "You fools are lucky to have ever done the business for me!" and ended the call.

The two men at the desk glanced up at Svetlana and then away quickly again when they saw her swivel toward them.

The tall Asian man said, "My staff is transferring the crates into the luggage area now. They are to be loaded onto the plane by ten am. I will leave by noon."

"Yes, Mr. Zing."

"Zin. It is Zin."

"Very well, Zen. Sign here." The attendant pushed a piece of paper to the man and pointed.

"Now what?" Jak said, hiding the harpoon behind him, as Milo had suggested.

"Now we wait," Milo answered.

"For what?" Svetlana tapped her high heeled toe on the cracked marble floor.

Milo leaned over and whispered, "Them."

"What about them?" Jak said loud enough that the attendant and Zin both glanced back at them again.

Talk about fools, Milo thought, my brother could sometimes be the prince of them. Milo leaned over again, "If you shut up long enough, perhaps you will find out."

Jak shrugged. "I will concentrate on my newest poem then."

"You do that."

"Can I see it?" Svetlana peered at the journal in Jak's hand.

"Not yet."

"What is it about?" she asked.

"Feliks."

"Who is Feliks?"

"The only pet I ever had." He looked at Milo. "Isn't that right, brother?"

Milo waved a hand.

"I will read it to you," Jak said to Svetlana. "It goes,
the brilliant Feliks,
left for death, by Milo's hand

We all miss his licks."

"Who is we?" Svetlana asked.

Milo shook his head. "The little people crawling in the simple man's head."

"You don't know genius when you see it." Jak closed the journal.

"I see genius every morning in the mirror." Milo shrugged.

"The two of you fight too much. You are brothers, da? You should not treat each other like this."

Milo said, "What do you know of brothers?"

"I know a lot about men."

"You know a lot about one aspect of men." He pointed to his groin.

"Perhaps this aspect tells me all I need to know." Svetlana fished in her purse and drew out a tube of lipstick.

As she smeared her lips with the bright candy red color, Milo watched the man named Zin leave. Dressed in a tailored suit, he obviously had tremendous wealth. Milo wondered what he was doing on such a miserable island as this. He walked to the desk and peered at the manifest the attendant was preparing as he asked, "How long of a flight is it to Melbourne from here?"

According to the manifest, Zin was headed there tomorrow. No doubt to see some of the tennis tournament himself. It was a wealthy person's event, of course. And Zin was wealthy, evidenced by the listing of his plane.

A Lear Jet.

Milo moved closer and read a notation next to the tail number that said *Long Range*. Perhaps this meant the jet was fitted with an extra gas tank for—

The attendant moved the sheet away from Milo. "A bit longer than six hours on most private jets, why?"

"I was curious, as we, too, are arranging for a charter."

The attendant looked Milo up and down and smirked. "I'm sure you are."

"You think I cannot afford one? I am Russian oil magnate. I can afford a lot of things."

"Mmm. Hmmm." The attendant placed the papers into a large metal stapler, and with a loud *THWACK* he stapled them together. Then he reached under the counter to retrieve an envelope. As he folded the sheets into the envelope, he said, "You let me know just as soon as you expect your plane to arrive and I'll arrange everything you need from here. If there is a plane that is…" He whispered the last part.

"It will come later tonight."

"Well I suggest you find someplace to wait nearby. This terminal closes in five minutes."

Milo had a plan that required access to the luggage area after the attendant left. After all, this airport was not like the large commercial ones in New York or Moscow. He said, "We will stay here. It may not arrive until the morning."

"You can't sleep here."

"We are not bothering anyone. It is just us." Milo pointed at Jak, who was mired in his journal and Svetlana, who sat straight up, sunglasses on with bright red pouty lips.

"This is not allowed. The security patrol will come as soon as I leave this station. So you must go now."

As Milo was about to respond to this, Jak approached the side of the desk. He placed a hand on the stapler and said, "I need an envelope. Do you have an extra one?"

"If I give you one, will you leave?"

"Absolutely." Jak nodded while glancing at Milo.

"Alright, then." The man bent over to reach for an envelope and, in one fluid and lightning fast motion, Jak took hold of the metal stapler, swung it up in an arc and back down on the little man's head. With a simple *oof*, he collapsed behind the counter.

"There," Jak said.

"That was good thinking," Milo said. He put a hand on his brother's shoulder. "I am proud of you."

Svetlana walked over and peered behind the desk. She said, "I don't think I should be associating with you two. It is bad for my reputation as a professional athlete."

"Do you want me to finish, then?" Jak asked, holding up the harpoon.

Yes, but not with that," Milo said. "Too much blood and the guards will soon be making their rounds."

"OK. I have the better idea." Jak grabbed the man by the ankles and dragged him to the men's room.

"What is he doing? This does not help." Svetlana pouted.

Milo reached over and took the envelope off the stack that the attendant had placed it on. Reading the manifest, he said, "I told you, we are not leaving."

"You did not tell me this. You told that man who is with Jak."

A lot of flushing sounded through the door and then Jak came out, his arms wet up to the elbows. "Now we can stay."

Milo said, "We should go to the luggage area. The security man will surely not check in there at this late hour." He replaced the envelope in the stack.

Svetlana stood up and said, "I hope they have a sofa or a lounge area in this place."

"It is not going to be like a Vegas nightclub. It is a luggage area."

"You can sleep on a suitcase," Jak said, wiping his arms on his pants.

"Disgusting."

"Come. It is this direction." Milo pointed to a set of three metal doors that led to an area adjacent to the runways outside the shitty window.

Four minutes and a broken door later, the three of them wandered through the luggage area.

"I cannot see a thing," Svetlana stood in the open doorway.

"Fix that," Milo said to Jak, pointing to the door.

Jak pushed Svetlana aside and wedged the door closed,

bending the metal lock mechanism with his bare hands.

"You are strong," Svetlana said.

"Da."

"I like that in a man."

Jak glanced at her and away.

Milo flipped on his cell phone light and wandered around the dark area, searching for the right luggage, hoping the attendant had written it down correctly.

"There!" he said, pointing to the crates. "Now we have a ride to the mainland."

"You are kidding, yes? I would not climb into that with even the Brad Pitt." Svetlana pointed. Stuffed with large brown coarse-woven cloth sacks of what appeared to be that awful jackfruit, the crate was large enough to fit Jak.

"Good," he said, nodding at the second crate. "Because you will be in that one…

"With me."

CHAPTER EIGHTEEN

EVERY TIME FELIKS MADE A RUN FOR it, the damned thingy that the big funny sounding guy had looped around his neck yanked him back up onto the porch. He couldn't remember what it was called. Not quite a leash. Too long and too thick. A mope? No that wasn't it. A clop?

Nah.

In any case, whatever it was it had caused Feliks to almost pop his own head off, like one of those mice who'd been half eaten by an owl. Running around in circles looking for its own behind.

Not Feliks. No way.

So he sat on his back paws while he fed the long, thick leashy thing up to his mouth with his front paws. This was definitely a time to be a human, or any other animal for that matter who had those elusive opposable thumbs. Yeah, a couple of those would be great right now. Because then he wouldn't have to taste the oily grimy sludge on this mope thingy. *Yuck*.

But his teeth were sharp enough.

Didn't take but a few minutes to gnaw through that thingy and be on his way. Now he could follow that road, the same one that took him all the way out here to this place, and get back to that house with the cheese in the kitchen. *Yummy*.

And as he had that thought, a *whizz* and then a *thump* sounded next to him. The *whizz* so close it almost took off his ear.

Feliks looked at the culprit on the ground. A large nut of sorts.

A big, hairy nut. Gross.

But wait. That was the victim. Because…

He peered up the tall tree from whence it came. And there, at the very top, a huge, monstrous-sized crustacean of some kind used his opposable claws to pinch off leaves and…

Feliks darted left.

Whizz.

Thump.

Another close call.

Another nut. Another victim.

Because the crab was the culprit. And it would be up to Feliks to stop him. So, he dug his right claw into the base of the tree and then his left. And he darted straight up the trunk. The cheese could wait a few minutes. But first.

A little seafood.

Vanessa lay in not quite a deep slumber, but rather the kind of sleep that you know you are in, not quite dreaming, not fully lucid, yet unwilling to wake, nearly unwilling to move. Almost the perfect state.

And in her dreamy vision, she saw herself bathed in sunlight, a warm white glow about her like an enormous halo. One that blocked out any other landscape or object. Much like a cloud of perfect milky light. One so thick that it could hold her, yet fluid enough that it radiated and moved about her as well.

It was almost as if she were touching the creamy gates of Heaven itself.

And as Vanessa soaked in the comfort, the warmth, the utter perfection of the moment, she heard a rustle. And then a groan.

And stumbling into her vision, she saw Chadwick. Well, not the man, but rather the essence of the man. He was shaped as he should be, all tall and purple and throbbing. That head was now beautiful. It was a cone of pleasure, really.

But it was muttering something.

Vanessa told him to quiet down, not confuse the matter. Stay as he should be.

But he mumbled again. And then he groaned.

And Vanessa saw a six-legged woman appear from behind The Essence of Chadwick, and skitter about him like a god-awful, sex-crazed spider. Then another appeared. And another. Dozens of the leggy creatures circled him, sized him up. Then that first spidery lady—a wee bit larger than the others—gingerly placed each of her legs up and around the thickness of Chadwick. She squeezed just hard enough to climb him. And then, no sooner than she had glanced at Vanessa, the sex-spider darted up the Chadwick Shaft and nestled herself around the head.

That glorious, wonderful—

WAIT!

That is mine! Vanessa shocked herself with the thought. She was so angry that she was yelling it in her dream.

Chadwick moaned.

Then the creatures began circling Vanessa. They peered at her, *wondering, what kind woman was she?*

I'm not *that* kind of woman, she said.

And one of them tested her with a touch. A long spindly leg against her own. Oozing with want and need and hope. Hope to take advantage. Need to have her.

She yelled this time, *We don't want your sort. Leave us. Leave us be!*

But was it heard? Was Vanessa still asleep? She had to wake.

The creatures skittered back and then sized up Chadwick again. They watched their leader take him. They watched her legs stroke and grind.

Vanessa had to pull herself through and up and out of the murky depths to take action. To stop this creature—all these sex-starved creatures—from mounting her man.

And Vanessa willed herself to wake. To push through the slumber-mud. To find lucidity.

Chadwick moaned louder. And louder.

That bitch!

And he moved. He moved with the creature.

Stop that!

And he groaned an awful plea of pleasure and pain.

I SAID, THAT IS MINE!

And Vanessa shot through the paralyzing force of sleep, straight up into herself and into this hot, bright reality.

The beach, blurry in her new-found vision. The sand and the waves. And Chadwick.

Vanessa felt behind her, his leg. "Wake up. Wake up Chaddy, you're dreaming."

He moaned louder.

Vanessa pinched her eyes.

He groaned.

"Chadwick!"

She blinked her eyes to see and then turned, and jumped to her feet and stared.

At the dozens—no, hundreds...maybe thousands—of crabs crawling across the beach.

Crawling across Chadwick. Crawling across his face.

"Chadwick!"

Chadwick shot straight up and the crabs fell and skittered away. All of them except one.

The one on his face.

Chadwick gave a muffled scream, "Get it off! Get it off me!" He spun in a circle, slapping at the creature with limp hands.

Vanessa grabbed a branch and swatted at it but missed, striking Chadwick's head instead.

"OW!" He wrestled with the creature. Both hands.

Vanessa swatted and missing again, she'd left a bright red mark across his neck.

"OW! OW! OW!"

"Sorry!"

Chadwick spun and spun and spun.

"OW. OW. OWWEEE!"

Chadwick, like a white-bread man trying to move to an unheard techno-beat, lifted his knee high and bent his back, kicked the foot out and thrust a fist in the air. All the while, gripping and pulling and twisting the creature that had locked onto his face.

A Monty Python episode, Vanessa mused, too mesmerized by the millions of crabs around her. A giant beating heart of them. Throngs and veins and waves of them. They literally colored the beach red.

And a crab skittered across her foot, waking her from the trance. Vanessa saw now that they were going to the water. They were…she stared at the small waves pushing the crabs back as they ran into the water and stopped for a few moments and then skittered back onto the beach. Spent. Their mission accomplished. All emptied now.

Of eggs.

My God, Vanessa thought. It's trying to impregnate him.

And she ran to Chadwick and with all her might, she gripped the little creature's back and she yanked.

"VANESSA!"

And the crab gave way just long enough for her to pry it off of Chadwick's nose. But then it snipped at Vanessa's fingers, cutting into her.

"Bloody hell!" She smacked it and stepped back.

The creature fell from Chadwick's face, and with one claw outstretched, in a final attempt of saving itself from the fall, it pinched one last time.

"OWEEEE!"

Onto Chadwick's ear.

Milo felt the first bite at what he estimated to be the halfway mark of the flight from Christmas Island to Melbourne. A nibble on his calf is all it was, but it had kicked off the ensuing feast. Svetlana, who had curled herself into a tight ball to keep warm, was barely breathing in her sleep.

He wasn't sure if they'd invaded her sack, too.

The little critters must have been hiding in the wood of the crates. They smelled the human sweat and ventured out for a meal. Probably came from those sacks of awful jackfruit that had been in these crates. What kind of millionaire was this guy, anyway? Even Milo, a man who had grown up in Communist Russia—no fresh fruit for the first seventeen years of his life— wouldn't waste the time and effort to purchase a single piece of that junk fruit. That guy had diverted the plane to that crappy little island to load up on two crates full of it!

Imagine how pissed he'd be when he found out it was all stuffed in the trash back in the baggage area.

Another bite and Milo slid his hand down his leg, scraping it on the inside of the crate, and he itched the spot. Then another bit his elbow. Before he knew it, one had crawled into his armpit—he jerked his hand up to stop the little mite.

Svetlana yelled, "Son of bitch!"

"Shh! You must keep it down," Milo said.

"You are punching me."

"There are bugs!" Milo whispered loudly.

"I am feeling it, too," Jak called.

About seven feet from them, Jak was in his own crate, locked tight when the baggage handlers had loaded them onto the plane in the morning. Milo couldn't see, but the locks sounded pretty hefty on these shipping crates.

What the hell did they need to lock up fruit for, anyway?

What a fool, Milo thought.

Svetlana said, "I feel none of these bugs you speak of. Stop kicking!" She kicked his leg.

"Stop that, and be quiet!" Milo said, nudging her. He couldn't see her in the darkness of the plane's luggage hold, and his back was pressed to hers—the only way they would both fit in the crate.

She said, "Stop kicking and I will stop yelling!"

"Don't be stupid." Milo gritted his teeth. "They cannot know we are here until after they unload the crates."

Jak said, "Why are they not biting Svetlana?"

"I smell too good. I use the lotion, not like you pigs!" Svetlana yelled the last word so loudly this time, he was certain they would hear them from above. Even above the roaring buzz of the engines.

"That's it!" Milo wriggled and pushed his leg up, untied his boot.

"What are you doing?" Svetlana said.

"I told you to shut up."

"I am not shutting up."

"She is not shutting up, brother," Jak said.

"I know this. That is why…" He slid his hand lower and under his sock. The only skin protected from these tiny beasts. But this was serious. If they were ever to find Vladimir and the tape and become rich, Milo had to shut this bitching woman up. Otherwise there would be a team of police waiting for them on the tarmac.

"You kicked my back." She elbowed him in the ribs.

"Shit!"

"See? It hurts."

"Why are you hurting her, brother?" Jak called.

"Milo ignored them and slid the sock all the way off. Then he twisted and bent and squeezed his arms and legs in rotation.

"What are you trying to do?" Svetlana kicked again and said, "Ouch! That hurts!"

"Stop kicking." Milo forced his shoulder to turn all the way until he was spooning Svetlana.

"You are the one kicking," Svetlana yelled.

"Why would you kick her, brother?"

Milo pushed both knees up and under Svetlana's, immobilizing her legs and feet.

"Are you trying to have the sex with me now? I am not in the mood." Svetlana elbowed him in the ribs.

"Oof." Milo reached his arm up and across his body. He squeezed it against the inside of the crate until it was across Svetlana's chest.

"I am not having the sex. Stop this. Stop this!" She was all out screaming now. Milo had to hurry.

He reached up, his closed fist pushing against her breast.

"What is this smell? What are you?"

And Milo found her face, her mouth.

She bit his hand.

"OW!"

He jabbed her ribs with a thumb from his other hand.

She bit again.

"Why are you raping her, brother? She does not want this."

"I'm not—"

She bit again.

"Ow!" And he turned his wrist and shoved the sock into her mouth.

Svetlana screamed a throaty, muffled, what would have been a blood-curdling cry, but it was silenced with the polyester and cotton blend of the stocking.

But then Svetlana bucked. And she thrust her skull back, colliding the back of her head into the front of Milo's. He first saw a bright yellow star in the shape of a giant rooster. Then blackness spilled over the vision.

Svetlana fell limp, having knocked herself out.

Milo felt woozy. The bugs kept biting.

The blackness closed in, bleeding over every edge of his vision.

He tried to move to itch his knee, but the buzz of the airplane faded into silence as Milo slid into blackness with it.

"Brother?"

Ten minutes later, and after navigating the sea of red pinchers on the beach, Vanessa and Chadwick walked along the road in silence. No cars, as this road and seemingly most others had been closed for what the signs declared *Crab Migration*. Strange people here, Vanessa mused as they crunched across the stones and gravel in otherwise silence. Chadwick didn't feel up to chit-chat and for fairly good reason.

She stepped over a huddle of crabs and glanced at him. "Want to try again?"

"No."

"Are you sure?"

"I am."

"Well." She stared at the creature dangling from his ear. "We'll have to do something at some point."

"It doesn't hurt anymore, I'm fine."

"It looks like it hurts."

"It's on the lobe. Like an earring, I imagine. Though I've never had a piercing, myself."

"So that's it. You'll just wander around with a crab dangling from your face…for the rest of your life."

"I suppose so."

"Brilliant."

"Besides." He reached up and patted the creature on the back. "We've reached a truce, haven't we, Hot Stuff?"

"Hot Stuff? What does that mean?"

"It's her name."

"You've named her."

"Hot Stuff. Like that Lil' Red Devil in the comic. Don't you remember? By that Australian chap. What's his name?"

"I've no idea."

"Well you should remember. It was a very popular comic when we were children."

"I'm sure."

"I believe it was Harvey Comics."

"Chadwick?"

"Yes, mum?"

"You can shut it now."

He muttered, "You're so unpleasant to be with sometimes." Then he reached up and stroked the crab. "She's not so bad once you get to know her, Hot Stuff. Don't you mind."

And thank the good Lord that's all he said for the next thirty minutes, as they made their way back to the house where Chadwick had seen Finn and company.

Feliks crossed the final ravine and scaled the rocky cliff, emerging on the side yard of The House With The Cheese. He canvassed the site for interruptors, those who may once again try to restrain him with that mope-thingy, but saw no-one. The pool water was flat, no persons in the water. Or animals, for that matter. Though Feliks doubted the sharks would show themselves if they were living in The House With The Cheese's pool. No no, they would stay well hidden from sight of passers-by. Though Feliks had heard once that some sharks could jump from the water and clear a whole boat to get to their prey.

So it couldn't hurt to check. Carefully, of course.

Feliks crept up to the poolside, slowly, peering at the blue water. Unnatural, it was, with the sorts of chemicals that these silly humans put into the water. Silly, really, if you think about it. I mean, what were they trying to do with all those chemicals? Make it smell worse? Would that keep the sharks out?

Who knows what these humans think.

But, as Feliks figured, there were no sharks. At least none visible from here. See what the chemicals do? Ruin the whole ecosystem of that little man-made pond. Still, Feliks wanted a better look. So, he stepped onto the mini blue pier—bouncy, it was —and peered deep into the water.

Not a single fish. Just a large painting of lady with a fishtail at the bottom of the pool. Was that supposed to be scary? She looked like a meal to Feliks. Well, if she didn't appear two-dimensional, she would anyway.

Strange, these human people.

At the very best, the image was making him hungry, not scared.

Cheese.

Feliks carefully backed off the pier. He didn't want to get wet today. Not if there was no meal promised at the other end of the water torture.

And as he placed his back paw on the concrete edge of the pool, he caught a movement from the corner of his eye.

He froze.

There. Two humans on the path to the house. A woman walking first, ahead of a man. A very tall man. With a large thingy hanging from his ear.

Was that a crab? Was it attacking? Why was the man not fighting back? Those claws hurt!

Another note of evidence to log into the files of human strangeness, Feliks thought. But this man would then be very strong and a formidable opponent to Feliks. He would go straight to the cheese and take it first.

A cheese thief.

Feliks crept backwards, one step at a time, smooth and easy. He didn't want to be seen. He needed to stay quiet and calm. He needed to remain hidden. He needed to retain the element of surprise on these two. He would use every advantage at his disposal, he would. Because this cat was no pushover. This cat was no chump. This cat would do what it takes. Whatever it takes.

To win that cheese.

CHAPTER NINETEEN

FINN WOKE TO THE SLOSHING SOUND OF waves hitting the hull of the yacht mixed by the buzz of the motors. Though the ride was smooth in such a large boat, Chart must've been pushing it close to full throttle, as the steady, deep hum was as loud as any marine motor Finn had ever heard. Meanwhile, Lindsay slept like a passed out sailor, head tucked under the pillow and unmoving.

Finn eased his leg out from under hers, and she didn't as much as stir.

He climbed out of bed, holding onto the ceiling of the stateroom and steadying himself with a knee against the bed frame. He glanced down at Lindsay. Still no movement. If he didn't know better already, he could mistake her for dead.

This girl acted like a guy all the way up until she didn't.

The image of her placing both feet flat against the headboard last night as she rocked on top of him, like some sort of yoga-karma-sutra super-move, flashed in his mind.

Finn had almost hyperventilated just trying to keep up.

He tip-toed to the doorway naked, grabbing a pile of clothes from the floor on the way. Then he slid the door open with an elbow and stepped out. Sliding it back closed, he almost jumped when a voice sounded behind him.

"Holy grail, you've got the ass of bison."

Jon stood with his head tilted to the side, a hand on his chin.

"Good morning, Jon."

His eyes went wide. "It is now."

Finn kept his back to Jon as he tried to slip a foot into his boxers. The tight corridor made this just about impossible though, and Finn fell to the side, his shoulder breaking his fall against the far wall.

"Easy big fella, I won't bite," Jon paused, then said, "too hard."

"Not your type, Jon, you should know."

"Don't you want to try? See if it…sticks…so to speak?"

"I'm good." Finn got his other leg into the boxers and pulled them up.

"I'm certain you are."

Finn turned to face him and then stepped into his shorts. "Sleep well?"

"Once all that the rocking and knocking stopped, I slept like a puppy."

Finn glanced up the stairs. "Yeah, the water was pretty choppy on the way out last night."

"I'm talking about your roommate." He winked.

Oops.

Finn said, "Anyone else up?"

"I'm not sure, but I don't think little Nikki ever made it to bed last night." He held up a limp wrist. "At least not to her bed."

"Really." Finn stared up the flight of stairs. "Where was she?"

"I think she's taken a bit of a liking to the captain."

"Well then." Finn pulled the t-shirt over his head. "Let's have a peek at their progress, then, shall we?"

"Sounds scandalous." Jon followed Finn up the stairs, making a *hmm, mmm* sound behind him. Then he whispered, "Let me know if you change your mind."

Sure enough, Nikki was still up in the wheelhouse with Chart. But now she was seated in front of him, hands at the wheel. Chart stood behind her, both hands over hers, whispering in her ear.

Interesting.

Finn cleared his throat.

"Jesus, Finn." Nikki jumped out of the captain's chair, almost knocking Chart over.

"Interrupt something?"

"Fuck are you to talk? We heard you and Lindsay trying to crack the hull of the boat for an hour last night."

Chart said, "Not to worry, this baby is solid. Even the tamed bear here couldn't break through with a little everyday hanky panky."

Jon shook his head with a finger to his mouth. "I don't know what you all heard, but there was nothing everyday about it from my listening vantage."

"Alright, enough." Finn climbed up and settled into the second captain's chair. "So what's our ETA, deckhand Nikki?"

She deferred to Chart, who said, "Still have a solid eight hours. Why don't you guys stir up some food?"

"Thought you'd never ask," Finn said.

But as he moved to stand, a phone began to ring. Knowing his cell phone—or any of the others' for that matter—would be useless all the way out in the ocean, Finn looked around. "What the—?"

Chart reached across the dash and slid a handset off a cradle. "Chart here."

"Who?" He strained to listen and said, "Oh yeah, sure. Right here." He held the receiver out to Finn. "For you. Heck of an accent." Then he pointed down the stairs. "There's a handset in the bar area if you want some privacy."

Finn stared back for a moment, processing the likelihood that he'd be getting a phone call out here and for the life of him he couldn't imagine who it could be other than Australian police or authorities. Then it hit him.

"Good idea," he said, making his way down the stairs to a glossy teakwood bar, stocked full with every liquor imaginable and a set of crystal highballs, martini, and lowball glasses. Place was like a beach house on Cape Cod, Finn thought. He found the phone on the underside of the bar, settled onto a tan leather stool, and answered, "Hello?"

"You're a difficult fuckin' man to find, Finn," one of the Beran twins said with a Boston accent that destroyed every vowel of the sentence.

"How did you...?"

"Never mind that, listen. We got the information for you. You get the tickets?"

Tickets. Baseball. He'd have to remember to get on that if the Sox actually got back to Fenway. "Sure, sure, I got 'em. What's up?"

"Four seats? Touching the dugout?"

"Sure."

"Red Sox dugout? I got no interest seeing those retarded birds from St. Louis."

"Yeah, yeah. Whatever you want. Just...tell me what you know."

"Ok, then. Here's Bobby, he knows the details." There was a shuffling noise in the background and then the other brother's voice came on the line. "Finn, that you?"

"One and only."

"Got that right. Nobody's ass is as big as yours and still muscle."

Finn glanced back up the stairs with Jon's comment in his mind. "So I've heard."

"Right. Anyway, you know that little schmuck actor? That Dillon West guy?"

Finn peered through the slit of window that looked out to the bow of the boat, where Dillon had splayed himself out 'for the rays', and said, "Yep, all too well."

"Right, well it all comes down to him and his psychotic fantasies."

"His what?"

"Of the sexual nature, you know?"

"No. I don't."

"Well you don't want to know. Trust me, brother."

"Then…?"

"But you're gonna have to hear it if you want to know the connection here with your tennis gal, that Svetlana chick." He blew out a breath and said, "Now that little number. She is smoking hot. Like a fucking pipin' hot iron skillet, that one. I'd like to—"

"Bobby."

"Right. Anyway, so this Dillon is at the club, right?"

"Club Red Eye. The Russian's place."

"Yeah. And he's dancing and chattin' it up with the ladies."

Finn looked out at Dillon who was now turning over and pulling his shorts down, most likely to eliminate an obvious tan line. "I can picture it, yep."

"And he snares one of 'em in his little actor trap, right? She's all hot and bothered and wants to do the nasty with little Hollywood here."

"The nasty."

"Sex, brother. But the kind where she doesn't care where or how, just the *now* part."

"So…"

"So he takes her to the restroom."

"Mens' or Ladies'"

"They're the same at this club. One restroom, fogged glass for stalls. Everyone mixin' it up."

"The nasty."

"Now you're gettin' it." He whispered something to his brother and continued, "So this chick and Dillon go into the restroom and find an empty stall."

"And?"

"And the dumbass even gets some of it on video." More whispers and he said, "Right, except the video was actually just audio, 'cause Dillon the camera man was so drunk that he put his phone back in the pocket of his jeans after he started recording."

"Awesome."

"Yeah, like a rockin' night, you know?"

"I can imagine."

"Yeah, so this is the way it goes down, according to the court-sealed documents."

"The ones you got unsealed."

"Nah, man. We just got access, you know?"

"Lovely."

"You want me to read this or what?"

"Please. Continue."

"Right, so here goes, exactly as it's written by the judge, reviewing a discovery deposition." He cleared his throat and continued, "The defendant Dillon Carnegie West blah blah blah... legal bullshit...blah...ok. Here it is." Another throat clear. Then a smack sound, and, "Fuck you do that for?"

"You want me to fuckin' read it, or are you going for an Oscar here?" Billy said in the background.

"I'm fuckin' gettin' to it. I had a frog in my throat."

"I'll put a frog in your throat."

"And I'll shove a—"

"Guys!" Finn said.

"Sorry, Finn," Bobby said. "Anyway. Here goes." He cleared his throat. A triple clear and a little laugh. Then a "fuck you" whispered in the background. And Bobby continued, "Said defendant, a one Dillon Carnegie West entered the restroom with a one Betsy Waller Jones, whereby the defendant and Ms. Jones entered into a union of sexual nature. Ms. Jones attests to kissing and foreplay of the *'petting zoo variety'*, whereby she urged the defendant to *'move it along'*. When pressed to articulate exactly how Ms. Jones urged the defendant, Ms. Jones attests that she told the defendant to *'stick her like a spit-roasted ham, and do it now'*."

"Classy gal," Finn said.

"Yeah, you should see the photos of this one. She looks like

Britney Spears the morning after New Years, if you know what I mean. Except not as clean."

"If that's even possible, I get the picture."

"Right. Anyway..." he continued reading, "said defendant then retrieved a tube of ointment from his back pocket. The defendant declared the substance was something called Fire Stick and was given to the defendant by a good friend named Chase. When Ms. Jones asked the defendant what the ointment was for, he replied, *'Ever been shot with a flaming arrow?'* Ms. Jones attests she then said, *'No, I've never even seen one before'*. The defendant then said, with no irony, *'y'all watch this'* as he proceeded to cover his penis with a condom and then lather the condom with the ointment. When Ms. Jones inquired what he planned on doing next, the defendant whipped out a book of matches and *'lit his cock up like Noah's burning bush'*.

"I think that was Moses, actually."

"Told you, she's a dipshit. Have to be to wind up with this braniac."

Finn stared out at Actor Dillon, who had rolled his pant legs up to the knee and was now tanning his calfs. "And then?"

"Right. So it continues...said defendant then screamed in what appeared to be serious pain and quickly pulled the condom off his penis and threw it in what he believed to be the toilet."

"But...?"

Bobby continued, "Ms. Jones witnessed the flaming condom missing the toilet and landing on a stack of toilet tissue instead. Thereafter, Ms. Jones' memory is fragmented, as she attests she fled the restroom and the mounting flames up the wall, as the defendant was busy relieving the burning sensation of this lower region by placing his penis and balls in the sink and running cold water over them."

Billy was laughing in the background and saying something about Moses and the burning bush.

Bobby continued, "Ms. Jones then fled the club through the

front entrance, warning others of the fire. Ms. Jones attests the smoke and fired grew too fast, because in Ms. Jones' words, *'it was probably made of cheap poster board…all those SoBeach clubs are'*, and thereby she never saw the defendant flee the club. By the time she had reached the outdoors, the roof was already ablaze."

"Jesus. The kid burned down the club," Finn said.

"Yeah, and guess what? Little Ms. Jones was right. The club was way out of compliance of fire codes. Judge finishes with this… though the defendant has obvious mental and social issues that must be addressed separately, the fire was accidental and not the result of malicious intent or gross negligence on his part. Failure to have proper fire safety devices and procedures caused the fire to consume the premises, not the errors of the defendant. The court of Miami-Dade, District 23 hereby clears the defendant of wrongdoing and fault in all matters financial, criminal, and civil with respect to the lawsuit filed by Milosevic and Jakov Popov seeking damages and relief from the defendant. No damages are to be rewarded, and the defendant is not found at fault. Because of the intimate nature of the details of this lawsuit, the findings are hereby to remain sealed and part of court evidence and discovery, not a matter of public record."

"Stellar. Who the hell was the kid's lawyer?"

"Oh yeah, says here it was Marco Doegreen."

"None other."

"Yeah, I think he was Hugh Grant's lawyer at some point. But apparently he fired Dillon for non-payment for services," Bobby said. "Anyway, what're you going to do with that info?"

"I think little Dillon and I need to have a word, though it's now obvious what's going on here." Finn looked out at the dipshit, who had decided that it would be a good idea to go ahead and get some sun on his unsheathed and now not-so-private package. He chose to not interrupt that for a bit, and said, "but first a little strategy session with my team here."

"This is it? Are you certain?" Vanessa stared up at the glass and metal structure. It was like a contemporary oasis in the middle of the otherwise rubbish-heap of an island.

"Certain. Yup." Chadwick nodded his donkey-head up and down, making the crab sway back and forth with the movement. It held tight to his ear, though.

Amazing.

"You hear something?" Vanessa spun around and scanned the landscape.

"Don't think I can hear out of this ear. Can I Hot Stuff?" He reached up and tapped his left ear, the one with the creature. "But I didn't hear anything with my good one either."

Vanessa ignored him and scanned again. Nothing in sight and no movement to speak of, she turned back around. "Anyway, let's find a way in."

"Yes, let's. I'm famished."

Vanessa walked up and tried the front door. Locked.

Chadwick reached up, rapped his knuckles twice on the door, before Vanessa could take hold of his arm, stop him. "What are you doing?"

"Seeing if anyone is home, of course. Why?"

"Did it occur to you that we may not want them to know we are here? That we may want to sneak inside before alerting the owner and the others of our presence?"

"What do you suggest?"

"Stay here."

"Why?"

"Just—" and she cut herself off and wandered to the other side, where the garage lay wide open.

She walked into the huge garage and past a disabled Vespa bike, the tires flat. Bending to inspect the damage, she determined that the tires had been sliced wide open by a knife of sorts.

Sabotaged beyond repair.

The owner must have had his own run-in with the crab vigilantes.

"What'd you find then?" Chadwick's booming voice echoed on the garage concrete, and Vanessa startled.

"For God's sake! I thought I told you to stay put. You nearly gave me a heart attack!"

"I don't know why. We can be of considerable help." He stood there with the crab hanging from his head. She wondered which of the two creatures before her had the larger brain.

"We?" She made a face. "Now you are considering you and that crab a *we*?"

"Yep. We're a team we are. Come as a package now."

The crab clawed at the air with his free arm, as if in agreement.

"I must be bloody fucking starkers here."

"Might be."

"Well you're in no position to judge, are you?"

"Why not? I know you as well as anybody."

"Which is not saying much."

"You're mean, Vanny. A spiteful mean, old—"

"Don't." She held up a single finger. "Say another word that you *will* regret."

"He mumbled something to himself and looked away."

"Let's go search the house."

Another mumble, and Chadwick followed her to the door and inside the house, which appeared to be empty. Leaving Chadwick in the kitchen, Vanessa searched the rest of the downstairs and then upstairs. Also empty. She returned to the master bedroom, which was outfitted like a pleasure palace, complete with dark red velvet throws and billowy white blankets on a poster bed.

Vanessa walked to the corner of the room, where she found a large screened Macintosh computer. She touched the mouse and the screen clicked on for a moment—showing a schedule and a bracket of competitors, with the word's Australian Open at the top

—and then flickered to a screensaver that showed a photo of Svetlana the tennis star bent over and retrieving a ball. The shot looked to have been taken from the corner of the court at a major tournament, as the blurry stands in the background appeared to be full. The focus of the lens and the photo, however, was on Svetlana's bright white panties beneath her skimpy little skirt.

"Pigs."

She touched the mouse again and a password box showed up. She couldn't get back to the Australian Open screen.

A quick search on her phone showed the tournament was underway and would last the next two days, when the finals were set to be played. Of course. That's why they were all here this week. Svetlana had most likely not qualified for the competition. From what Vanessa had read in the Daily Mail the Russian model was having too much fun in Miami to be bothered with practice anymore. So she must be headed there to participate in some sort of publicity event. That's what this was all about. Who knows why they stopped here on this godforsaken—

And as she had that thought, a howling, terrorizing cry sounded from downstairs. Chadwick. And then a growl and a scream. But not a human scream. No, this was like a leopard or maybe...no!

Vanessa bolted downstairs, grabbing a wooden chair from the hall on her way to the kitchen, where she found Chadwick, his back pinned to the open refrigerator, and a cat—no, a bobcat—THE bobcat, crouched in the corner, ready to pounce.

The crab was swinging wildly from Chadwick's ear, snipping and snapping the free claw.

"What in God's name?"

"It's him, Vanny! It's Boblet!"

"How on earth—?"

"I don't know, Vanny, but he's found us. He's still angry for me sending him all the way here!"

"That's not possible—"

"Or maybe he's angry for me sealing him in that crate with you. He didn't like you, did he?"

The crab swung and clipped at the air.

"Chadwick,' Vanessa said, holding the chair in front of her, legs out like four little wooden stakes. "He's an animal, a wild animal. He doesn't like any human, you nitty! Least of all, one that he's stuck in a box with!"

"What did you do? What did you do to him, Vanny?"

"Oh, do shut it, please."

"He hates us, Vanny!"

And then, the now-quite-large bobcat darted forward in a flash, up over Chadwick's shoulder, swiping at the crab, and chomping down toward Chadwick's ear. Chadwick slid sideways, narrowly missing the lunge, and ran to the other side of the kitchen, behind Vanessa.

The cat then darted out of the kitchen. He didn't turn, he didn't lunge at them, he just bolted out.

In his mouth, a hunk about the size of a toaster, of cheese.

Finn stood off to the side, a cold Hop Hog brew in his hand, as he watched Nikki and Lindsay grill the little puke named Dillon.

Nikki said, "So let me get this straight, Bug Nuts—"

"I said stop calling me that!" Dillon stomped his foot on the floor of the boat. Sitting alone in the crescent-shaped tan leather booth, shoulders slumped and no drink, he looked like a busted teenager in front of a school detention committee.

Lindsay and Nikki stood shoulder to shoulder at the bar, Nikki drinking a Corona light, Lindsay a Perrier water. Jon stood on the other side of the bar, far from the conflict, a Mai Thai in hand, complete with rainbow colored umbrella.

Nikki said, "Oh right, it's Toasted Nuts. I forgot, sorry."

"Not that either!"

Lindsay said, "Dillon, come clean. We heard the whole conversation on the second handset while Finn was talking to his source."

"Exactly. His source broke the law. The record was sealed, you guys. As soon as I get home, I'm calling my new lawyer! The Winkle will press charges! You'll go to jail for it. You all will!" On that, he swept a finger around the room and then crossed his arms and made that scrunched up face again. Like he'd just licked a turd.

"Someone's a little testy." Jon sipped his Mai Thai with a loud slurp at the end.

"The Winkle?" Finn leaned forward a few inches and said, "You mean Elliot Winkledink? I thought he was serving time for smoking pot with a thirteen year old girl."

Dillon said, "No. That's all in the past. He's out now. Besides, it was medicinal marijuana, and the girl was almost fourteen."

The four of them looked at each other, and Dillon continued, "Duh, she's anorexic. He said on record that smoking the marijuana was to fix that. You know, munchies."

They all fell silent on that one, and Finn said, "Dillon, back to your situation."

"What about it?" Dillon asked.

"The way I see it, and tell me if I'm wrong here, is that you sold Svetlana out to these Russian thugs to save your own ass." Finn took a gulp of the beer.

"Look. It's not my fault those geniuses never hooked up the water supply to the fire sprinklers. It's their own doing that the club got torched."

"Forget about that," Finn said. "I'm more interested in discussing the aftermath."

"What aftermath?" Dillon said.

"The one where you told the Russians about the sex tape, Roasted Bug Nuts." Nikki pointed the bottom of her Corona at him.

"They made me, okay? They kidnapped me. They threatened my parents!"

"They do that," Nikki said, taking a gulp. "It's in the Russian mobster playbook."

Finn said, "So then what? You tell them about the tape and…"

"Look, they think they're going to be able to take the video and sell it themselves. That's the plan. That's all I know."

Nikki said, "Then what does Vlad have to do with all this? Is he one of them?"

"No way," Lindsay said. "He's probably the mix-master. He's cutting and producing the video. Right?"

Dillon clapped with a shitty grin. "You guys are all so smart. Like I said, this video is going to be epic, dudes. Like Svet is hot as shit. Like *shit-hot*, you know? And me. I'm behind her, gettin' my groove—"

"Enough." Nikki held up a hand. "Before I vomit on Chart's yacht here."

"Whatever," he continued, "people are going to pay big money for this show."

"So what was the plan, originally?" Finn said. "Before your nightclub pals showed up."

"It was like this, okay?" Dillon sat forward, all animated now. "Svet was going to send the tape to her buddy Vlad here. But then the Russians attacked us and Svet accidentally killed one of them —"

"With a mango pit," Nikki said.

"Crazy, right? Like a total a mind-fuck!" Dillon held both his hands up in utter disbelief.

"Go on," Finn said.

"Anyway, right. So then they take me, threaten me, and Svet bolts."

"And you knew she'd come here."

"No place else to go, big dude." Dillon picked at a fingernail. "She had to get the video edited and ready for prime time."

"And what exactly is prime time?" Lindsay said.

"All the right outlets. Everything but the bigscreen."

"Bloggers, triple-x sites, porno producers," Lindsay said.

"Of course. All the major players. Vivid, Penthouse, all the satellite TV channels. Anything that charges viewers a fee and pays her a royalty."

Finn said, "But then the Russians decided to hijack that plan and earn back the money they lost on the club you burned down."

"I already told you. It wasn't my fault. Ask the Miami-Dade court system."

"Old reliable, that circuit." Lindsay laughed.

"The hell does that mean?" Dillon asked. Then, "Hey can I get one of those beers now?"

All four of them answered in tandem, "*No.*"

Then Finn circled back around to a comment made earlier. "Dillon, you said *anything that would charge viewers a fee and pay her a royalty.* Her."

"Yeah, so?"

"So what was in it for you? Tell me you didn't agree to make the video for free," Finn said.

"Are you stupid? I get to tag that ass? And have it shown across the world? Every chick sees how good I am in bed. Every movie producer, all of Hollywood gets a look-see. It would completely amp up my acting career."

"Let me get this straight," Nikki said. "You think that by starring in a sex tape with Svetlana, you can revive that dead-dick career of yours in acting?"

"Ha ha, very funny," Dillon said, glancing around at them. "Haven't you all ever heard of a lull?"

"No offense, Mr. Dill Pickle," Jon said. "But you'd need to star as Lucky Pierre between King Kong and Godzilla to wake up your acting career."

"Who's Pierre?" Dillon said.

"Okay, okay." Lindsay stepped forward and started pacing the small space between the booth and the bar. She said, "We need a plan for this whole videotape situation." She looked at Finn. "You really think we can get to Vlad before the Russians?"

"Not likely, no," Finn said. "But we can get the tape from them if they reach him first."

"You mean, you can," Nikki said.

"I wouldn't tussle with this buffalo," Jon said.

Lindsay continued, "Okay. So we get the tape, we save Svetlana. Then what?"

Nikki said, "We leave Scorched Bug Nuts here out in Kangarooland."

Dillon said, "Fine. Whatever. You guys are all a bunch of everyday citizens anyway. I need to find some celebrities to hang with."

"Who are you calling everyday?" Jon said, wiping the lapel of his jacket. "This is Canali."

"Tell me this," Nikki said. "Fuck are they all going to the Aussie Open for anyway? Not like Svetlana can compete there. She missed the cut by a few hundred players."

The whole boat fell silent, except for the buzz of the motors and the slosh of the waves around them. Then a voice echoed from up above, as Chart said, "I know exactly what their plan is."

CHAPTER TWENTY

MILO WOKE TO THE SOUND OF A small engine or motor and the smell of natural gas fumes burning. The crate was pitch black again, and Jak's whispers were barely audible.

"Milo? Milo where are we?"

Svetlana moaned as she woke, too.

"Shh." Milo listened. "I don't know."

"At least the bugs stopped biting me. I thought it would never end," Jak whispered loud again.

"I said shush."

Two voices echoed outside of whatever room they were in. The motor revved and came closer. The voices echoed closer, too, and then a loud banging sounded and Svetlana jerked.

The sound of metal grinding on metal echoed into the room and light cut across the crates. The motor revved again and came closer. Then the crate was bumped and raised, and Milo reached across quickly to put a hand over Svetlana's mouth.

She gave a muffled cry.

He whispered, "They are picking us up with a forklift. We are in the back of a truck and being moved."

She nodded and he released his hand.

Milo felt sensation of being moved through the air by the fork lift and a few moments later the crate was dropped to the concrete floor of what must have been a warehouse.

"Get ready," he whispered to Svetlana. "They will be surprised by us."

A creak sounded right next to Milo's ear as the end of a crowbar was jammed into the crease between the wooden slots of the crate. The crowbar was worked around the edge of the top until the wooden panel was lifted off.

Milo popped upright, fists raised.

"What the—?" A man holding the crowbar stood next to the crate. Behind him, two men dressed in suits peered into the crate. One was a rotund man, his suit looked custom made. The other was Zin, the owner of the jet.

"What is this?" The rotund man said.

Zin answered, "Where is the jackfruit?"

The man with the crowbar said, "What's on your face, mate? Looks like the inside of a pomegranate."

"Where is my cocaine? This is not—"

"It is in the jackfruit! Where is my fruit?" Zin stepped in front on the rotund man and drew out a black pistol, pointing it at Milo.

Svetlana pushed up and gasped when she saw the gun.

"A woman, too!" The man with the crowbar gasped and stepped backwards.

"Open the other crate," The rotund man said. "It must be in there."

Milo said, "The fruit. It was filled with cocaine?"

"Ten million dollars of street value. Where did you put it?"

"Oh shit," Milo said.

The crowbar man pried open the second crate, and Jak exploded out of the box with the harpoon drawn. In one sweeping move, he shot Zin, and the steel harpoon arrow plunged straight through the skinny Asian man's chest and into the rotund man's, pinning them together and killing them both instantly.

Svetlana shrieked.

Milo launched from the box and took hold of the crowbar with both hands, swinging it into the back of the man's head. He crumpled to the ground with a whimper.

Meanwhile, the forklift jerked forward and the two blades spun over Milo's head as he ducked.

Jak walked over and worked the arrow out of the dead men. Then he re-loaded the harpoon.

The man on the forklift yelled something and then turned the forklift around and fled. He floored the engine, but the machine was slow.

Jak walked forward and shot the harpoon.

Svetlana shrieked again.

The arrow fired straight through the small window at the back of the forklift and split the man's ear, then clanked across the warehouse floor.

The man screamed, holding his ear and peering back at Jak.

Jak ran forward, catching up to him, and jumped on the back of the forklift.

The man yelled then jerked the wheel of the machine back and forth.

Jak held tight with one arm and reached through the opening to control the wheel.

The driver attempted to pry Jak's grip off the wheel, but it was a feeble attempt at best.

Jak pointed them straight ahead. Toward the back wall.

The driver moved to bail out the side of the forklift, but Jak held him in the seat with his other arm.

The forklift barreled forward, and at the very last second, Jak pushed from the back of the machine and rolled off to the side, as the forklift crashed into the concrete wall, crumpling the lift teeth upwards and crushing the cage and the man inside.

"Ouch," Milo said. Then he walked over to Zin and took the SIG Sauer 9mm pistol from his limp grip.

"Ouch? This is all you can say?" Svetlana climbed out of the crate and looked at Milo and Jak and then around them. "You kill too many people. Look at all of this blood."

"Yes," Jak said, dusting off his arm and retrieving his harpoon and arrow. He stopped, surveyed the scene around them, and continued, "I must write another poem."

Finn stood at the bow of the boat, staring out at the streams of white water waves created by the double sets of outboards on the yacht. Nikki stood with him, silent, waiting for Lindsay to finish her phone calls and join them for a quick strategy session.

Finn said, "So what's the deal with you and Chart?"

"Relax, Patrick, nothing is going on."

A thin glow of light from the sunrise appeared on the horizon, like an orange rind floating in green tea.

"You can be honest with me."

"Oh, in that case, we pretended we were the last two people on earth. You know, keep the civilization going and all that."

"Really?"

"No."

A long beat of silence passed between them, and Nikki said, "What about you? Don't you think it's a bit irresponsible for you to be hooking up with Lindsay like this?"

"Why do you say that?"

"Cause it won't last?"

"Why not?"

"Ever heard of the concept of compatibility?"

"We're totally compatible."

"Patrick. Her idea of a full meal is a single gluten free cracker with a spritzer of non-fat coconut oil topped with a cube of tofu. Yours is three double-meat cheesesteaks with a side of fries and onion rings, maybe a chili-dog as a chaser."

"What, no dessert?"

"I'm serious Patrick."

"Well, this relationship is *not* serious. So you can relax, too."

"Be careful, is all I'm saying. I know women, and she likes you.

A lot."

"She knows the deal. Just a little fun on vacation is all."

"That what this is to you? A vacation?"

"You know what I mean."

"Tell you what, Patrick. The woman sure does seem to make a lot of private phone calls."

"Maybe she's shy."

She gave him a look that said, *gimme a fucking break.*

She had a point.

And with that, Lindsay walked up, hooked an arm into Finn's and leaned all the way up to giving him a big kiss on the cheek. "Gorgeous sunrise." She smiled big. A bit too big.

Nikki raised her brow at Finn. *See?*

He rolled his eyes at Nikki and turned to Lindsay, who said, "We ready to strategize? Head this mess off?"

Finn asked, "What do you suggest?"

"I think we should put out a public statement as soon as we have Svetlana back in our care. We need to say she is co-operating fully with the authorities in the investigation of the death of the Russian man at Dillon's condo."

"But she's not co-operating," Nikki said.

"We all know that cases are made and won in the media, not the courtrooms. Trust me," Lindsay said.

"And the police? What do we tell them?" Finn grabbed the railing with both hands and leaned down.

"We tell them that Svetlana was terrified for her life and so she ran. She believed she was being targeted by Russian mobsters in a classic racketeering scheme. We use Russian NHL stars like Pavel Bure and Sergei Federov as examples. Svetlana was terrified for her life, so she fled the States before she ever knew the police were looking for her."

"You should have been a lawyer," Nikki said.

Lindsay smiled. "And then, we release the tape."

"We what?" Finn said. "Why would we do that?" He looked at

Nikki who had twisted her face with a sudden look of skepticism.

"To get all the attention off her self-defense technique and back onto her perfectly sculpted ass."

"That could work," Finn said.

Nikki elbowed him. "With men, maybe. The women of the world, though…"

Lindsay said, "They'll be apt to applaud her technique of self-defense."

"And who do we release this tape to?" Finn turned around and leaned back against the railing.

"That's the critical part. We need to get it out through social media, not traditional channels."

"What, like Twitter and Facebook and that crap?" Nikki asked.

"Exactly. Make people talk about it, want to see it. Make it go viral," Lindsay said.

"And if we fumble?" Finn said.

"Well then you'll be out one of your clients, she'll be in prison, and all that debt she owes you will have to be written off."

"No stakes there," Nikki said.

"And if Svetlana refuses to go with our plan?" Finn asked.

"Not an option," Lindsay said, staring out at the sun, now shining bright streams of light over the water, like endless shards of gold-tinged glass.

"You of all people know how stubborn Svetlana is," Nikki said. "She doesn't do anything she doesn't want to."

"I'm not worried." Lindsay turned back to Finn. "I'm sure Patrick here can convince her somehow."

Nikki leaned forward. "You don't mean—?"

"I do." She smiled and smoothed a hand across Finn's chest as he hid his face. "One taste of this man, and she'll do anything."

Vanessa put a finger to her lips as she tiptoed to the front door, one hand holding a small metal cleaver she'd found in the kitchen, the other hand gripping a handful of Chadwick's shirt to keep him close behind her. She needed some sort of layer of protection against that vicious beast of a bobcat.

Chadwick would have to do for now.

He whispered, rather loudly, "Perhaps he's fled the scene."

"I'm not so sure." She peeked out the glass entry, scanned the front yard and drive.

Nothing.

"Follow me." She eased open the front door.

"Where're we going?"

"Away from here." She stepped through the doorway and onto the porch.

"Right, but to where, I mean."

"I told you, Finn and his friends are headed to the tennis tournament."

"But we can't walk, Vanny. It's all the way across the ocean. Melbourne, is it?"

She turned and raised the dull edge of the cleaver to his face, then pulled back when she caught sight of that stupid crab hanging off his ear. She said, "Of course we can't walk, you dolt. We'll need to catch a ferry or something. But first, we'll need to get to the ferry. So I ask, did you see any vehicles here we can take? Hmm?"

"Well." He glanced at the cleaver and then stared straight up to the sky. "I recall a Vespa in the garage."

"A Vespa with no usable tires, you mean?"

"Perhaps there's a service station nearby. Someplace—"

"Shut it."

As she turned back to the drive, Chadwick whispered, "No mind, Hot Stuff. We'll find a way with or without Vanny."

"You and that crab of yours couldn't find your way out of a shopping sack without me."

"You underestimate us, Vanny."

And as she was about to respond to that, Vanessa heard a low rumble of a vehicle approaching the drive. At the bottom of the hill, the nose of a truck appeared. A rubbish vehicle.

"Quick," she said. "Hide."

"Where, Vanny?" Chadwick spun around like a schoolboy looking for a dropped penny.

"There." She pointed to a row of hedges at the end of the drive, and darted toward them with Chadwick following close behind.

Ducking low, she was amazed that someone had found a way to grow such beautiful bushes in a place like this.

Chadwick whispered, "Why are we hiding?"

"So we can overtake that vehicle. Watch." She peered between the branches as the large truck squealed to a stop at the front of the drive.

A man jumped off the back bumper and started toward a line of rubbish bins at the end of the drive.

Chadwick whispered, too loud again, "But how do you suppose we are going to get the driver out?"

"I said watch. I'll distract him. And when I do, you take the wheel. I'll jump in after."

"Brilliant."

Vanessa moved to hand Chadwick the cleaver but then thought the better for it and hid the weapon behind her back instead. Then she unbuttoned the top three cinches of her blouse as she approached the driver's side. She said, "Pardon me, but can you please help? My...kitty is stuck in a tree, around back."

The rubbish man and driver exchanged looks. The driver stayed put behind the wheel.

Vanessa continued, "Please? There's a reward in it for you." Then she reached up and opened another cinch.

The driver slid out, "My pleasure. Where is it?"

The rubbish man wiped his hands on his overalls. "I can help, too, you know. Specially if there's that kind of reward."

"I assure you, the reward is worth it." Vanessa winked at him and turned, walked back up the drive toward the house, careful to keep the small cleaver pressed against her leg and hidden from view.

The two men followed her up the driveway and to the back gate, which Vanessa opened and stepped into the back yard. The men walked so close behind, that she had to hold the cleaver against the front of her thigh. She could feel the breath of one man and smell the salty, sweaty skin of the other.

Then, the moment she stepped foot into the back yard, a growl sounded. A deep, rumbling, threatening growl.

The bobcat.

Brandishing the cleaver, Vanessa darted back behind the men and through the open gate.

The rubbish man said, "What's that?" And stared at the cleaver.

The driver turned and looked at the bobcat at the far side of the pool. "That's no kitty."

"And I'm no prize." Vanessa slammed the gate shut on the men and sprinted back down the drive.

The bobcat made an attacking sound and Vanessa peered over her shoulder to see the damned thing hurdling the fence.

Bloody hell.

Swinging the cleaver blindly and wildly behind her, Vanessa ran. She ran as fast as she ever had, as fast as she ever could. "Chaddy!"

Chadwick yelled, "Look out! It's Boblet!" And he slammed the driver door shut as he revved the engine.

The truck lurched forward and picked up speed.

"Chadwick!" Vanessa ran past the driver door to the back, swinging the cleaver.

The bobcat leapt clear over Vanessa and slammed into the side of the truck.

Vanessa hurled herself into the trash heap at the back. She readied herself with the cleaver as she yelled, "Go, Chadwick!

Floor it!"

The bobcat rolled across the gravel and climbed back to all fours as it ran and jumped again, this time slamming into the bumper and giving a screech before rolling off the road.

"Faster, Chaddy!"

The truck sped around the corner, kicking up dust and crabs in its wake. And the bobcat, who sat back on its hind legs now at the edge of the road, licked a paw and then chewed on a mangle crab.

Vanessa pushed herself up on a plastic bag that smelled like rotten fish. As evidence, a fish spine poked through the bag and stabbed her hand like a thick needle.

"Bloody hell." She yanked her hand away and fell backward, landing on a large cloth sack full of something squishy.

Ready to find a way out of the rubbish, Vanessa repositioned herself on her knees. All she had to do was ease her way to the back of the truck and she could climb out onto the bumper, yell for Chadwick to pull over. She glanced up at the road.

Boblet was long gone.

Lifting a leg to step toward the back, she slipped, ripping open the cloth sack with her heel and falling over again.

"To all hell!"

Then, when she turned to right herself again, she saw it. A jackfruit split open and a cellophane baggie inside, the size of a fist. The baggie was filled with some sort of powder. White powder.

"What the...?"

Vanessa tugged the baggie out and shook it.

The truck roared and turned hard, flinging Vanessa against the siding.

She banged on the steel side. "Slow it down, Chadwick!"

"Wha--?" he yelled from the cab.

"I said slow down. I've found something!"

"Yes, mum!"

Vanessa reached down and took hold of another piece of fruit, tore it open. Sure enough, another white baggie was tucked inside. Another fruit, another baggie. Then another.

And another.

The whole sack was full of them. Bags and bags of the white powder. It could have been cocaine or heroin, but she was sure of one thing. It was drugs of some sort. Looking around, she realized that there were three more cloth sacks. All full of fruit. All full of the powder.

To be certain, she tore open the corner of one of the baggies, took a sniff.

"Good God."

She dipped a pinkie into the powder and inspected it. Then gave a lick.

Her entire mouth went numb.

"My Lord," she whispered, "I believe we've stumbled upon a million. Perhaps millions of dollars in street value here."

"Chadwick!" She banged her hand against the siding. "Chadwick! Stop the truck. Stop the vehicle this very instant!"

She felt the truck stutter and slow. It veered to the shoulder of the dirt road, a wake of crushed crabs in the soil behind them.

And then she heard the grind of motors again. *What was he doing?*

She banged the siding, about to say, "Stay stopped," when she felt the floor below her pitch backward. The trash. It was moving beneath her. The hopper was pushing her back into the truck. It was compacting the load.

No!

No! No! NO!

"Chadwick, stop the compression! Stop the motors! You'll ruin it, you'll..." And she screamed, "YOU'LL KILL ME!"

Vanessa jumped forward and clawed, clutched, fought her way to the lip of the hopper floor as it rose high and forced her further back.

"NO!"

Vanessa took hold of the edge of the metal panel as it pushed toward her, pressed her against the already compacted heap inside the belly of the truck. She pushed forward and hurdled a leg over the lip. She launched her body over the side. She screamed as the plate cinched lower, closing out the light of day.

"CHADWICK!"

And Vanessa rocketed her body out of the back of the truck and to the ground below with a thump and another yell.

"You idiot!"

Exhausted and unsure whether she'd broken an ankle or a leg or something, Vanessa pressed her hands against the dirt road as her chest heaved for air.

"Mum!" Chadwick appeared in her vision above her. "Are you —"

"Hurt? Dead? What?" She kicked at him.

Chadwick hopped back. "Vanny!"

"You imbecile!" Vanessa kicked again, missing. "Do you realize what you've done?" She kicked and kicked, missing and writhing and yelling.

When she stopped, he stood there, hands on his hips, staring at the back of the truck for a good long while with that stupid crab hanging from an ear, and then he said, "I believe I've compacted the load."

"Compacted the load?"

"That's right."

"With me as part of it?"

He shrugged. "You seem to have gotten on all right."

"You almost killed me!" She pushed to her feet.

"Right. Sorry about that."

"Sorry? That's all you can say?"

"All I can think of."

"Ugh!" She dusted herself off, and said, "And it wasn't just me back there, Chadwick."

The motors whined and creaked as the hopper plate eased its

way back to the rear of the vehicle.

He peered up into the truck. "Was Boblet with you?"

Vanessa said, "No, not the stupid bobcat! There was an entire shipment of cocaine in there. Millions and millions of dollars worth, maybe more!"

Chadwick scratched his chin. "Is it alright, you think?"

Vanessa pointed to the compacted load, oozing orange and green, popped plastic bags and white gooey powder intermixed with the rotten fruit and rubbish. "What do you think?"

"It may be all right." He frowned with those fleshy jowls and said, "Perhaps we could sell it as a tropical flavored drug. You know, like fruity meth or something of the sort."

"Fruity meth?"

"Or something of the like."

And Vanessa stared at him. Stared straight through him. If her eyes were Department of Defense lasers they would burn a hole straight through that lizard brain of his and kill him on the spot. In fact, if the moronic, half-wit uttered one more word, one more syllable even, she would kill him with her own hands.

And then he said, "Mango-caine. That has a nice ring to it."

And Vanessa pounced.

She ripped the crab off his ear, taking a chunk of flesh too, and beat him over the head with it. *Whack! Whack! Whack!*

"Vanny! Oww! My ear! Stop it!" Chadwick yelled as he fell to the dirt road and covered his head with both hands. "You'll hurt Hot Stuff!"

Whack! "Stupid!"

Whack! "Insect-brained!"

Whack! "No-excuse!"

Whack! "For a human!"

Whack! "Being!"

"Vanessa!" Chadwick howled. "Please!"

Then a siren sounded. And another.

Vanessa crumpled to her knees beside Chadwick, and dropped

the dead crab. Exhausted from the beating, drained from the day, absolutely sapped of every single ounce of energy left in her body, she watched.

As one Christmas Island policeman exited his vehicle, weapon raised, and zipped her hands tight with a plastic cuff. Then he did the same to Chadwick, all the while asking if either of them had identification, or a place of residence, relatives of family, or even a purpose to be on the island.

Of which neither of them had any.

Then a second policeman clicked on his CB radio and said in a perfectly clear voice and to Vanessa's ultimate horror, "Two illegals coming to Detention Center One."

CHAPTER TWENTY-ONE

WHILE JAK AND HE PILED THE BODIES into the crates, Milo had found two sets of keys. One of them was clearly designed for a boat of some sort. He'd also found several thousand dollars in cash in the rotund man's wallet, and he'd taken the pistol as well as Zin's iPhone.

Now, as he creaked open the warehouse door, bright sunlight spilled inside, nearly blinding him. As suspected, they were mere yards from the water, a number of boats docked just outside.

Jak thrust a hand over his brow. "It is daytime."

"Yes, and now we can see your bug-bitten face," Svetlana said as she slipped on her enormous sunglasses.

"We must find the boat and..." he swiped the iPhone to life and re-read the ESPN page he'd found about the Australian Open, then said, "we have less than an hour to find this Vladimir before the final match begins."

"We don't even know where this match is," Jak said.

Milo turned and thrust the iPhone upwards, into Jak's view. "We have the GPS, remember?"

"Oh."

Svetlana dusted herself off and said, "This better be a nice boat. We cannot arrive in a small...how you say...dingy?"

"Nobody will recognize you, trust me." Milo said.

Svetlana pursed her lips and spun around. "This ass, they will recognize. The moment it is shown on the screens."

"We will see of that." Milo exited. "But first, we must hurry or we will miss our chance."

Jak was messing around with his pen and notebook again. Milo slapped it from his hand, sending the pencil across the pavement.

"Why have you done this, brother?" Jak said, bending to pick up the pencil.

"And this." Milo picked up the notebook. "It is filled with garbage."

"How can you say this? These are works of art from my heart." Jak stood and held out his hand. "Give it back."

"Not until we finish this. We need you to be focused on business, not your so-called art."

"Brothers." Svetlana pushed her sunglasses tight to her face. "Always with the arguing."

Milo stuffed the notebook in his pocket and strode ahead, toward the docks. "You are sure he is in the media village, this Vladimir?"

"I told you," Svetlana said, following Milo as Jak sulked slowly behind both of them. "He must find a place to use the wiring of the stadiums. I don't understand why, but this is what he has said to me."

"Is he in a van?" Milo said.

"No. You will see, Vlad is a refined Russian." Svetlana waved a hand. "Not like you two."

"I will show you refined." Milo stopped at the edge of the dock and looked out at the slips. Seventeen boats in total, most were obviously made for shipping small cargo. But one stood out among them. It was bright red and small, a speedboat.

"I think that might be the one," Jak said.

For the last two hours, Finn had stood at the wheel with Chart as

Nikki, Lindsay, and Jon stood looking out from the port side and Dillon stood alone looking out starboard. After negotiating Hobson Bay, at the edge of Melbourne, Chart guided the yacht through the mouth of the Yarra River, a channel rimmed with factories, warehouses, and storage facilities. Stacks and stacks of rusted and various-colored shipping containers towered on one side, and rows and rows of white colored Subaru cars and SUVs stretched across endless parking lots on the other side. Being a Sunday, the channels were quiet, except for a lone container ship being unloaded by an enormous crane right at the mouth of the river. The whole area smelled like a mix of natural gas and carbon monoxide.

Hard to believe that the Yarra would wind up past all these outer facilities and into the mainframe of Melbourne, literally dumping them to the edge of the tennis stadium. And, according to Chart's contacts, they could dock within a mile of the tournament complex without a problem. The plan was to locate Svetlana using Finn's network of industry contacts who would be at the tournament. Then they would intercept the Russians before they found Vlad. A thin and flimsy plan, at best, thought Finn, but what else could they do?

And before Finn had a chance to make his first phone call to a sportswriter buddy, Nikki burst into the wheelhouse and yelled, "Turn this shit around!"

"Where's the fire?" Chart said, spinning the wheel and lowering the thrust of the engines to a lull.

"Svetlana and the Russians aren't at the tournament. At least not yet."

Lindsay burst in behind her. "Yep, no doubt. It was them."

"Where the hell are they?" Finn asked.

"Leaving some warehouse." Nikki pointed across Finn and behind them, to the nearside bank of the river, where a row of warehouses bordered a small dock full of flat transport boats. "Back there!"

Dumbfounded, Finn said, "You're sure?"

Jon sauntered in and said, "They were sunburned or something, but it was them. I'd recognize that platinum hair anywhere."

"I can pull us in there." Chart pointed to an empty pier about two hundred yards away.

"Go for it," Finn said. Then he turned to Nikki. "What were they doing?"

"The Russians were fighting about something, who knows," Nikki said. "Svet was watching them like it was a mildly interesting sitcom."

"Alright, look." Finn pointed at Lindsay and Jon. "You two stay here with Chart. Nikki and I will slip off the boat and grab Svetlana."

"And just how do you plan on doing that, big bear?" Jon asked.

"I'm coming with," Lindsay said.

"No way," Finn answered. "These guys are psychotic. Can't let you anywhere near them. Just stay here on the boat and be ready to bolt."

She crossed her arms and tapped a foot. "Don't treat me like a dog, Patrick. Sit, stay and all that. I'm a big girl."

Finn glanced at Nikki, who shrugged and said, "Whatever."

"Fine," Finn said, as Chart threaded the yacht into a slip, barely touching a rubber bumper attached to the concrete wall. "You and Nikki be ready to grab Svetlana. I'll distract the Russians."

"Ooooh. This could get good. Have any popcorn on board?" Jon said to Chart.

"How about Skittles?" Chart smiled.

Jon made a face and shook his head.

"Ready?" Finn asked the girls, noticing Lindsay fumble with the back of her sweatshirt.

After a moment, she said, "Ready."

Finn hopped up onto the landing and reached down, hauling Nikki up first and then pulling Lindsay to the concrete dock.

"Christ Patrick, you almost dislocated my shoulder." Nikki rotated her arm and massaged her elbow.

Lindsay dusted herself off and winked at Finn. "Thanks for the boost, hon."

Nikki rolled her eyes again.

"OK, look. You two plant it right here." He pointed to a tall pile of shipping pallets. "I'm going around the front of this building. When you see me come out the other side, get ready to pounce."

"Got it, boss."

"Be careful, Patrick," Lindsay said, touching his arm.

"Oh for fuck's—" But Finn took off before Nikki could finish her sentence.

It turned out that the warehouse he decided to jog around was about four times the size he'd figured. That, and Finn seemed to be in worse shape than he'd remembered. He'd have to start hitting the gym regularly again when he got back to the States. But first, he had to find a way to keep breathing all the way to the other side. For Christ's sake, it felt like he was carrying two bags of cement and a baby rhino on his back.

Pacing himself for the last hundred yards, Finn started to feel lightheaded. Then, finally reaching the corner of the building, he noticed the Russians had moved and were now in-between Svetlana and the girls. Even if he was successful in getting the Russians' attention, there was still no way for the girls to get to Svetlana.

Looked like Finn would have to step it up a bit and force them to come after him.

First, though, he needed to catch his damned breath. So, as he stood bent over with both hands on his knees, his chest heaving, and his head still foggy…he watched the Russians argue. Now would be a good time, but he just needed a little more oxygen first. Maybe Nikki was right. A lower-fat diet may be necessary soon.

Then he saw that the big Russian named Jak, was still holding the harpoon. The arrow was dripping a thick ooze of blood onto the concrete.

What the hell was wrong with his face?

And as he had that thought, a flicker of yellow caught his attention from the corner of his eye. Then he saw the figure approaching, bold and arrogant. And loud.

"Hey, ass-tards! Over here!" Dillon strode across the pavement.

"Dammit," Nikki said loud enough for Finn to hear.

The Russians turned, Jak's arm and the harpoon raising in one fluid motion. He said, "Stop there."

The smaller guy, Milo, took Svetlana from behind and raised a flat black pistol to her temple. He glanced around quickly and then yelled, "You two. Come out! I see you behind the crates!"

Shit. Finn had little choice but to sacrifice himself now. But first, what the fuck was Dillon the Dipshit doing?

"What, you think you're getting all the profits? I'm in on this, remember?" Dillon kept walking forward. "And what the hell is going on with your face, dude? You look like a teenage pimple farm."

"I said stop there!" Jak yelled.

"How about you stop pointing that thing at me, I know you aren't going to shoot me. You need me."

And oh so wrong he was.

Jak stiffened his arm, lowered his aim, and fired. The arrow exploded from the harpoon's barrel and thrust straight across the dock and buried itself in Dillon's right thigh.

"Motherfucker!" he screamed, falling backwards and hitting the pavement on his elbows. "You fucking shot me, you god-dammed imbecile psychotic freak of a mother fucker!"

And that was Finn's cue.

"Come out!" Milo pushed forward with Svetlana in his grip.

She yelled, "Do what he says."

Finn darted, if you could call setting two-hundred and sixty pounds in motion a *darting* that is, out from the corner of the warehouse and aimed his trajectory straight toward the big guy.

Jak was busy yanking the thin rope attached to the arrow with both hands, reeling Dillon in to him.

"Ow! You're ripping my leg off!" Dillon writhed and hobbled on all fours, like a wounded crab, toward Jak. "Stop!"

"Jesus," Nikki said from behind the crates.

"Tell them now!" Milo said, "I will kill you all!"

"He will kill us all!" Svetlana yelled.

And Finn ambled across the dock, his footsteps heavy on the concrete, causing Milo to turn and Jak to pause.

"Jak!" Milo called, aiming the pistol at Finn.

"No!" Svetlana yelled as she stomped on Milo's foot and then elbowed him in the gut, causing the gun to discharge and Milo to fall back.

The bullet skipped off the concrete and pummeled Jak's ankle, shattering it and sending him to the ground. "Oh," he said. "Brother, you shot me."

"Ha!" Dillon yelled, "You idiots!" Then, "OWWWW!" And he resumed writhing on the ground.

"Shit!" Milo yelled.

"Jesus!" Nikki said again, as Jak gave a solid yank, pulling the arrow from Dillon's thigh and sending it clanking across the concrete as he reeled it back toward him.

Svetlana ran past Jak and hid behind Finn.

"What are you—" Milo said, watching Jak re-load the harpoon.

"Stop! Stop right there, FBI!" Lindsay came charging out from behind the stack of palettes, arm raised and holding...a gun?

"What the fuck?" Nikki said.

Everyone turned, except Jak, who was still focused on setting the harpoon and aiming it. Right at his brother.

"I said stop! Put down the weapon!"

Finn stepped forward and stopped when Jak said, "Don't make

me shoot you instead."

"Put down the weapon, Mr. Jakov Popov!" Lindsay said.

"This man, has shot me. And now he must pay." Jak, on one knee now, aimed the harpoon at Milo.

"Jak it was an accident." Milo put a hand up.

"I am sorry brother, but it is eye for eye." And he fired.

"No!" Lindsay, who had been directly behind Milo, dove to the concrete.

And the arrow sliced through the air, through Milo's hand, and then through his shoulder, sending the pistol clattering across the dock.

"Brother!" Milo crumpled to the ground, hit his head, and was knocked out.

Nikki darted forward, much faster than Finn ever could, and grabbed the pistol.

"Imbeciles," Dillon said, then passed out.

"My hero!" Svetlana kissed Finn, square and hard, on the lips. "You are so strong! So fast!"

"Oh please," Nikki said.

Lindsay took two thick nylon Zip-ties from her pocket and cuffed the Russians hands. Then using two more, she cuffed their legs. She said to Nikki, "You can put down the gun now."

She turned to Finn. "What are you waiting for? The match has already started. If you're going to stop Vlad, you'd better hurry. Jon will escort you."

Finn stood there, confused, mesmerized.

"Another fucking FBI agent, Patrick? You really know how to pick 'em," Nikki said.

"He didn't pick me, darling. I picked him…and the rest of them." She stood and put both hands on her hips, no longer a yogi. She looked like a cop. A damned sexy beast of a woman.

Finn asked, "Why now? Why not at Chart's house or earlier?"

"Think about it," Lindsay said. "Jon and I were separated. That left me with one gun against these two maniacs, one with a harpoon. Could've gone nuclear in a heartbeat, gotten us all killed. No, I needed them off guard, distracted. Dillon here ended up being the perfect foil."

"I'm no foil!" Dillon yelled.

"Shut it." Lindsay kicked his leg and he howled. She continued, "Anyway, we've been following these clowns for years. This is the least of their corruption. Believe me." She turned and kicked Jak in the leg this time. "Isn't that right, Jakov?"

Then, eyes rolling to the back of his head, Jak mumbled, "This is going to be longer than a haiku." And he passed out too.

CHAPTER TWENTY-TWO

"THAT WAS ONE HELL OF A SHOW, Patrick. One hell of a show!" Chart navigated the yacht, headed toward the stadium.

Patrick shook his head, still glancing back at the docks, at Lindsay standing over the wounded Russians and Dillon.

"Don't worry, Patrick. I'll pay for the therapy when we get back to the states." Nikki patted his shoulder.

"He does not need the therapy. Perhaps just a little love, yes?" Svetlana stroked his chest with a hand.

"Our first task is to locate this Vladimir Konstantinov," Jon said, his accent now tinged with a Midwestern accent, not a hint of a lisp. "Svetlana, are you certain he will be in the Airstream trailer at the north end of the stadium?"

"I don't know which end it is, north, south, northeast, who knows this thing?"

"That is where the trailer village is, where the media is stationed," Jon said. It was hard to take him seriously as an FBI agent while he was dressed like a Vegas showboy.

"So I take it you're not…" Nikki eyed him and continued, "you know." She made a twinkling face.

"I'm as straight as a harpoon." He winked at her. "Actually, I'm partial to short athletic girls with foul-mouths."

"Too bad you are not athletic," Svetlana said, pursing her lips toward Nikki.

Nikki was about to show Svetlana some athleticism when Finn

caught her raised fist. "Easy."

"Bottom line is, this video tape is evidence. We will need it for proof of the extortion scheme of the two Popov brothers," Jon said.

"Sure you don't want to just have it for your home office files?' Chart asked.

"I am certain, Mr. Westcott."

"Can I get a copy? You know, as a memento?"

"I'm afraid that can't be—"

"Don't worry," Svetlana interrupted him. "Patrick and I can make you a new one."

"Jesus, I need to go barf overboard now." Nikki turned to leave the wheelhouse.

"Before you do that." Jon took her by the arm. "Let me explain the plan first."

After shooting both Russians, Lindsay dragged and then dumped their bodies into the river. Walking back to Dillon, she discovered he had awakened.

"Well, well," she said. "You decided to join us for the finale."

"You almost killed us all, you crazy bitch."

"Ah, but I didn't. Did I?"

"I need a doctor. I'm bleeding to death here."

She bent down, inspected the wound through the tear in his shorts. "No." She stood back up. "It barely hit a vein. Almost missed the leg, actually. It'll stop bleeding all by itself in a bit."

"It hurts!"

"It's going to hurt a hell of a lot more if you don't just hand over the tape. I know where it is. Svetlana came clean with me."

"How the hell should I—"

She raised the pistol, waved it. "Do you think I got you all alone here because I'm waiting for backup?"

"Wait, where are the Russians?" He glanced around nervously. "What did you do with them?"

She nodded toward the river, and shrugged. "Didn't need them anymore."

"Jesus, wait, wait, wait." He put up both hands. "You're not FBI, are you?"

"Of course I'm not." She stepped forward, gun raised. "Now. The tape?"

"I don't—"

"We can do this the easy way, where you reach up into your asshole and you pull that little baggie out, or…" She pointed the pistol at his face. "I shoot you, then cut open that little anus, and pull it out myself."

Dillon stared at Lindsay for a few seconds, then stared at the pistol. Then he groaned, as he turned onto his good leg and pulled down his pants.

CHAPTER TWENTY-THREE

WITH NO FEWER THAN TWO-HUNDRED MEDIA trucks and vans clustered in a makeshift village, loosely connected by a tangle of multicolored wires, it took a good twenty minutes for Finn, Nikki, Jon, and Svetlana to locate the Airstream that Vlad was supposedly inside. Made of shiny aluminum, it looked like a gigantic silver bullet.

Meanwhile, Chart stayed back at the boat, just in case the authorities questioned the validity of their docking rights.

Over the loud hum of generators and the nearby crowds, Jon said, "Now remember, he should be expecting you, so just act normal and get him to open the door. Then once it's open, step in past him to clear the way for me to come in behind you."

Svet rolled her eyes and put the sunglasses back on as she said, "I am not an idiot. I am knowing of what to do."

Jon made a face that refuted the idiot comment and turned to Finn and Nikki. "You two cover the exterior. If anyone tries to barge in, stop them."

"Shouldn't be too difficult," Finn said, watching a blimp float far above the center court stadium.

"Explain again why you aren't enlisting the kangaroo cops on this one, getting some backup?" Nikki said, tapping a foot.

"Look, this is more than a little out of American jurisdiction. We don't want it all balled up by red tape this side of the pond or even state-side. Vlad here has been in my personal sights for a certain hack he performed on our website a few years ago."

"Wait, was that the one that replaced the Top Ten Wanted fugitives with the Top Ten All-Time Playmate models?" Finn asked.

"That was him?" Nikki pushed Jon, who almost fell over. "Get out!"

"None other than Vlad." He shook his head.

"Impressive," Nikki said.

Finn shrugged, "I'm not sure I agreed with the methodology of the voting on that list."

"Yeah, well. You're the only one in the free world who would've voted for Marge Simpson as a Top Ten Playmate of all-time." Nikki waved Finn off.

Finn said, "Hey, I thought it was clever. You know, shook it up a bit."

"I think this Mrs. Simpleton looks like the shaved cat with a blue lamb on the head. This is not sexy for me." Svetlana shined her fingernails on her sleeve.

"That wasn't the point you guys," Finn said.

But before he could explain, Jon said, "OK, look, we're off topic here. Is everyone ready?"

Svetlana adjusted her skirt—tighter than a safety wrap on a pill bottle—and pushed up her breasts. Then with a firm nod, she said, "Now I am ready."

Jon and the rest of them hid around the corner of the Airstream, as Svetlana knocked.

A few moments later, Vlad answered from inside. His sharp Russian accent was muffled by the aluminum door. "Who is it?"

"It is me, Svet."

"And?" Vlad yelled from inside. The drapes moved, but there was no way he could see them from his vantage on the inside.

"And..." Svetlana said. "There is nobody with me."

Jon swatted her from behind.

She spun and gave him an evil look.

Jon whispered, "He must be asking for a password, did you agree on one?"

"Oh." She turned back around and said, "And…I have no Moscow Mules with me."

The door swung open and Vlad swept Svetlana up the two steps and inside. But before he could close the door, Jon hopped to the entry and shoved his leg in the way.

The door slammed on his foot.

"Ouch!" he yelled. Then he pushed the door, but it wouldn't budge. Surprisingly, Vlad was too strong for Jon.

"Go away!" Vlad called.

Jon eased a hand inside his jacket and pulled out a Beretta pistol as he said, "Vladimir, let me in and we can talk. That's all I want to do."

As Jon drew his Beretta, Vlad thrust a flat black Uzi out the door.

"Uh oh." Nikki ducked and Finn moved forward. One long and fast step, and he barreled into the door with his shoulder as he thrust Vlad's arm upward.

Vlad yelled as the door popped open and he fell backward. A spray of bullets erupted from the Uzi, punching holes in the Airstream's ceiling.

Svetlana screamed as she was dumped into the narrow bathroom and to the floor.

Jon fell off the steps then jumped back up and dusted himself off as he pushed inside.

Nikki followed and jammed the door closed behind her.

Finn, who was now kneeling on Vlad's chest, took hold of the Uzi and held it out as he leaned a forearm on Vlad's throat. Swiveling his head, Finn took in the design of the Airstream's interior. No ordinary trailer, the living area was as wide as a New York hotel room and outfitted like a Vegas lounge, complete with a sleek dark gray leather wraparound sofa, shiny chrome tables, mirrored walls, and what looked like gems set into the siding.

And it all reflected the soft purple lights glowing from beneath the sofa and tables.

"I feel like I just stepped into Larry Flynn's Hollywood trailer," Nikki said.

"Except for the NASA workstation," Finn said, nodding toward the end of the trailer, where four LCD televisions sat atop a semi-circle desk, also chrome. Tennis matches and commercials played on the screens with no sound. A pair of headphones dangled off the side of the desk.

"I had this all under control, you ape." Jon held out a hand. "Give me the gun."

"You have your own," Finn said. "And no, you had none of it under control. Someone was about to get shot, and likely you."

Vlad tried to say something, but it came out garbled and unintelligible.

"Finn, ease up. You're killing him." Nikki pointed out.

Svetlana called from the floor of the bathroom, "You have made me bump my head. Now I am need of the medical care."

"Shut it, Slutlana." Nikki pointed to Vlad. "Finn? Guy's turning purple."

"It's just the lighting," Finn said.

"Then why is he wheezing like that?"

"Alright, alright." He pushed off Vlad, who gasped then turned onto to all fours and coughed.

"See?" Look at that," Nikki said.

"He's fine," Jon said. "But so was I. You can all go in the corner now, while I take care of this, thank you very much."

Finn flipped on the Uzi's safety and shoved it in the back of his shorts. Then he and Nikki moved to the bedroom end of the trailer. Finn was careful not to touch the sheets as he leaned against the wall.

Svetlana turned on the water in the bathroom and immediately yelled, "Ouch!"

"It is boiling hot, be careful," Vlad said. "It was hooked to the wrong line."

Svetlana shook her burned hand and then made herself busy trying to clean the lenses of her sunglasses with the corner of the bedroom curtain.

Nikki made a face of disgust and moved to the left of Finn.

Jon nodded, motioning Vlad to the kitchen area. "Sit."

Vlad did as told and Jon pointed his Beretta at his chest. "OK. Now, where is the tape?" Jon's eyes darted around, nervous, not composed.

Finn didn't know why, but he wasn't quite ready to relax yet. He felt like there was something he was missing. Something he couldn't put his finger on. In his mind, all they needed to do was collect the tape and be sure that there were no copies left out there to be used against Svetlana. Nothing else that could ruin her branding or endorsements.

In other words, his investment.

Why had Lindsay suggested releasing it on the internet?

Vlad nodded toward the desk. "There."

"Where?" Jon asked.

"Under the desk," Vlad said with a shrug.

"Nikki," Jon said. "Check it out, I don't want this guy grabbing a gun from under there or something."

Nikki glanced at Finn and pushed off the wall. Then, as she walked toward the other end of the trailer, and before Finn could reach back and pull the Uzi—as the scheme, the whole picture came to his mind—Jon stepped forward and curled his arm around her throat.

"What the—?" Nikki moved to thrust an elbow into Jon, but he jammed barrel of the Beretta into her skull.

"Don't even think about it," Jon said.

The smugglers' speedboat was a Wahoo Powerboat Phantom 15, a rocket on water that boasted 70 horsepower, according to the dash display. Lindsay revved the engine to the maximum tilt, the moment she cleared the docks.

Dillon, leg oozing and still dealing with a bruised ego from having to fish the thumb-drive with a real thumb from his anal cavity, sulked at the back of the boat, arms crossed and looking away.

Dead weight, anyway now, Lindsay thought, *I should just dump him overboard with one good turn.*

But that would prove counterproductive for her long-term profitability with Svetlana's sex tape. Having Dillon alive and hopefully back in the acting circuit upon their return to The States would be beneficial to all parties. The tape would be much more popular if it had two stars in it and not just one.

So, Lindsay kept the wheel steady and eased into the boat-staging area at the docks just outside the tennis grounds. When she located Chart's yacht, she pulled up behind it.

"Ahoy," Chart yelled from the deck above her.

Lindsay smiled and gave a wave.

"Don't believe her! She's a traitor!" Dillon yelled to Chart.

"We talked about this," Lindsay said. "Not another word." She tapped the pistol under her jacket.

"What's the problem?" Chart called down.

"You'll kill me anyway, won't you?" Dillon said. "Admit it!"

"If you shut up, you'll get your end of the deal." Lindsay raised a brow.

"I don't believe you. I don't believe any of you!" Dillon crept up to the bow of the boat. "I think you're all in some sick cult that kills everything in its path. Svetlana included!"

"Dillon. Relax." Lindsay glanced back up at Chart and back to Dillon.

"What's he talking about?" Chart said.

But Dillon didn't relax. Instead, he skittered backwards on the back of the boat. "Sick! You're all sick!" And he dove overboard, into the murky river water.

"I wouldn't do that if I were you," Chart yelled.

"Yeah? I'm outta' here!" Dillon yelled back and turned to swim away.

Chart pointed at Dillon. "No, I mean it. There are giant—"

But before he could finish that sentence, an enormous light brown creature emerged from the depths below Dillon. So large, that it looked like a baby whale. But it wasn't a baby whale, it was a fish. A giant fish. The biggest that Lindsay had ever seen.

It opened its mouth and swallowed Dillon.

Whole.

"Grouper," Chart said.

"Slide it on the floor, nice and slow." Jon now held the Beretta's barrel to the underside of Nikki's jaw. Even if Finn could get a shot off, and if he only hit Jon with the wild spray of bullets, he risked throwing Jon's hand into spasm and twitching his trigger finger.

It would kill Nikki.

So, Finn held the Uzi by the barrel and eased it down to the floor.

"Now kick it to me." Jon nodded.

Finn toed the Uzi toward Jon, and the gun spun on the Airstream's hardwood floor.

Jon caught it with his foot.

Vlad picked up the Uzi, pointed it at Finn.

"Hands behind your back," Jon said to Nikki.

She complied, and Jon pulled a baggie of thick zip-ties from his ridiculous suit pocket. Fishing one out, he strapped it tight around Nikki's wrists. Then he shoved her forward.

Nikki bumped into Svetlana, who fell back into the bathroom and on the floor.

"Son of bitch!" she yelled.

"You next," Jon said to Finn. "Turn around and put your hands behind your back."

Finn looked back and forth between Jon and Vlad. If he charged them, he could clear the seven foot distance in less than a second. A Navy SEAL would struggle to get a shot off in that instant. But that would just take care of one of them. The way they were positioned, Finn couldn't knock one into the other, at least not in a straight shot. That would leave the second gun live and still pointed at Finn.

Suicide.

So, Finn turned around and put his hands behind him.

Nikki said, "Let me get this straight, then. You aren't FBI and neither is Lindsay."

Jon laughed.

Finn said, "My guess is you cut a deal with Vlad here out at the pool. When Svetlana and I were talking at the front of the house. You two are what, simple grifters?"

"We are not simple." Jon glared at him and then smiled. But you are a clever one, Patrick, I'll give you that. Too bad we'll be dumping you overboard in an hour."

"Perfect," Nikki said.

Jon stepped forward and Finn asked, "So why the charade? Why play act all this time?"

Jon said, "First, we had to win over Svet's confidence, of course, while we figured out just what kind of scheme they had going. But then it fell right into our laps, see? So it was time to act. He pulled a zip-tie tight around Finn's wrists.

Svetlana, who had moved to the corner of the bed, said, "Everyone wants to profit off of this body." She kicked a heel up into the air and traced her long leg with a fingernail. "And yes, it is superb. But it is mine and I shall profit from it first. Da?"

"Not da," Jon said. "Vlad here gets a cut for the production."

Finn started forward but Jon held his wrists. "Wait." Then he pulled not one, but two more zip-ties around Finn's wrists.

"Done?" Finn said. "We'll need a chainsaw to get these off."

Jon pushed him forward and Finn stumbled to avoid knocking into Nikki.

Vlad said, "Yes. I added the music, the lighting, the setting. Without me, you would have nothing to go to market with."

"Jesus, you guys make this sound like a Sundance film." Nikki grimaced.

"It is better than Sundance. It could be part of the Cannes Festival. Tell them, Vladimir." Svetlana eased her leg down.

"It is true." Vlad nodded.

"So where's the damned tape now?" Finn asked.

And before Jon could answer, there was a knock on the Airstream door.

"Sorry I'm late," Lindsay said, as Jon let her into the Airstream. "It's hot in here, can we open a window or something?"

"It is from all the hot water. I will raise the air-conditioning." Vlad flipped a few switches on the wall and a hum sounded, then cold air streamed in from vents in the ceiling.

Nikki said, "Well, well, well. If it isn't the lead agent from the Fucking Bitch Institute."

Lindsay said, "Coming from you, I consider that a compliment." Then she walked to Finn and sized him up. "You were the best part of this little operation. No hard feelings, ok?"

Finn said, "Yeah, right. Namaste."

Nikki leaned over and whispered loudly, "Seriously, boss. What is it with you and psycho chicks?"

"Maybe I should get a bumper sticker, you know, *Sick-Chick Magnet* has a nice ring to it."

Nikki said, "How about, *I like Whacko Women*?"

"Not bad. Or maybe *I Ride the Crazy Train*?"

"Enough," Lindsay said. Then she turned to Vlad. "How much time until the main spot?"

Vlad said, "The Coco-Cola commercial is airing after the first set. It is still four games to two, we have time."

"This will be over fast," Svetlana said. "Djokovic is too good for Nadal."

"Your opinion is very insightful," Nikki said.

"OK, look. Here's the deal." Lindsay stepped to the side of Vlad and out of the path of the Uzi. "Svetlana, we will air this tape at the right moment here. Then we will distribute the video using an encrypted video streaming site and charge $9.99 per viewing."

"And what is my percentage?" Svetlana said.

"Wait, wait, wait!" Nikki turned to Svetlana. "You're in on all this?"

Svetlana frowned. "I am businesswoman. I need the money to keep up with my lifestyle of the luxury."

"See? Piece of ass equals piece of work. Please acknowledge, Patrick."

"Duly noted," he said.

"You can keep twenty-five percent," Jon said.

"Forty," Svetlana countered.

Jon glanced at Lindsay, who nodded. "Thirty percent for Svet."

"Forty-five." Svetlana crossed her arms.

Lindsay held up a hand. "Hold it, you're going the wrong way. You need to come to the middle for a deal."

Svetlana gave a face. "I came beautifully on this video. That is all the coming I am doing."

"Gross," Nikki said.

"Why don't you give Svetlana some optionality on the back end?" Finn said, "You know, if you sell more than a million copies, she gets to keep a higher percentage on everything after that."

Nikki gave him a look of crazy.

Finn whispered, "I'm just trying to get my investment back."

"We'll all be dead, Patrick," she said.

"Nah," he answered. He knew that once the three dipshits were focused on getting that video onto the screen, he'd have his chance to get free. All he needed to do was find something sharp. And waist-high. And he needed to do it fast.

He looked around while the others bartered.

"I like this idea," Jon said. "But let's do it this way. Svetlana gets twenty percent for the first million, and Lindsay, Vlad, and I split the other eighty. Then it goes to thirty-seventy until the next million, and forty-sixty on the next, and then fifty-fifty, where it remains forever."

"Deal," Svetlana said. "This will sell ten million copies, minimum, maybe twenty-five."

Lindsay nodded, and Vlad shrugged. "Fine."

"By the way, where is Dillon?" Jon asked.

"Oh, him," Lindsay said. "He went for a...swim."

"You got the tape...out of him, first?" Jon scrunched his face.

"Don't worry, it was in a baggie. All clean, see?" She fished the thumb drive from her pocket.

"I don't even want to know," Nikki said.

"No different than a drug mule," Lindsay answered. Then she turned to Vlad. "What's the viewership estimate?"

"Twelve to fifteen million."

"Not bad," Svetlana said. "This is a good marketing start."

"And you're inside?" Lindsay said to Vlad.

"I have hacked into the main network. We will reach viewers world wide."

"Excellent," Jon said. "Let's load it up."

And then it hit Finn how he could free himself, how they could escape. He said, "While you guys are busy doing all that, can I go to the men's room? Feel like my bladder's going to explode here."

"Make it fast, and don't miss the toilet," Vlad said.

"I'll do my best." The moment Finn shut himself into the bathroom, he turned on the hot water. Sure enough, the stream came out boiling hot, pouring steam into the tiny space. While it was still heating, Finn turned and wiggled his body up and onto the counter.

Careful to keep his hands from the water, he pushed his arms as far up behind him as his shoulders allowed, which was just high enough to be above the faucet. Then he swiveled his body a bit and eased them lower toward the scalding metal. Unfortunately, he couldn't do this without also burning his wrists. He grimaced as he held his arms—and the zip-ties—tight to the metal.

"You OK in there?" Jon called.

"Fine, almost...done," Finn said, steam billowing in his face. He kicked the handle of toilet, causing it to flush loudly.

His hands burned, being seared on the faucet. He held them tight to the metal.

Finally, one zip-tie melted enough and snapped off. Then another.

The third snapped off, and Finn yanked his hands from the faucet.

Two thick red lines glowed on his wrists. *Damn.*

Squinting in the hot fog, Finn rifled through the drawers under the sink for something sharp.

At the back of the bottom drawer, and under a pile of Russian magazines, he found a new Gillette disposable razor. He stepped on one of the plastic razor head casings, but it just split open and five tiny blades fell out, all but useless to help Nikki get free.

"That's enough!" Jon banged on the bathroom. "Come out now or I'm shooting through this door!"

"Hey, that is fine walnut. Don't hit it," Vlad said.

Unable to find any other sharp objects, Finn resolved that he'd just have to do the best he could. Because Nikki was right. As soon as they could dispense with Finn and the others, they would.

So, Finn slipped his hands behind his back and pretended to open the door awkwardly.

Jon stepped back and waved his hand at the steam. "About damned time. What were you showering in there?"

Finn winked at Nikki and angled his body for her to see his free hands. "Not easy to get your pants up and down with no hands."

Jon seemed to consider that, and then he grabbed Finn's shoulder and said, "Yeah, how did you—"

And Finn swung his two closed fists around and clobbered Jon's head on both sides, dropping him like a broken puppet.

Nikki, timing her cue perfectly, darted forward and head-butted Lindsay in the stomach.

Lindsay gulped a gallon of air as she was sent flying into Vlad, who was bent over the keyboard.

Finn took hold of Jon's Beretta, aimed it at Vlad. "Don't even."

Vlad glanced back at Finn and straightened.

Nikki rolled on the floor, slipping her hands to the front of her as she came back up.

Lindsay, looking bleary-eyed, coughed and stood as she tried to aim her pistol at Nikki.

But Nikki was too fast, swinging her hands upward and into Lindsay's jaw.

Lindsay's head snapped back and she dropped the pistol.

Nikki darted forward and took hold of it, aimed it at Lindsay, who was now crumpled on the floor next to Jon.

"Get your shit-ass over here," Finn said to Vlad.

Vlad stepped over Jon, who was knocked out cold, hands above his head like a good little captive.

"Nice moves," Finn said to Nikki.

"Not so bad yourself," she said.

"Hey, now that we can cut these jokers out, maybe we should just let Slutlana and Vlad air the tape. It's possible she could get her own reality show like the Kardashians."

Finn shook his head. "It'll never happen with a Russian. Plus, I just lined up four endorsements. She can pay me back over three years. If this tape came out, those would be gone and she'd be kicked out of the WTA. Never play another a match. My way is a safer play."

"Yeah, you're right. I didn't want to see that show anyway."

And as the two of them contemplated that, Finn realized that Svetlana had been unusually quiet the whole time.

And that was because she had snuck over to the computer.

"Don't!" Finn said.

Svetlana turned. "I am to be a star of the big screens."

And she pressed *Send*.

Finn, Nikki, Vlad, and even Lindsay gawked at the monitors, where instead of a Coca-Cola commercial appearing, the image of Svetlana in all her glory played on both the gigantic in-stadium instant replay screens and all the major cable networks. But on this edited version of the tape, Svetlana was not having sex with the one they all had expected.

Finn glanced at Vlad. "What happened to Dillon?"

Vlad shrugged. "He's a terrible actor."

As he said that, the door to the Airstream burst open and a man in an Australian policeman's uniform yelled, "Hands up, everyone!"

His partner said, "Whoa." Then he took off his hat and stared at the spread before him, so to speak.

And Chart said, "Hey, I'm even bigger on TV!"

And this time, Nikki vomited for real.

CHAPTER TWENTY-FOUR

FINN SAT OUT ON his back porch, a bottle of Corona Light in his hand, the cool ocean breeze touching his face. A thick fog covered the water today, extending up into the clouds and hiding the sun like a light bulb behind a shower curtain.

Hobie, unaware of the muted beauty above him, held his own head halfway into a hole he'd been digging for the last hour. He looked up at Finn every few minutes, gave a *woof*, and then went back to work.

He wondered what that dog was thinking sometimes.

Finn laid his head back and closed his eyes, and his phone began to vibrate in his pocket.

Fishing it out, he saw the number and answered, "Svetlana."

"My Patrick, how are *the* you?"

My Patrick. Ever since she dodged jail time with Finn's testimony, Svetlana had called Finn that. "How are *you*, you mean?"

"I am good. Very good. Thank you for asking."

Finn was about to explain his correction, but let it go. "Yeah? Tell me."

"I have a new line of perfume to come out in the next month. They are very hard at work with the perfecting of the scent, but it is near finishing."

Wow. A lingerie line, a swimsuit label offshoot, sunglasses, namesake tennis rackets, a full modeling schedule for the next eighteen months, and now perfume? At last count, she'd bagged a whopping six million downloads of her sex tape after dropping the price to $7.99. Finn was kicking himself for refusing to take his agent's fee off of that. Svetlana was rolling in it.

And then some.

"Great," he said. "What's it called?"

"That is what I am asking you for, I am wanting your opinion."

"I don't think I—"

"It is for a woman, but a strong woman. And as a man who likes the strong woman, one who can handle the strong woman, you are the perfect test group for my naming of this product."

"Okay…what are the choices, then?"

"Yes, here they are. GunSlick, IcePick, RazorCut, PistolWhip, or Man-Izer."

"Geez, that's…those are…tough choices, yeah."

"See? This is why I need my Patrick."

"What does it smell like?"

"What does this matter? It is the marketing, you know this."

Right. Could smell like a donkey's ass, but it's all in the packaging. He said, "I say you go with PistolWhip, that sounds original."

"Great, I will tell them straight away."

"If that's all," Finn said.

"Yes."

He was about to hang up, when she said, "Wait. I almost forgot. Have you received the check?"

"Not yet."

"Well, I sent it and I think this is fair. You saved my life and all."

"I don't think I saved your life, I think I saved mine and Nikki's."

"Well. You came for me, and this is enough. You deserve a little more than what I owe you."

"Thank you Svetlana, but that's not necessary."

"OK. We can have alternative plan. I will give you a different payment…in person. I will even let you choose what positions you—"

"No, no, no. That's OK. I'll keep the check, I appreciate it very much."

"Someday," Svetlana said. "I will make you have the sex with me. You will see."

"OK, Svetlana."

"Goodbye." She hung up.

A warm and nurturing gal, that Svetlana. Like a perfect little Susie Homewrecker.

Finn heard a rumble behind him and turned to catch Nikki's truck appearing over the crest of the hill, heading for his drive.

Hobey pulled his head out of the hole and gave a good loud *WOOF* this time. Then he galloped toward the driveway. A minute later, Nikki walked around the side of the house with Hobey wobbling next to her, trying to bite the newspaper in her hand. "Yes, boy, good to see you too."

"Well, well. Thought you were on vacation this week. SoCal." Finn stood and gave her a hug.

"Leaving now, just had to drop this off." She reached in her pocket and unfolded a check then handed it to him. From Svetlana, it was written out to Finn…for *One-Hundred and Fifty-Thousand Dollars.*

"Wait, wait, wait. She said more, not twice what she owed me."

"Dude, that chick has taken in tens of millions in the last three months. I told you. You should've agreed to an agent's fee on that video."

"Yeah, yeah. I wouldn't have felt right about that."

"I would have."

"She said she was sending more, but this is too much. Maybe I should send half of it back."

"I think you should tell her to cut you in on a new video deal. I hear Johnny Depp is looking to get back on the big screen."

"That's disgusting."

"Just sayin'." She looked around. "Besides, this place could use a tune-up."

"What's wrong with my house? It's cabin-chic."

"More like cabin-shabby. Anyway..." she held up the newspaper. "See this yet? Fresh off the press."

"Haven't looked at a paper all weekend."

"Well this one takes the cake. Here." She opened the paper to the second page, where there was a spread on the ongoing saga of poor Lobster Kratt's legacy. Or more to the point, his inheritance.

The article read:

OFFICER FLOODED IN LOBSTER ESTATE

In an extraordinary finale to the Lobster Estate Saga, Judge Grant Hall has now ruled on the substantial estate of late Larry Kratt, known as 'Lobster' for his affinity of the spiny creatures. Having no children, and being a widower himself, Mr. Kratt had designated his prized forty-eight pound lobster named Linda as the sole heir to his estate upon his death. However, it was reported that Officer Tony Flood had found both Mr. Kratt and Linda dead last month. In an amazing twist, though, Mr. Flood also found seventeen baby lobsters taking refuge beneath Linda. Having been confirmed through DNA testing—ordered by the State DA—the lobsters were determined to be the descendants of and therefore the rightful heirs to Linda the Lobster's newfound estate. After much controversy and a week of hearings, Judge Hall ruled that the moment Officer Flood had assumed natural custody of the orphaned lobsters he became the immediate and uncontested trustee to the riches which are estimated to be worth over one-point-four million dollars. When asked about the luck and timing of the fortune, Officer Flood said, "I just wanted to give them a good home, one they deserved. And now I'll have the means by which to do just that."

It is said that Mr. Flood has since retired from active duty as a police officer and has bought a house on the water in Yarmouth, where he founded a boat charter service called Flooded with Fish. Here, customers can be 'virtually guaranteed to land all kinds of Sea Bass and Striped Bass, Bluefin Tuna, and Bluefish. We like 'em fast and we eat what we catch!' Declared Flood.

What a country, Finn thought.

"Hell of a thing," Nikki said. "If I knew how rich that old guy was, I would've been nicer to him."

"No you wouldn't have."

"Yeah, you're right." Nikki stared out at the fog. "So, anything you need me to do before taking off, then?"

"Well. There is one thing."

"Don't even think about asking me to clean up that home office." She thrust a thumb toward the house.

"No, no, not that. I got a call for a new client last night. May need you to swing by, get some papers signed."

"Yeah? Tell me it's a he and not Russian."

"Actually, you're in luck. His name is Haystack Williams, no tennis involved."

"Haystack? Sounds like a corn-fed, Midwestern linebacker from Kansas. NFL first rounder?"

"Not exactly. But his sport did recently steal prime time on ESPN from the NHL."

"Shit boss, if you're talking about what I think you are, that is neither a good city nor a reliable sport for income."

"You got it, the PPT." Finn sipped his beer. "He's a professional poker player."

"God help us both."

"Hey, he made over three million last year on winnings alone, that's not counting endorsements."

"What, Ray Bans? Hair gel?"

"He's apparently got beautiful hands. I've got a call into Lancome. Oh, and he likes colorful shirts, so Robert Graham may be the next call."

"I can picture him already."

"That's the spirit. I haven't even told you the best part yet. I mean for you."

She looked up at him, and Finn gave her his best predator smile. Total shark.

She tilted her head, raised a finger. "Don't you fuckin' say it."

Finn nodded once. "Yep. He insists on having female representation."

Nikki took the beer from Finn and slugged the rest as he said, "Ever been to Vegas?"

EPILOGUE

VANESSA INHALED THE FINAL puff from her cigarette, held the smoke in her lungs like it was from the last bong hit in the world, and exhaled. Then she extinguished the spent stub into the dirt at her side.

"That was fast," Chadwick said.

Leaning back to back to the man, with nothing more than a chain link fence separating them, they had sat like that all morning, as they had every day since they'd arrived at this hellhole called *Detention Center Number One*. Vanessa was getting tired, though, she considered going back to her room for a bit and laying down to recharge her batteries before the next disgusting meal.

Amazing how tired one can get when there was nothing to do but sit around all day.

She said, "It was my last one, too."

"I'm sorry to hear that."

She reached up, touched his shoulder through the fence, and said, "Will you give me one of yours?"

"Not likely."

"Come on, Chaddy, we're a team here. We must help each other when we can."

"No."

"Just one."

"No."

"Chaddy."

"I'm using these for a trade tonight. It's steak and mashies, my favorite."

"Steak?" She pressed away from him just far enough to peer at the side of his face. "They serve steak over there?"

"They do."

"What's it look like?"

"Well, it's all ground up and it has a ketchup sauce spread on it."

"That's not steak, that's meatloaf." She slumped back to the fence. "And it's tomato sauce, not ketchup."

"Well it's delicious. In fact, I believe it's the best meat I've had in years."

"Oh Christ, then you've been going to the wrong butcher. That's not even beef."

"Of course it is. What else would it be?"

"Goat? Kangaroo? Sheepdog?"

"That's disgusting, goat."

Vanessa said, "Look, I'll add another favor to the list for when we get out of here, alright? Just hand me another ciggie."

"No, it's not alright. At this point, you're into me for seventy-seven sexual favors. I couldn't possibly cash in on all of those in less than a week."

"A week?" She pushed off again, this time far enough to see him in full.

He turned, too. "What, you think it'd be shorter than that?"

"Good god, no. Do the math. That's eleven favors a day for a week. You'd die of dehydration, emptying yourself like that." She glanced at his crotch and back to his face. "If you could even get it up that much."

"I could take pills."

"It would fall off." She turned and slumped again, crossing her arms this time. "Something I'm not willing to risk. That skin rocket of yours is far too valuable to me."

"You do love me, don't you?"

"I say *it*, not you."

"See? You treat me like that and expect me to do kind things in return."

He moved to stand up, and she said, "Wait, wait. I didn't mean that, Chaddy. I'm just not feeling like myself today."

"I see that." He looked around, smiled at a tiny Asian man walking past him, and turned back to Vanessa.

"Please accept my apology."

He fell back to the ground, slumped against her. "Accepted."

"There, there. That's better." She patted his shoulder with two fingertips through the fence.

A minute passed and she said, "Now. How about that ciggie, then?

He sighed. "You're going to keep asking, aren't you? Until I give you one."

"Yes I am."

"Fine." A rustling noise sounded as he fished the pack of cigarettes from his pocket and drew one out. He slipped it through the fence. "Seventy-eight, then."

"Seventy-eight." She snatched the cigarette and quickly lit it up, inhaled deeply. "Ah. That's so much better. No more salty air in my lungs, just the essence of tobacco and nicotine. My lifeline to pleasure in here."

"Say, Vanessa, did you receive a visitor today?"

"No, why?"

"Just wondering."

She inhaled, the nicotine streaming through her veins, stroking her synapses like little blood angels. "Chadwick, you don't wonder a thing like that. You must have a reason."

"Right, well. An interesting chap came to see me this morning."

Vanessa exhaled and then inhaled again quickly, so as to not allow the cigarette to be wasted between puffs. Sucking in, she said, "What sort of chap?"

"He said he was from the British Consulate in Sydney."

"Did he?" Vanessa felt her muscles begin to tense. The knowledge of something upsetting coming her way. Something that would not, could not be forgiven. "What did he want?" she asked, each syllable perfectly enunciated.

"Well," Chadwick began then paused, then began again, "He said he was helping two young English sailors who had gone off course, ended up here at Christmas Island. He was taking them back to mainland."

"And?" The word came out with a bitter spittle at the end.

"And..." Chadwick shrugged against her. "He said you and I could leave if we wanted. Today."

"He what?" Vanessa jumped up, turned. "He said that? When? Where?" She spun around. Suddenly the nicotine and the excitement were too much together. She felt vibrant, alive. She felt ecstatic. "Where is he? Let's go then." She turned.

"But."

"But what?" She sucked the cigarette deeply. The last rationed ciggie of the day, hopefully of her life. "What are you waiting for?"

"Well I told him that's alright. We weren't ready to leave."

"We weren't?" she stammered. "Wh...wh...why? Why would you say such a thing? Of course we are! We've been ready since the very first moment they locked us inside this hole of hell!"

"He said he'd be back next month."

"Next month?"

"Why would we stay here for another month? *WHY ON BLOODY EARTH WOULD WE WANT TO STAY HERE FOR ONE MORE NIGHT, LET ALONE ANOTHER MONTH?*" Screaming at the top of her lungs now. "*WHY? TELL ME WHY YOU WANT TO STAY!*"

The other detainees had crowded around on both sides of them now, watching the show. Chadwick glanced around and said, "Well, I thought you loved it too. Loved it enough to stay longer."

"*LOVED WHAT?*"

He glanced around, coming closer to the fence with each turn.

"*WHAT?*" she yelled again.

Finally, he whispered, "The meatloaf."

And Vanessa stared at him. Hands shaking, face so red, so full of blood, she could picture it, a giant ballon filled with blood. Furious, raging, incensed blood. Filling and filling and filling, it would soon burst.

She looked down at the cigarette, the burning ember in her hand.

"Vanessa?"

Then she willed herself to smile. A delusional, starkers smile probably, but one the same, as she whispered to him, "Come closer."

"What?" He leaned in.

"Closer." She glanced around, eyes dancing like crazy little wolves. Ravenous, violent, murderous little dogs.

He leaned all the way in, pressed his face to the fence.

"Darling?"

"Yes, mum?"

And she plunged the molten tip into Chadwick's forehead.

ACKNOWLEDGMENTS

To my first readers, the two VLs, you know who you are and what you mean to me. Your input, as always, helps steer me toward the vision for the story and I couldn't do it without either of you. To Tony Flood, for allowing me to use your name for the sake of humor, you have a great sense of it and I appreciate you always spreading the word about Patrick Finn. On that, for any mistakes here in law or law enforcement, those are mine and mine only, as I have taken ludicrous measures of literary license for the goal of a laugh. To my dedicated readers, thank you all so very much for your time and encouragement. It means the world.

ABOUT THE AUTHOR

Alex Cay is a former athlete, long-time artist, investor, and writer. Author of the Patrick Finn Island Thrillers, Alex was born in Upstate New York but now lives on the West Coast and escapes to the shore every chance he gets. If he's not busy as a husband or a dad, working, or writing, it's a darn good bet that you can find him seaside or on the ocean somewhere.

Connect with Alex online:
www.alexcay.com
https://twitter.com/AlexCayBooks
https://www.facebook.com/AlexCayBooks

If you enjoyed reading *All Tide Up*, I would appreciate if you would help others enjoy this book, too.

Lend it. This e-book is enabled for lending, so please share.

Recommend it. Please help your friends and family find this book by recommending it to them. Reader groups, social media, discussion boards are also great ways to spread the word.

Review it. Please tell others why you enjoyed this book by reviewing it at Amazon or Goodreads. When you do write a review, please send me an email at *alexcaybooks@gmail.com*, so I can thank you with a personal email.

ALSO BY ALEX CAY

A Patrick Finn Thriller by
ALEX CAY

MAN UP

"Laugh-out-loud fun..."
-Deborah Coonts, National
Bestselling Author of
LUCKY BASTARD

PATRICK FINN SERIES BOOK 1

MAN UP!

When former high-stakes bounty hunter, now professional sports agent, Patrick Finn and his NHL rookie goalie, Lew Kunkle, are attacked on Kunkle's new yacht, Finn brushes it off as a failed robbery. But then two more hitmen show up, along with Finn's ex-girlfriend who happens to work for the CIA.

Soon, a cast of characters that includes a billionaire team-owner's son, Finn's foul-mouthed assistant, two giant mastiffs, twin bail bondsmen from Boston, a bikini-model/shark-trainer named Manny, and her prized hammerhead named Elvis, all collide in a wacky escapade that spans the coast of Florida, across the Gulf Stream, and throughout Grand Bahama Island.

In order to save his client's life, and ultimately his own, Finn must stop the dimwitted hitmen and find the real killer, the chowderhead who hired them.

Available at *Amazon*.

A PATRICK FINN ISLAND THRILLER SHORT

ICY HOT!

Go for a ride with Vanessa and Chadwick.

In a short story that takes place soon after the end of MAN UP, bumbling British hitmen Vanessa Holmes and Sir James Chadwick are at it again. Just not in the way they ever thought.

Co-conspirator Stanley Cockburn made off with the cash at the end of Vanessa and Chadwick's last assignment, and now they're stranded in Jacksonville, Florida—out of money, out of gas, and all but out of options. So, armed with only an address and a bullet-less SIG, they decide to shake down Stanley's uncle until he gives up his nephew. Only one problem: They have to break into the uncle's pet shop to do it.

With so little to lose and so much to gain, the hapless hitmen take on a literal zoo of hurdles that includes water moccasins, a Komodo dragon, and a hungry school of piranha. It just takes is a handful of bad choices, unlucky timing, and a juvenile bobcat named Boblet for all hell to break loose—forcing the unlikely couple to fight for their lives, once again.

Join Vanessa and Chadwick in this Patrick Finn Island Thriller short - it's a quickie that you don't want to miss.

Available at *Amazon*.

www.ingramcontent.com/pod-product-compliance
Lightning Source LLC
Chambersburg PA
CBHW021229130626
46554CB00004B/1412